PARADISE BAY

'Look what I bought down in the village,' Liza said. She produced a handbag made from stiff brown leather, with a map of Frixos etched on the top flap. 'It's not very nice, but we aren't exactly spoilt for choice, are we?'

'No we're not,' muttered Alice, feeling like she had missed the punchline of a joke.

'What I liked about it was the strap,' Liza explained. She opened the flap and unbuckled the long leather strap, throwing the bag across the room, not even bothering to look where it landed.

'What about the strap?'

'I realised what a useful little thing it could turn out to be,' Liza said, advancing on Alice with the strap in her hand, her eyes blazing with excitement. Alice let Liza take her hands, allowing herself to be pulled to her feet, her heart pumping wildly. Liza grabbed Alice's hands and pulled them roughly, turning her around, crossing them behind her back and tying them quickly with the stiff leather strap. To all intents and purposes Alice was at Liza's mercy. The thought made her struggle, made her damp between the thighs.

'Why are you doing this to me?'

'I haven't decided yet,' Liza teased as she bent down and began to unbutton Alice's blouse . . .

A NEXUS CLASSIC

PARADISE BAY

Maria del Rey

This book is a work of fiction.
In real life, make sure you practise safe sex.

First published in 1992 by
Nexus
Thames Wharf Studios
Rainville Road
London W6 9HA

This Nexus Classic edition 2001

www.nexus-books.co.uk

ISBN 0 352 33645 5

Typeset by TW Typesetting, Plymouth, Devon

Printed and bound by Clays Ltd, St Ives PLC

To GP with all my love

one

It was a silly situation to be in. No matter how Joanne tried to rationalise, it was a silly situation. That was the trouble. What she felt was beyond reason; it was buried far deeper. Joanne had everything going for her: she was still only thirty years old, ran a successful design company, her husband was her best friend, business partner and lover rolled into one. She could find no explanation for the strange infatuation that had suddenly developed. It had come from nowhere, a sudden eruption of insanity from the depths of her soul. Here she was, the very epitome of the successful modern woman, madly infatuated with her young secretary.

She stepped out on to the hotel balcony, shielding the brilliant sunshine from her eyes. The hotel was high above a small Greek town, which lay strung out in a wide semicircle, falling away sharply from the hotel. The rectangular pattern of white-washed houses, so typically Mediterranean, shimmered in the heat haze of the afternoon. Beyond the town lay the Aegean, a deep blue band that rippled with golden points of light. On the horizon, in the far distance, the blue-white of the cloudless sky merged into the sea.

There were good reasons for the holiday, as Joanne had told herself repeatedly; for a while it had been important to prove to herself that the trip had nothing to do with her deeper feelings. And, for a while, she had almost succeeded. But now that they had arrived in Greece the justifications had become unfocused again. She wanted to believe that the trip combined an element of business with a much-needed rest, that it had nothing to do with the strange and overpowering attraction that she felt for Alice.

Standing alone on the balcony, gazing at the sleepy little town and the calm inviting sea, she realised that her justifications were nothing but pale excuses. She had only half believed them even before they left London. The real reasons were wrapped up in her unspoken desires, and intricately connected with Alice.

Joanne returned to the room; the heat outside was unbearable, with hardly a breeze stirring and the sea calm. The heat made it hard to concentrate, and the brightness of the sun seemed to block out all thoughts so that only shadows of sensations filled her mind. Inside, a fan chopped ineffectually at the air, but without the direct glare of the sun the heat was only just comfortable. She sat back at the desk, flicking inattentively through a pile of documents, all the time thinking about what lay in store for her and Alice on Frixos, the small island they were to visit for ten days.

Her thoughts were interrupted by a sharp knock at the door. 'Come in.' She turned to face the door expectantly, her heart beating just that little bit faster.

'Hi,' Alice said, walking casually into the room with a sheaf of documents in a blue folder. She wore a fashionable halter-neck dress, well above the knee and with a plunging neckline exposing the deeply attractive valley between her large firm breasts. Her long legs were bare and already sported a golden tan.

'Is everything sorted out?' Joanne asked, searching

2

Alice's dark eyes for some hint of recognition. Sometimes Joanne felt a little embarrassed, as if the way she was looking at Alice was so obviously sexual that it could not be interpreted in any other way. But if Alice ever recognised the look, she gave no hint of it.

'We leave by taxi at eight tomorrow morning,' Alice said. She sat on the edge of the bed, close to the desk, removing a neatly written document from the folder. 'The ferry leaves the port at eight-forty,' she said, reading from her itinerary. 'The crossing to Frixos usually only takes an hour. The harbour there is all silted up, according to the travel agent, so we'll be picked up by a motor launch that will take us ashore.'

'Good,' said Joanne. 'And the other matter?'

Alice closed the folder and plopped it down on the floor by her feet. 'You wouldn't believe how difficult that was,' she said, her oval face drawn in a bright attractive smile. 'I've had Caroline go through all the minutes of meetings, guest lists at garden parties and everything.'

'And?'

Alice leaned further back on the bed, crossing her legs and exposing the golden tan of her lithe well-shaped thighs. 'Good news,' she said. 'As far as we can tell there is no one at Paradise Bay who has ever met you. You're booked in under your own name, and we've avoided using the private airstrip so that we don't draw attention to ourselves.'

'Good,' Joanne said firmly. Alice's dress had ridden further up, revealing an enticing view of her seductive thighs. 'Nobody knows that I'm married to the part-owner of the hotel. We can check it out without worrying if things are being put on especially for our benefit. Have you phoned Philip to tell him?'

'I thought you might like to pass on the good news.' Alice bent down to flip through the blue folder; the fullness

3

of her breasts was fully displayed by the thin dress, and her decolletage was in Joanne's full view.

Transfixed by the sight, Joanne watched her scrabbling for the slip of paper with Philip's phone number on it. Her heart beat faster and she could feel the blood pulsing through her. Alice looked so beautiful, so innocent, so unintentionally seductive. Shaking nervously, Joanne stood up, uncertain of herself but moved by an inner compulsion that could not be resisted.

'Found it!' Alice looked up at Joanne and smiled, waving the pink slip of paper in her hand.

'You look so lovely in this dress,' Joanne whispered, stepping close to Alice. She stood over her, breathing in the soft scent of her perfume, aware that the moment had come to risk everything.

'Thanks, I saw it in the summer sales and thought it was just right for Frixos.' Alice continued to smile easily. She shifted round so that she was closer to Joanne, leaning forward slightly to give a fuller glimpse of her breasts.

'But you always look lovely,' Joanne smiled back. Tentatively she reached out and touched Alice's bare shoulder with the very tips of her fingers. She half expected Alice to recoil with horror, but instead Alice sat still, looking up innocently with her large brown eyes.

'I've got Philip's number,' Alice whispered, her voice losing its confident tone. She remained motionless on the bed, clutching tightly at the pink slip of paper with the phone number on it.

'I'll call Philip later,' Joanne said, taking the paper and letting it butterfly to the floor. She took Alice's hand and pulled her up so that they faced each other. She swept the long black hair away from Alice's face and stared into her large brown eyes. She felt that the two of them were wrapped up in a single magic spell, afraid that it would break in an instant and return them both to dull normality.

4

Alice looked away suddenly. Her soft lips were trembling and her eyes had filled with tears.

'Don't turn away,' Joanne said, taking Alice under the chin. She knew what to do. The doubts that had existed for so long were cleared away. She bent down and touched her lips to Alice's. She kissed her softly. Their lips barely touched, but Joanne's intention was clear.

Alice made no response so Joanne pressed forward again, taking hold of her shoulders and pulling her close. They kissed again, this time a more passionate searching embrace. Alice hesitated a moment then responded, opening her mouth to Joanne's searching tongue.

Joanne stepped back and carefully reached around Alice's neck. Quickly she undid the little catch that held the dress in place and let it go. The dress began to slip down but Alice caught it instinctively, holding it just below her chest, her large round breasts naked in the sunlight.

'You're beautiful,' Joanne said, noting with a little ripple of excitement that Alice was blushing, a pink glow lighting up her young face. Her eyes still carried the faintly demure look of innocence that Joanne found inexorably attractive.

'I ... I ...' Alice started to say something but stopped and turned away again.

'It's OK,' Joanne whispered soothingly. 'You don't have to say anything, everything will be all right. It'll be beautiful.' She began to massage Alice's breasts, large round globes of flesh tipped with copper-toned nipples. She squeezed the gorgeous twin fruits, then flicked her thumbs over the nipples to make them stand to attention. She kissed Alice on the mouth again, flicking her tongue in the other's cool receptive mouth, then bent down lower. Very slowly, paying reverent homage, she took each nipple into her mouth. She flicked her tongue over the nodes of flesh, tasting them as if they were the sweetest of buds.

'Please, don't do this ...' Alice murmured breathlessly.

She stood awkwardly, her hands holding tightly at her dress, legs parted slightly.

'I'm going to make love to you,' Joanne promised, strangely excited by Alice's reluctance. She could feel Alice trembling, her body shaken by nervous gasps for breath.

Alice closed her eyes when Joanne began to suck hard at her nipples. Her breathing was sharp now, gasping for breath and letting out little cries of pleasure. She took her breasts in her hands, cupping them and feeding them into Joanne's hungry mouth.

Joanne worked furiously, as the heat in the pit of her belly grew in intensity. She passionately attacked Alice's breasts, biting the erect nipples playfully and sucking them deep into her mouth. At the same time her hands worked the lovely round orbs, squeezing, rubbing, occasionally pulling at one nipple while mouthing the other.

They collapsed on to the bed. Alice lay underneath, her eyes opening and closing, her breath fluttering. Almost blindly she reached out and tried to massage Joanne's breasts, her delicate fingers moving gently towards their target.

'No, not now,' Joanne said hoarsely, pushing Alice's hands away. She pulled herself up so that they were face to face again, the look of confusion in Alice's eyes self-evident. There was confusion, but Joanne also saw a desperate longing, an aching desire mixed in with the clearest expression of innocence that she had ever seen. It was a beguiling mixture, and to her it reflected the deepest core of Alice's personality; it was a mirror to her soul.

Alice gasped. She and Joanne were kissing again, ardently sharing their hot breath, muffling unspoken sighs of pleasure. But now Joanne's fingers were exploring lower down, under the dress that had been pulled down to Alice's

6

slender waist.

Joanne thrilled to the feel of the smooth glossy thighs under her fingers; she slid her palm up and down the soft yielding flesh, enjoying the feel of the warm skin, knowing how sensitive a woman is just under the entrance to her sex. Very slowly, wanting to enjoy every second of the experience, she explored the unresisting body beneath her. She traced a finger up from the knee to the place where the thighs parted. She could feel Alice tense momentarily, whether from expectation or fear she couldn't tell; but her movement only heightened the pleasure of the game.

Joanne gently brushed her fingertips against the silky panties pulled deep into Alice's pussy. She played her finger in a tight circle, pressing the swollen pussy lips apart and forcing the silky material into the slit. She could feel the sticky dampness and the warmth of arousal. Alice sighed and parted her thighs, her hands clutching ineffectually against the bed, as if trying to stop herself from falling.

The dress was getting in Joanne's way so she tried to pull it down further, but Alice took hold of it and refused to let it be pulled down below the waist. No words were spoken, but from the imploring look on Alice's face Joanne stopped. The gesture seemed so odd that for a moment she thought that the spell had been broken, that the magic moment would suddenly turn sour. She seized Alice's face with both hands and pressed their mouths together, breathing life and energy into her. They kissed passionately, wildly, for what seemed an age, then Joanne pulled away.

Alice closed her eyes again and lay back, unable to smother the sighs of pleasure that escaped from her full red lips. Joanne touched her fingers to the mouth of Alice's sex once more, pressing against the sticky dampness of the panties. She wanted to see, to feast her eyes on Alice's lovely wet sex, but the dress obscured the view. She knew she could wait; from the ecstatic moans that escaped from Alice's pouting lips she knew that this moment, this moment that she had dreamed of, would be repeated. Her fingers slipped under the thin material and into the heat of the sex. She imagined the feelings that were pulsing through Alice, knowing that her own sex was aching with want.

'Oh God ...' Alice cried. Suddenly Joanne's fingers were deep inside her, pressing forcefully into the receptive warmth. She arched her back and pulled her thighs further apart, opening herself completely to Joanne. She thrashed her head ecstatically, gasping for air. Joanne's fingers were driving in and out, slippery with a coating of sex-honey, forcing wild pulsating surges of bliss at the very centre of her cunt-bud.

Alice cried out. Her body was seized with one immense spasm and then she froze, the breath escaping from her in a childish sigh of pleasure. Overwhelmed by the glorious orgasm, she fell back on to the bed, her body limp once more.

'Good girl, good girl,' Joanne whispered softly. She stood up and looked down at Alice, whose body was bathed in a glistening layer of sweat, the tanned flesh blushing a healthy pink.

Now was the moment of truth, now that the magic spell had worked its power. Joanne watched expectantly, nervously awaiting the moment when Alice emerged from the golden afterglow of her orgasm. She watched her awake from the dream, heard her breathing slowing gradually, regaining a natural measured rhythm.

Suddenly Alice opened her eyes as if the enormity of all that had happened had become apparent in one single awful moment. She pulled her dress up to cover her chest, obscuring the dark nipples with the haloes of red left by

Joanne's mouth. She sat up, moving slowly back, away from Joanne.

'Don't be afraid,' Joanne whispered soothingly, wiping the glistening drops of sweat from her lover's forehead. The force of arousal was still strong. She had taken Alice over the edge but her own desire was unquenched, burning intensely in the pit of her belly.

'I … I must go,' Alice whimpered, her voice trembling. Her eyes were dark with tears that threatened to fall down her face. Awkwardly she stood up, clutching at her dress tightly and pressing it against herself in a strange display of modesty.

'Don't worry, it was beautiful,' Joanne said, realising that she was rapidly losing control of the situation.

'No.' Alice looked around the room, seeking her bearings. 'I have to go.'

'Don't worry …' Joanne called. She watched Alice dashing clumsily out of the room, trying to put the dress back on and to regain some sense of composure.

She sat on the bed. It was not how she had imagined things ending, but then the experience had not been a disaster either. She closed her eyes and saw the image of Alice, thrashing wildly in the final throes of pleasure, her dark eyes blazing with an ecstatic joy. The image reminded her of her own arousal. She was keyed up, her belly tight with desire.

She lay back on the bed and parted her thighs; her fingers, still sticky with Alice's love juices, sought the mouth of her own sex. Urgently, not even waiting to pull her silk underwear off, she began to explore herself. The feel of her fingers entering her sex made her gasp with pleasure. It was a journey of rediscovery. She had explored herself many times as a young woman, but now she imagined that she was sharing the pleasure with Alice.

For a while Joanne knew she had been in complete

control. She had made Alice dance with the skilful play of her fingers. Alice, demure and innocent, had betrayed a raging passion that had climaxed in a screaming orgasm that had left her exhausted and confused. In some way the element of control made Joanne even more excited, driving her to press her fingers deeper into her vagina, searching for her secret place.

She finger-fucked herself furiously, driving herself forward with the skilful use of her fingers. The dreamy sensations from her pussy were too much and she cried out once, an aching cry that pierced the silence of the room. She climaxed and lost herself in the dreamy sensations from her pussy, still with the vivid image of Alice's eyes and lips firmly in her mind.

Martin dried himself casually, wiping away the cool, invigorating water. Frixos was hot and humid, and he woke every morning bathed in a sticky layer of sweat that made everything uncomfortable. The cold blasts of refreshing water had washed away the sweat, cleansing his body and clearing the darkness of mood that seemed to develop overnight.

Just as he finished pulling on his clothes he heard a sound coming from the bedroom. He padded barefoot across the light and airy bathroom, stepping casually on the damp towels that he had discarded, and pulled the door open an inch. Peering through the crack in the door he saw that a young woman had come into the bedroom. She was dressed in a thin white tennis skirt and matching white tee-shirt, casually carrying her tennis racket which she dropped on to the cane chair by the door.

She's got the wrong room, Martin thought. He made no move to enter the room, remaining rooted to his place by the bathroom door, staring in curiosity at the attractive young woman.

The young woman exhaled heavily. She was obviously tired out; her tee-shirt clung to her body, and dark patches of sweat were visible under her arms, down her back and between her breasts. She had long blonde hair tied in a single long ponytail. Her face was young but there was a sensuous quality to her, heightened by the way her full red lips were slightly parted. She wandered across the room over to the refrigerator, where there was a decanter with some glasses by the side. She poured herself an icy glass of water and then retraced her steps.

Martin watched her curiously. As she walked her breasts jutted tightly against the thin shirt, the dark patches of her nipples pressing visibly against the cotton garment. The short skirt, slit on one side to reveal a long elegant thigh, flapped gently over her round bottom.

She stopped by the dressing table and regarded herself in the mirror, putting the empty glass down. She bowed her head to one side and then pulled up her tee-shirt to wipe the sweat from her face. As she did so Martin caught a glimpse in the mirror of her firm round breasts, the tight nipples contrasting strongly with the pale white flesh of her chest. She wiped herself for a few seconds and let the tee-shirt drop again.

Martin felt his prick stirring, rising against the tightness of his shorts. The unexpected glimpse of the firm young breasts set his pulse racing.

The young woman turned away from the mirror and sat back on the bed, exhaling heavily once more. For a moment she seemed to be at a loss, sitting languidly on the bed, tiny beads of perspiration like jewels on her glowing pink skin. Eventually she bent down and pulled off her white sport shoes and ankle socks, letting them fall untidily on the floor. Next she removed the tee-shirt, pulling it high over her head so that her firm-fleshed breasts were naked in the bright sunlight streaming into the room.

She regarded herself in the mirror, sitting up straight, shoulders pulled back, chest pushed forward provocatively. The reflection appeared to displease her; she made a face at herself, twisting and turning, displaying herself from every angle.

Martin's prick was hard, pressing urgently against his clothes. From his vantage point he could see the woman's reflection completely, a vision of innocent loveliness captured in the long rectangle of the silver mirror. Her back was flawless, slender shoulders narrowing gently down to her petite waist. He was completely aroused by the view, excited by the look of her, and by the knowledge that she was unaware of his prying eyes.

She knelt on the bed, getting down on all fours and arching her back. She pouted seductively, blowing herself a kiss with her brilliant red lips and then laughing, her breasts swaying gently, the nipples tracing little circles in the air. Her short skirt was inadvertently pulled high around her waist, revealing her long supple thighs and a pair of snow-white panties pulled high into the cleft of her perfect backside.

From his place Martin could now see her pert backside and the beautifully proportioned pear-shaped breasts. She was close enough for him to discern a darker pattern in the panties, pulled tight between her arse-cheeks and soiled by a slightly damp patch at the entrance to her sex. Quickly he slid his clothes off, glad to let his raging hardness stand free.

She sat up on her knees and took her breasts in her hands, cupping them lovingly, covering the nipples coyly. She was caught up in a little game, posing seductively, enjoying the reflection of herself bathed in the golden rays of the sun. Her fingers began to play with the nipples, rubbing over the sore points of flesh, soothing and yet exciting herself. She pinched herself, forcing the tight points of flesh into erection, arousing herself at the same time.

She resumed her initial position, chest forward and shoulders back. But this time there was a difference. Her nipples were hard points of sensitive flesh, pressing forward invitingly. Her eyes were burning with a light that had been missing earlier, and her full lips were slightly parted. She lost the playful smile, and her expression was suddenly more serious, more intense.

She knelt down again, on all fours, unknowingly displaying her bottom to Martin. Very slowly, with cool deliberation, she slipped her hand down between her thighs. Watching her every movement in the mirror, she began to slide her palm up and down the inside of her right thigh, revelling in the feel of her muscular body. Her movements became concentrated higher up, just under the join in her thighs, where she pressed firmly with her fingers.

As she began to press her fingers inside her damp knickers, shuddering with pleasure when her fingers brushed against her cunny lips, Martin began to touch himself. He took his hardness in his hand, rubbing his fingers up and down the smooth pole of flesh. He imagined that the young woman's skilful fingers were touching him, caressing his firm hard prick.

She pulled her panties halfway down so that the thin garment was stretched between her thighs, almost as if it had fallen by accident. The pinkness of her sex was visible between the light patch of her pubic hair, the folds of flesh within seeming to glisten with the golden dewdrops of sex cream. Expertly she teased herself, playing her fingers tantalisingly across her pussy lips, threatening to enter but always withdrawing at the last instant. Her face was flushed, and her breathing had lost its rhythm as her eyes opened and closed with the dance of her fingers.

She cried out, gasping, when she pressed a finger deep inside herself, the force of penetration sending a ripple of pleasure echoing through her. Martin grasped his prick forcefully, rubbing himself, enjoying the vicarious pleasures on display. He closed his eyes momentarily, overcome with a shudder of pleasure, then looked again at the attractive young woman.

Her gasps of pleasure were clearly audible, a sighing accompaniment to the play of her fingers being forced into her sex. She had started with a single finger but was soon forcing three digits into her hungry sex, frigging herself with long slow strokes, bringing herself closer and closer to the moment of liberation. She switched hands quickly, managing to avoid losing the rhythm that had her pressing her backside in and out in rhythmic counterpoint to her fingers. She looked at the fingers of her free hand. The love juices were clearly visible: thick white drops of cream coated her fingers up to her knuckles. Without a thought she flicked out her tongue and lapped at her fingers, tasting herself, swallowing the drops of cream with evident relish.

Martin could hardly contain himself. He was using both hands to massage his prick, forcing tight fingers up and down the length of his hardness. His balls were aching, the pit of his belly was aflame with the swell of come ready for bursting. He was driven wild with desire by the glorious sight of the young woman masturbating herself with joyful abandon. All the time the pleasure was redoubled by the thought that he was invisible, that he was violating her space, invading her spiritually in some indefinable way.

'Oh Jesus ...' she moaned loudly, her voice trailing into delirium. Silver trails of perspiration were beaded all over her body, and her thighs glistened with drops of sweat mixed with the thicker emissions from her pussy. At last, on the edge of elation, she turned her head back, eyes half closed with joy. Her fingers sought their target eagerly, blindly. She screamed once, with pleasure, with pain. Two fingers of her free hand were pressed forcefully into the tight dark bud of her arsehole, three fingers of the other hand attacking the rosebud in her cunt.

Swept along into the valley of orgasm, her body alive with an unbelievable energy sweeping her into nothingness, she turned and looked Martin in the eye. For a moment their eyes made contact, but then they each lost control. She froze, her body locked into position, swept into the abyss. Martin gasped once, he closed his eyes and sighed, his prick forcing thick jets of come over his fingers and on to the floor.

Martin cleaned himself up quickly before emerging from the bathroom. The orgasm had been amazing, his prick seemed to have squirted thick wads of jelly all over the place. His face seemed rather tired, as if the intensity of the experience had robbed him of all energy. He padded barefoot across the room and collapsed on to the bed.

'Well,' said Liza mischievously, 'that was pretty good wasn't it?'

'Absolutely amazing,' Martin admitted, his voice slightly hoarse.

'Good. I told you everything would be OK. By the way, the manager was asking questions again.'

'You didn't tell him anything?' Martin turned over on his side and faced Liza in concern.

'Don't worry,' she said reassuringly. 'Andreas was just interested in your plane. He was asking how much you bought it for, the running costs, that sort of thing. I don't trust him. He knows you've got money and he keeps sniffing around.'

'I can handle that. That's no problem. Just don't tell him anything else.'

'I told you,' Liza repeated, 'I didn't tell him anything.'

* * *

15

Alice watched the motorboat draw up to the ferry, the air thick with the shouts of the Greek sailors and the roar of the outboard motor. She looked on passively, too tired to feel any excitement. She had been unable to sleep the night before, tortured by the traumatic memory of what Joanne had done to her. It was not something that she had ever imagined possible. Not with another woman, and especially not with Joanne, whom she had always admired. Working for her had been as much a pleasure as anything else. She liked her, certainly considered her a friend, but that had been the full extent of her feelings.

But at the time, drawn insidiously by the simple sequence of events, she had felt powerless to resist. Every touch of Joanne's hand or mouth had seemed to inflame her, passing jolts of electricity through her body, until she had been completely mesmerised. She hadn't wanted it to happen, but once it had started she had let it go, surrendering herself completely.

She listened to the motor launch banging gently against the side of the ferry, the metallic bang echoing noisily through the hull of the old ship in contrast to the gentle lapping of the water against the bow. The steps down from the ferry to the launch looked precarious; the old wooden slats were fit to collapse and the lower steps were already wet and slippery.

'I hadn't planned on going swimming this early,' Joanne joked lightly, pointing to her black high heels and breaking the nervous silence that the two of them had shared from the moment they had left the hotel.

'I'll go first if you like,' Alice offered, edging forwards to the first step. She wasn't sure how to handle herself any more; she had lost the confidence that she had always displayed towards Joanne. The memory of all that had happened was still far too strong. Every time she closed her eyes she could feel Joanne's lips on hers, or remember the feel of Joanne's fingers exploring the soft folds of her pussy. The memories were strong and embarrassing and Alice felt guilty and afraid. But worst of all was the memory of the pleasure; the golden moment when she had climaxed had been like no other she had ever experienced.

'No, it's all right.' Joanne stepped forward and took Alice gently by the elbow. They looked at each other for the first time since they had made love. Their eyes met and gradually they smiled. It was as if an invisible spark had jumped from one body to the next, and the nervousness dissipated at once.

Joanne stepped down towards the launch, her heels clacking loudly against the old steps, adding to the cacophony that filled the morning air. A uniformed sailor helped her take the last step on to the launch, she jumped on to the deck and the boat rocked gently beneath her. She glanced up and saw Alice following, inching her way slowly from step to step.

When the half dozen passengers were aboard the launch, it cast off and headed noisily away from the old ferry which creaked its farewell. The launch jumped bumpily through the undulating water, a white spray rising up and falling away behind them.

Frixos was a small volcanic island formed around a single round bay. In the fine haze the geology of the island was clear to see, with the dark volcanic rock rising high in the distance in strange geometric formations. The harbour village was spread before them like an off-white cloud low on the horizon, a small number of fishing boats a reminder of the thriving harbour it had once been. The sun was still low in the clear sky, casting long shadows in the frozen rivers of lava visible on the highest points of land.

As the launch drew closer it was possible to make out individual houses above the village, fine white structures

17

dotted amongst the grey-black of the rocks. Far to the left of the village was Paradise Bay, the only hotel on the island, built around the sandy beach of a small inlet.

Alice turned and found Joanne looking at her. She smiled nervously and turned away, feeling exhilarated and afraid. Turning back to look at the ferry disappearing over the horizon, barely able to see the mainland in the distance, she knew that things would never be the same again. Things were going to change for ever, and she felt powerless to resist, completely mesmerised by a wordless bittersweet joy she didn't understand.

two

The sun was still low in the sky, a nebulous golden jewel shimmering like a mirage over the distant Aegean horizon, casting seeds of light that danced on the rippling surface of the sea. From his seat by the hotel pool, Martin had earlier watched the tiny fishing boats edge out across the bay and out into the wider sea, casting their tiny nets into the green-blue waters.

He liked being by the pool. It gave him a chance to look around, to watch everything and everyone. He wore dark mirrored glasses that gave nothing away, reflecting instead two pointed shafts of light, like a pair of lasers scanning the horizon. From his place he could watch the young women sunning themselves, their beautiful bodies almost naked, offering irresistible displays of their firm tanned flesh. He had watched a young married couple playing in the water, laughing joyfully and splashing noisily at each other, the woman emerging from the water like Aphrodite, her body glistening in the light, drops of water beaded over her like jewels.

All morning he had been in torment, aroused continually by the glorious bodies on display. Earlier one of the guests, a woman in her thirties, had gone for a swim. She wore a single-piece swimsuit made from a glossy material that clung tightly to her body. Her breasts were well covered, but the fullness of the shape and the largeness of her nipples were moulded into the material. As soon as he saw her Martin had become hard. She walked with poise and dignity; there was a seriousness about her, something a little stern, that he found immensely attractive. She walked to the edge of the pool, her firm breasts jigging lightly with every step, then stopped. For a moment she looked into the water with dark intense eyes, then she dived in gracefully, hardly raising a ripple on the silvery surface.

Martin had followed her with his eyes, tracing the shimmering vision as she swam under the water halfway across the pool. She resurfaced for a second, drawing a fast breath, then continued below the surface. She swam several lengths of the pool, always swimming under water, propelling herself with deft kicks of her long shapely legs. At last she stopped and sat in the water until she regained her breath, then pulled herself out. The water splashed from her body, leaving her dark skin glistening in the sunlight. The water had permeated the material of the swimsuit and it had become semitransparent, like an almost invisible second skin.

The woman became aware of her near-nakedness at once and looked round furtively, checking to see if she had been noticed. Martin had turned away at the right moment, avoiding her searching gaze. The poolside had been relatively empty. Coolly she headed slowly back to her room, all the time keeping her eyes lowered. Martin was fascinated. The dark mound of her pussy hair was clearly visible, indicating the entrance to her bulging and generous sex. The dark aureoles of her breasts, as big and as dark as ripe black cherries, had puckered from the shock of the cold water. As she disappeared from view he was able to admire the fullness of her backside. The two round cheeks were almost bare and moved together seductively as she walked.

Martin had been hard all the time he had watched her, excited by the curves of her body and by the perfection of her face. He had wanted to take his prick in his hand, to close his eyes and express his admiration for her, to imagine her playing up and down his prick with her full generous lips. But, lying in the sunlight, out in the open, he had been unable to, and concealed the bulge in his shorts with a casually draped towel. The torment had been delicious, part of the strange game that he played.

Martin's thoughts were suddenly interrupted. He turned to find Andreas Karaplis, the hotel manager, silhouetted beside him, his tall thin frame blocking out the sun.

'May I join you?' Andreas asked, his voice betraying only the faintest hint of an accent.

'Sure,' Martin said politely, sitting back up in his seat. He smiled superficially, the dark glasses concealing his irritation at being disturbed.

'A drink?' Andreas asked, waving a waiter over at once.

'A scotch, thank you, plenty of ice.'

'A scotch and an ouzo,' Andreas ordered, then turned back to Martin with a relaxed and friendly smile.

'This is a lovely place,' Martin murmured, feeling obliged to make at least some effort at conversation. All the time he scanned the poolside, on the alert in case some new woman should come into view.

'Thank you. Do you know Amanda Trevelyan?'

'The travel writer?'

'Travel writer and television star,' Andreas corrected with a short laugh. 'She's staying with us at the moment, you might meet her some time. Well, Amanda told me that it has taken thirty years of tourist development to achieve Paradise Bay. Can you imagine that? Thirty years of mistakes before we got it right!'

'I suppose she knows what she's talking about,' Martin said sourly, taking his drink from the waiter with scarcely a glance at the man.

'Oh she does,' Andreas continued blithely, ignoring the sullen remark. 'You said yourself that this is a lovely place. Have you explored the island yet?'

'No, not really.' Martin imagined that Andreas was doing his duty and playing the part of hospitable host, and he hoped that the single drink would be enough hospitality for the day.

'Oh you should,' Andreas urged enthusiastically. 'There is so much here for the discerning visitor. Up in the hills there are some very interesting archaeological sites, very interesting. There is a ruined temple to Diana. The frescoes there are unique, absolutely unique. And of course the village has a lovely atmosphere, unspoilt.'

'Yes, I'm sure we'll get to visit there soon.' Martin's rising irritation was plain. He finished his drink and turned away sharply, facing the pool once more.

'I can see you are tired,' Andreas said, preferring to ignore the discourtesy. 'Perhaps you have come here for a long rest?'

'Yes, that's right, a long rest. And some peace and quiet,' Martin said pointedly.

Andreas started to make another remark but was interrupted by the arrival of Liza. Martin's smile suddenly returned in relief.

'Hello again.' Andreas stood up, offering his seat to Liza. 'Would you like a drink?'

'No, we've got to … er … go somewhere,' Martin said coldly, cutting off Liza's intended reply with a sharp glance.

'Yes, that's right,' Liza apologised. 'Another time perhaps.'

'Yes, definitely.' Andreas brightened at the prospect. 'One evening perhaps, I could show you round the old village.'

'Yes, yes,' Martin repeated impatiently.

He stood up and took Liza by the arm, ignoring the fleeting look of anger on Andreas's dark face. He led her away quickly past the poolside bar and towards the room, aware that Andreas was watching them go, his anger replaced with an unconcealed look of desperation.

'Well?' Martin asked expectantly as soon as he and Liza entered his room.

'I want you to know this wasn't easy,' Liza told him. She opened her bag and took out a pair of black silky panties.

Martin took them from her excitedly. For a second he fingered the smooth glossy garment, then brought it up to his face, breathing the pungent bouquet as if it were the most heavenly perfume. He walked across the room and sat back on the bed, not bothering to conceal the growing bulge in his shorts.

'I had to sneak into the staff quarters,' Liza added. 'I had to find the maid's room and then search through her things. God, that would have been hard to explain away.'

'But no one saw you.' Martin smiled, clutching the soiled garment close to his skin, a dreamy look in his light brown eyes. The room was full of blazing sunlight, focused in the mirror on the wall and then cast back in all directions.

'What did Andreas want?'

'Just being a pain in the butt.'

'Let me get changed,' Liza said, unbuttoning her white cotton shirt. It was hot, and the garment had started to stick to her soft smooth skin.

'Change in the bathroom,' Martin suggested, looking Liza directly in the eye.

'No, I'll change here,' she replied coolly, continuing to undo her buttons.

23

'All right, change here, but turn around,' he compromised.

Liza smiled. She knew Martin's ways. He loved to look at women, and she knew that for him there could be nothing more erotic than catching a secret glimpse of a beautiful woman undressing. But it had to be right; it was the essence of the moment that charged it with such erotic power. A fleeting glance, an unguarded moment: that was the aphrodisiac that made it so good for him.

She turned round and unbuttoned her shirt, knowing that he was spying her reflection in the mirror, feasting his eyes on her. It was strange; she knew that if she turned around and stripped off in front of him it would have little effect compared to stripping off in secret, trying to shield herself from his burning eyes.

She unbuttoned the shirt but did not remove it fully, letting it hang loosely, her breasts only partially covered. She unclipped her simple loose skirt and it fell to the floor around her ankles. When she stooped down to pick it up her pear-shaped breasts were fully revealed. For a second she caught his eyes in the mirror, watching her greedily, drinking in every image. She smiled at him mischievously, knowing that the look would disturb him, unsettling him in a way she didn't fully understand yet.

Martin smiled back nervously, doubt clouding his eyes momentarily. His hand was rubbing up and down the bulge in his shorts, enjoying the feel of his hardness, working himself up to a greater level of arousal.

In a moment she had slipped off her panties and turned to face him, the white shirt hanging loosely on her shoulders. She was naked apart from the shirt and as she moved, the sunlight caught the shifting garment, revealing her firm breasts and smooth belly.

She sat on the bed beside him, careful not to touch him, but close enough so that he could feel the warmth of her body and breathe the faint scent that she was wearing 'Lie back, right back, that's it,' she directed, pressing his shoulder down with the very tips of her fingers.

Martin lay flat on his back, holding the stolen panties close to his face like a powerful talisman. His prick was still hard, and the silver drops of fluid dripping from the glans had formed a damp patch in his shorts. She had calculated that the way her shirt shifted as she moved, as if blown by a non-existent breeze, would add to his excitement. He closed his eyes and lay back passively, stretched out completely on the bed.

Liza carefully edged his shorts down, releasing his stiff shaft of flesh. In an instant he was naked, his pale body bathed in the golden light playing through the room. His long hard prick looked delicious, the hard smooth flesh crying a single tear of silvery fluid. Her first instinct was to bend down and take the hardness deep into her soft receptive mouth, to taste the silver fluid on her tongue, to explore the sensitive dome with her lips.

'The maid enters the room,' she began, her voice soft and soothing. 'She is wearing her uniform. Frilly white cap. Black silk shirt with a white collar. Short black skirt with a slit. Black seamed stockings. Black high heels. The uniform is smooth and glossy in the light. It looks like it's made of rubber or PVC.'

She waited for a moment, Martin had closed his eyes, she wanted him to picture the scene in his mind. She knew the image she wanted to project; she wanted him to see the maid in a tight black second skin, with an innocent angelic face and the body of a goddess.

'She doesn't see you, you are in the room next door,' she continued softly. As she spoke Martin's eyes were closed, but she could gauge the effect of her words by the way he shifted around on the bed. It was obvious that he was dying to take his thick hard cock in his hands. It twitched and flexed instinctively, the silvery fluid smeared already on to his belly.

'I've just come out of the shower,' Martin suggested eagerly, wanting to hurry the story along.

Liza complied. 'Your body is still wet,' she said. 'The water is dripping down your naked body. You go to the door to see what the noise is. You look out and see the maid. She is making the bed, she is on her knees at the foot of the bed. Her skirt is very short, you can see her long thighs, see the tops of the stockings, the dark suspenders.'

'I can see the suspenders are made of black rubber, pressing into her skin,' Martin added hoarsely, his hand moving towards his prick, touching it gently with his fingers but not taking it in his hand fully.

Liza wanted his obvious torment to grow so that the vivid picture in his mind, painted by her soft whispered voice would begin to drive him mad with desire. She moved his hand away from his prick gently, and then continued the story. 'I want you to see it all, the way the dark glossy uniform clings to the fullness of her body, the way that she moves, totally unaware that she is being watched by you. She bends down lower, humming a tune to herself. Her black panties are visible now, tightly pressed into the folds of her cunt, the dark hair peeking through.'

Without pausing Liza took the dark panties that he still held tightly. She brushed the knickers across his face for the last time. His body stiffened all over as soon as she took hold of his prick, using the dark silky panties to touch him where he was most sensitive.

'You walk into the room, she doesn't hear you. She spots that the bin by the desk has been knocked over. She crawls along the floor. You can see the skirt riding higher. The black panties are deep in her cunt. Your prick is hard.' She worked her hand up and down his hardness, wearing

26

the panties over her hand like a glove. The feel of his prick under her fingers made her hot with desire. The story was affecting her as well as him.

'Her panties slip down . . .' Martin started to say, but his voice trailed off into a sigh of pleasure, jerking his pelvis higher to meet the downward stroke of Liza's fingers.

'The maid turns around and sees you,' she paused momentarily, knowing that Martin's fantasy and her story would diverge from here on. 'She looks at your hard prick, at the water dripping down your naked skin. You can see that her blouse is low cut, she has lovely dark tits.'

'No, I'm still in the bathroom...' Martin moaned, his face twisting with confusion.

Liza knew that the story was going wrong for him, as if his script had been replaced by another. From the way he caught his breath she was certain that the feel of her fingers must have been ecstatic. She lowered her voice a notch, bending down to whisper breathily in his ear. 'She smiles. You take her hand and put it on your prick. She smiles, she plays her hand up and down your prick. You move to the bed. She takes your cock into her mouth. She is moving up and down your cock with her mouth.' She was working her hand up and down rapidly, driving his prick harder and harder. From the pained expression on his face it was clear that he was nearing the end.

'She sits on me . . . I . . .'

'Yes. She sits on your prick,' she improvised, working his words into her fantasy. 'Her cunt is warm and inviting, it feels like heaven.'

'No . . .' Martin gasped furiously, opening his eyes, a look of confusion etched on his face.

Liza saw that he was fighting back, trying to twist the story his way once more. She leaned forward quickly, knowing that she had little time. Urgently she slid her hand under his balls, searching with her fingers the space between his muscular buttocks.

'She's sitting on my face ... Pissing on me ... Pissing on me ...' Martin whispered, wearing an expression of distant surprise, as if his fantasy had turned out strangely without his intervention.

Liza forced her middle finger up against his tight arsehole. In other circumstances she was certain that he would have resisted, but now he moved down, parting his thighs a little, so that her finger passed some way into his bumhole. He closed his eyes at once, fell back on to the bed, parting his thighs even more. 'She is riding up and down your prick,' she persisted, wanking him in the arsehole with one hand and his prick with the other. 'You are fucking her. She is fucking you. Up and down your prick. It's heaven. She is crying out with pleasure. Pleasure that you are giving to her. Pleasure that you feel as well.'

Martin cried out once, his body stiffened and then relaxed. Thick wads of creamy spunk jetted out on to his belly; wave after wave of unbridled joy convulsed his sweating body. At the moment of release Liza had ensured that the image in his mind had been of the maid sitting over his lap, with him forcing his hard prick deep into her wet pussy.

The restaurant had been almost full when Joanne arrived. She glanced around the tables, wondering whether Alice was early. The restaurant was on a high terrace at the back of the main hotel complex, the beach stretching out far below, the golden sands forming an amber crescent around the calm waters of the bay. It was the bay that had given its name to the hotel; the natural beauty of the inlet had been untouched by all the development around it.

Joanne stood and watched the scene below: the gentle rise and fall of the water along the sand, the white spray

28

foaming like champagne. The very naturalness of the landscape was easy on the eyes, as if the hand of man had yet to defile the gentle contours of land and water. The restaurant was cooled by a gentle breeze that blew up from the shore, the air tangy with the taste of the sea.

It had been a busy morning in an unhurried sort of way. The ostensible reason for visiting Paradise Bay had been to make a discreet check on the hotel. Check-in had been very relaxed, the practised informality of it all a testament to the professionalism of the staff. Joanne had been a little tense, afraid that through some oversight she would be recognised. It was not so much that recognition would destroy any chance of making a real inspection, but that it would destroy the very privacy that she sought so desperately with Alice.

The hotel manager, Philip's partner, had introduced himself briefly. Joanne had been impressed by his angular good looks and by his genuinely pleasant manner. It would have been so natural to find Andreas condescending and his easy charm a facile show put on for the guests, but there had been none of that. When he smiled it was obvious that the smile was real, and the light in his dark eyes could not be faked.

In keeping with the natural low-key surroundings the hotel had been constructed around the landscape. The main part of the hotel complex, housing the pools, the restaurants and the main bar, was constructed on a promontory to one side of the bay; the steps leading down to the beach were cut straight into the hard volcanic rock. The rooms themselves were in two smaller buildings, spurred off from the main complex and set in lush vegetation.

The rooms were spacious, the sun streaming in through the large windows and door opening out on to a small balcony. Joanne had stayed in more extravagant hotels, where the rooms were furnished with an eye to luxury,

29

and a panache that only the more exclusive interior designers could supply. But here the rooms were decorated with a simplicity and sparseness that was entirely fitting.

Alice's room was next door, and they had agreed to meet in the bar after freshening up. They had spent the morning exploring the hotel, visiting each of the two pools in turn, spending a little time drinking in the bar. At first they were interested purely in the geography of the complex, finding their way from place to place. As the morning wore on they became aware of the less obvious things: the general tidiness of the place, the way the staff conducted themselves. In every case Joanne had found nothing to fault, nothing at all. The standards of Paradise Bay were the highest that could be expected.

She sat at a table by the edge of the terrace with an unimpeded view of the beach below. She ordered a glass of mineral water and waited patiently for Alice. Their relationship was still uncertain, and during the morning their conversation had been light and inconsequential, carefully skirting around their previous encounter. They had even avoided looking at each other too closely, afraid of the emotional fall-out that could result if their eyes met and locked.

Alice arrived a few minutes later, dressed in a simple loose blouse and matching skirt.

'I was beginning to wonder whether you were going to have lunch at all,' Joanne laughed, relieved that Alice had finally appeared. She had begun to wonder whether Alice was going to stay in her room, avoiding lunch completely, knowing that the small talk could not last forever.

'I'm sorry.' Alice smiled, her full red lips drawn to reveal fine white teeth. 'I couldn't remember what time we said we'd meet.'

'It's OK,' Joanne said, reaching out and taking Alice's hands in her own. 'It's just that I'm starving! What would you like to eat?'

'I'm not sure,' Alice shrugged. 'Whatever you want. You choose.'

'Shall we have some fish? It's caught locally so it's guaranteed to be fresh.'

'If you want,' Alice smiled.

Joanne ordered for both of them, privately wondering at the wider significance of Alice's inconsequential acquiescence in the matter. She shook the thought from her head, afraid to read too much into nothing. 'Well,' she asked, deciding to remain on a neutral topic, 'what do you think of Paradise Bay?'

'I think it's great,' Alice said, her dark eyes glittering girlish delight. 'Everyone's so friendly, and the hotel is brilliant. I don't think Philip's got a lot to be worried about.'

'I'm inclined to agree,' Joanne admitted. 'I haven't seen anyone put a foot wrong so far. But still, let's see how things go over the next few days, maybe the effect will wear off.'

'How come you've never been here before? I would have thought that you and Philip would have been regular visitors here. I would be jetting out here every weekend...' Alice stopped in mid-sentence, glancing across to the next table where a young couple were being shown to their seats by a waiter.

Joanne looked across to the table, smiling politely to the attractive young blonde and her companion. The woman was striking in her good looks, her long blonde hair catching the golden rays of the sun; but the man looked dour, his pale face turned down in a sombre frown. The woman returned Joanne's smile but the man simply looked away, his cold stare directed out across the sea in a deliberately unfriendly gesture.

'It's OK.' Joanne turned back to Alice. 'They won't hear

31

us. Philip owns about sixty per cent of Paradise Bay, it was one of his wild schemes to diversify a few years ago. My husband, being the sort of man who likes to think he works with cool logic, put his money into it on impulse.' She laughed curtly. 'He met Andreas in Copenhagen, at the airport bar of all places. They got chatting and before their flights departed had already sketched out the deal.'

'But it looks like it's all worked out OK.'

The food arrived, freshly cooked red mullet with a simple Greek salad, accompanied with a fine chilled white wine. Joanne paused while the waiter served, then continued easily. 'Well, the hotel looks fine, I'll grant you that. But it's never made the sort of return that it promised to.'

'If it's always this full then I can't see why.'

'The accounts look OK, but the money just hasn't come in. Don't get me wrong, Philip hasn't lost a penny. He was always smart about that sort of thing, even when acting on instinct. But on paper Paradise Bay should have made him an awful lot of profit.'

'But why haven't you ever visited?' Alice repeated, picking gingerly at the fish.

'At the time he made this deal I was busy setting up my studio. It was an exciting time for me, and I'm afraid that Philip and his work took a sort of back seat for a while.'

'I'm sure Philip didn't mind,' Alice said, taking a sip of the wine.

Joanne glanced round and saw the man at the table opposite staring, his eyes boring directly into her. Their eyes met for only an instant and then he turned away, a look of barely concealed disdain on his stern face, his thin lips pressed together disapprovingly. As she turned back the woman next to him smiled to her, a friendly open smile in contrast to his cold stare. Joanne smiled back, then

32

turned to her food.

It looked as if the rest of the meal would pass in silence, the fund of small talk exhausted for the moment. Joanne noticed that the man opposite kept looking at Alice, his sharp brown eyes on her all the time, scrutinising her constantly, searching greedily up and down her body. Alice noticed him too. She kept turning away, but again and again she caught his eye, and always he glanced away with a sneer. His beautiful companion, her long hair swept by the breeze, kept smiling back at her reassuringly, as if counteracting the icy influence of her partner.

'Ignore him. Every time you look at him he gets a kick,' Joanne finally broke the silence.

Alice looked up at her. 'He keeps looking at me all the time,' she complained. 'It makes me feel uncomfortable. There's something about that man that I don't like.'

'Of course he's looking at you,' Joanne told her. 'You're a fantastic looking young woman. He's looking at you, his girlfriend's looking at you, the waiters are looking at you. I'm looking at you.'

'That's different,' Alice whispered, blushing faintly.

The atmosphere lightened only when the strange couple at the next table departed. The sun was at its zenith and the breeze had stilled; the air hung heavily, damp with the taste of the sea. The restaurant emptied suddenly, and the motionless air and the sun directly overhead signalled the onset of an inescapably languid mood.

Joanne and Alice walked arm in arm through the hotel, sharing a close and unintentional silence, wrapped up in the same feeling of easy contentment. They passed Andreas in the lobby, looking slightly tired and agitated, he almost walked right past them, but at the last moment he snapped back to life. He paused for a moment to exchange a few pleasant words, asking about the meal and their plans for the day. He looked tired, the first few beads of sweat gathered under his hairline. He smiled amiably, but his eyes seemed to be looking into the distance, his mind elsewhere.

'You'd think he'd be used to the heat,' Alice remarked as they stepped out from the lobby into the searing heat.

'I think he probably is,' Joanne said, steering Alice towards the small whitewashed complex of hotel rooms. 'That's plain exhaustion, nothing to do with the heat. I'd recognise that look anywhere.'

Joanne stepped into her room, leaving the door open behind her. Alice stood by the open door for a moment, not knowing what to do. She had not been asked in, there had not even been an inviting smile. But Joanne had deliberately left the door open. Alice walked hesitantly into the room, closing the door behind her. She stood shyly by the door, hardly daring to walk fully into the room. Her eyes were downcast, hands clasped together in front of her. It was so difficult to know what to do.

Joanne stopped and turned back. She smiled and walked up to Alice, taking her by the hands and pulling her gently into the centre of the room. Alice gradually lifted her gaze, till she faced Joanne fully.

She stood passively for a moment, arms by her side, until Joanne stretched forward an inch and pursed her lips. For a fraction of a moment the soft petals of their lips touched. Alice could breathe the soft scent of Joanne's skin, taste her lips and mouth. The time for words had passed.

She looked at Joanne with dark wide eyes, her heart pounding and breath racing. The simplest touch of flesh on flesh had been enough to melt her, to dissolve any fears and misgivings. She closed her eyes to give herself fully to the sensation, knowing that what was to follow could only be beautiful, even if it was an intense and painful kind of beauty. Her heart jumped, and she opened her mouth to Joanne's searching tongue, feeling the breath sucked out of her. She twisted her head, giving herself completely to the long passionate embrace that fuelled the fire starting to burn deep inside her.

Joanne explored Alice's mouth, using her tongue and lips to the full. With her hands she began to undress herself, unbuttoning her simple dress and letting it fall off her shoulders into an untidy bundle by the bed. She stepped back, letting the last kiss linger for an instant extra before pulling away.

She was dressed only in black silk bra and matching panties, the dark red nipples made darker by the thin filmy garment. Her breasts were small perfect fruits, the upturned nipples massive in proportion, already erect against the bra that offered them up so temptingly. Her black knickers were almost opaque, but even so the hair about her pussy mound was hardly visible, the wispy blonde hairs obscured by the shiny blackness of the silk.

'Now you can touch me,' she whispered, unclipping her bra and letting it drop. The sunlight cast shades of light and dark against her chest, her breasts casting shadows against the smoothness of her skin.

Alice stepped forward awkwardly, unable to keep her eyes off Joanne's lovely nipples. The way that Joanne had spoken, the strange choice of words, the husky whisper, had stirred something deep inside her, as if a hidden switch had been thrown and a dim light cast on a strange new world. She took Joanne's waist in her hands, pressing her fingers into the soft warm flesh, pulling the two of them closer. She kissed her on the neck, planting sensitive lips on the subtly perfumed skin, working her way down slowly. It was a journey of exploration, discovering the feel of a woman's body under her lips. The two of them slipped on to the bed together, wrapped in each other's arms.

Alice's mind spun, overwhelmed by the wealth of sensations. She planted soft fleeting kisses down Joanne's neck, down between the tight firm breasts, marking the smooth skin with a livid smear of scarlet lipstick, a map of her hesitant journey. Her eyes marvelled at the flawless skin, tanned with a golden sheen that seemed to radiate in the brittle sunlight. She took Joanne's breasts in her hands, squeezing the firm flesh with her fingers, palming them tenderly. The very tips of the nipples were tinged with a delicate pink flush, contrasting with the darker-skinned aureoles.

She planted a final kiss between the breasts, feeling the lovely globes on either side of her face, then took one of the nipples in her mouth. The feel of the erect teat in her mouth was delightful, a hard little button between her lips and teeth.

Joanne sighed, closed her eyes, cradling Alice's head in her hands. The dampness between her thighs increased, reflecting a growing arousal, an excitement that became stronger with every moment that passed.

Alice opened her mouth wide, drawing in as much of Joanne's breast as she could, sucking the nipple into the back of her throat. Hungrily she kept up the attack, creating eddying pulses of bliss when she used her tongue to soothe the roused nipples. While she devoured one breast with her mouth she used her fingers to touch and explore the other, flicking her thumb roughly over the cherrybud to excite it to attention.

'Inside me now, touch me there,' Joanne gasped, parting her thighs.

Alice pressed her palm directly between Joanne's thighs, palming the hot damp patch where Joanne's honey had begun to flow. She moved her hand back and forth, eager to explore the forbidden territory. She traced a finger round from the valley between the buttocks to the entrance to the sex, her eyes closed, seeing the journey in her mind's eye.

Joanne lifted herself, raising her backside so that Alice could slide the wet panties off completely. In seconds she fell back down, shivering with ecstatic pleasure when Alice's gentle fingertips brushed the lips to her pussy. She opened herself, using her fingers to part her pussy lips damp with oozing sex cream.

Alice moved down. She wanted to look, to see fully Joanne's nakedness. The pink cunt flesh glistened, jewels of pussy cream coating the quivering walls of sensitive tissue. She slid her middle finger into the parting, pressing gingerly deep into the sex. She smiled when she saw Joanne swoon with pleasure, closing her eyes, an involuntary look of delight twisting her lips into a half-smile. She slid her finger back and forth, then slipped a second finger into the wet hole, increasing the speed of the motion.

Soon Joanne was writhing, twisting her head from side to side, jerking her hips up to meet the downward stroke of Alice's hand. She was breathing fitfully, her face twisted by fleeting expressions of ecstasy, her mouth opening and closing wordlessly. The pressure went up a notch when Alice began to use her mouth again, returning once more to the divinely erect nipples.

Alice could feel the pleasure she was giving reflected back, aware of the stickiness between her own thighs, her clothes constricting her like a snake. She wanted to free herself, to be naked beside Joanne, to feel once more Joanne's searching tongue on her breasts. But she put these thoughts away, concentrating instead on Joanne's exquisitely beautiful body. She wanted to make her scream with pleasure, to explode into a rapturous orgasm.

'I'm going to come in your mouth,' Joanne said

hoarsely, hardly finding the strength to utter the words. She sat up, pushing Alice flat on to the bed with her hands, kissing her on the mouth at the same time. Moving quickly she straddled her, sitting directly over Alice's face.

Alice stared open-mouthed. The wispy blonde hairs around the open sex were dappled with little drops of cunt cream. She flicked out her tongue, tasting Joanne's essence for the first time. In response Joanne sat lower, forcing her sex directly over Alice's eager mouth.

Instinctively Alice used all of her mouth, the lips, tongue and teeth to mouth-fuck Joanne in the cunt.

Joanne gasped. Alice had speared her tongue forward, in a single movement flicking directly to the centre of her rosebud. She pressed down lower, prising herself open with her fingers, riding up and down with the motion of Alice's mouth.

Alice sucked deeper, taking Joanne's cream into her mouth and swallowing it as if it were sweet honey, increasing her own arousal. Her pussy was wet, driven by an aching want deep in her belly, her whole body aflame with desire.

Joanne climaxed and her body was seized by a powerful shudder; she froze like a marble statue caught in the midday sun.

Alice cried out at the same instant, burying her head deep between Joanne's thighs. The climax made her head spin and her heart beat wildly. There was a timeless blur, then she found herself lying beside Joanne, her body bathed in sweat, tingling with the afterburn of their passionate lovemaking.

'Good girl . . .' Joanne told her, pulling her close and kissing her softly on the lips. The simple words, spoken tenderly, made her ripple with pleasure. She realised that she had taken Joanne to the limit, that she had tasted Joanne's secret place, that her mouth was still perfumed by Joanne's creamy elixir. The feeling of wrongness was pushed back below the surface, buried by the knowledge that she had served Joanne so well.

Andreas stood at the balustrade at the end of the verandah. From there he had a clear view of most of Frixos, from the gentle curve of the beach right around to the village on the other side. In the mid-afternoon glare, standing alone in the blistering heat, he felt as if he were the only person alive on the island. The listlessness that fell over the island with the afternoon heat had sent everyone scurrying for shelter and for sleep. That was the only respite from the oppressive atmosphere, the still air immoveable, untouched even by the faint breezes carried by the calm sea.

He felt trapped, caught by the dead weight of the air and the merciless beat of the sun. The time for laughter had gone. There was only so much that he could do to charm his way out of the hole he had so skilfully dug for himself.

Resolved to failure, but mindful of the desperate nature of the situation, he turned and made his way through the hotel, towards the guest rooms.

Martin had been on the border between sleep and wakefulness, drifting in and out of consciousness at random. His eyes were closed, his face bathed in a bright orange glow, beads of sweat forming on his face. The steady rhythm of Liza's breath was matched by the timeless hiss of the sea lapping at the distant shore. This was a special kind of silence, the steady rhythm of breath and ocean, the backdrop to so many wordless dreams.

He had been disturbed at some point. He had heard distant voices, siren songs carried with the sound of water and sand. The sound rose and fell in intensity, a different and discordant rhythm that had pulled him almost to wakefulness. He had listened, catching the song, recognising the distant cries of pleasure that floated through the air. The siren song had ended suddenly with a shattering cry, a strangled gasp of ethereal pleasure, an orgasmic sigh, and then the sea, sand and Liza's breath.

A sudden knock at the door forced Martin awake, dispelling the calm peace with which he had lain. Quickly he pulled on a pair of bermuda shorts and staggered to the door with rising anger.

'I'm sorry to disturb you, but I must speak with you,' Andreas said quietly, a rare sense of urgency making a nonsense of his apologetic words.

'Now? Can't it wait?' Martin said brusquely.

'I'm sorry, but this will all be in your interest, I assure you. It won't take long, we can work out any arrangements later.'

'Five minutes.' Martin opened the door and Andreas slipped quietly into the room.

He took a few faltering steps then stopped. Liza was lying naked on the bed, her body bathed in bands of light and dark. She was sleeping on her stomach, her pert round backside offered invitingly, one knee pulled up slightly, exposing a rear view of her sex.

'Do you want to cover...' Andreas started to say, turning to one side. He was excited by the unexpected view. Liza's backside was eminently fuckable in the prone position in which she slept. But he didn't want to offend Martin, and stood away, embarrassed by the awkward circumstances.

'What do you want?' Martin asked. He went and sat on the bed beside Liza, but made no move to cover her up.

'I won't waste your time or mine,' Andreas began. He turned to face Martin, but his eyes kept straying to Liza's nude body. 'I think that you are a shrewd man, you have money, you own your own jet. This island has yet to be developed properly. Paradise Bay is the one and only development here. But there is a great potential for expansion here. There is the airfield, the ferries to the mainland and other islands. Our island has many beaches, antiquities . . .'

'Yes,' Martin interrupted, 'but what is your point?' He stroked Liza's thigh with his palm, stroking the warm flesh from the knee up to her arse-cheeks. He broke into a sickly sneer, revealing sharp uneven teeth. His face looked like a pale mask.

Andreas paused. He couldn't help himself; his blood was racing, his heart pounding. What had promised to be a tricky situation had become impossible. His prick was hardening, Liza's nakedness and the sexual way that Martin was handling her, were distracting. 'The point is,' he said, 'that I can offer you a chance to invest in Frixos. Not just any chance, but the chance to get in on the ground floor, if you'll pardon the expression.'

'Not interested,' Martin said flatly. 'Why should I invest in a nowhere place like this?'

'Because it can make you a lot of money. There can be no other reason, none of any value anyway. Look it's simple. I have bought many of the best plots of land on the island, absolutely the best. Some of the land I have makes Paradise Bay look like ... like ... I have bought the land, I have a brother who works for the government and can arrange for all development licences and planning permission. We can't lose.'

'If you can't lose, why ask me?' Martin was now gently caressing Liza's backside, massaging her pert round buttocks with his fingers. All the time he watched Andreas, aware that his eyes were straying all over the sleeping beauty.

'I ask you because I have a temporary problem,' Andreas laughed nervously. 'You could say it's a cashflow problem. I have bought the choicest plots of land, but not all of it is paid off yet. We can become partners, that's how I built this place. I have a partner in London, he gets a share of the profits of this hotel and for what? I do all the running of the hotel, I do all the work, and we share the profits. But I'm not complaining, don't get me wrong. That's the way business works. I offer you the same deal.'

'Then why don't you ask your partner in London to help you out? He can be your partner in these other ventures. Unless there's a problem?'

'No problem!' Andreas said sharply. 'I offer you a good deal, a very good deal. If you want I can take you to see these other places tomorrow. What do you say?'

'I told you, I'm not interested. I came here to get away from it all. If I wanted to do business I would have stayed in London or gone to New York.'

'Please, just think about it.' Andreas dabbed at his face with a white handkerchief, his desperate eyes fixed on Martin now, completely ignoring the arousing view of the woman.

Martin shook his head firmly. 'No means no. To be honest, I think you're in the shit in some way. I can tell. I can read people, it's in your eyes. I never trust people who are in the shit, it's bad business.'

'Just let me show you . . .'

'No,' Martin stood up, finally throwing a cover over Liza. 'I think this interview is over now. I would threaten to call the manager, but that hardly seems appropriate here, does it?'

Andreas turned sharply on his heel and left the room, taunted by Martin's derisive laughter.

three

When Alice awoke she found herself naked on the bed, her sticky body bathed in a thin layer of perspiration. For a moment everything was blank, the room looked strange and the light much brighter than it should have been. She lay still, closed her eyes once more and let herself float dreamily in the state just beyond sleep. Without turning she became aware of Joanne sleeping beside her, her breath rising and falling rhythmically.

Alice suddenly felt elated; a tight ball of excitement welled up inside her. Everything had changed, irrevocably. It had happened without warning, but now she was glad that it had. The edge had been taken off her initial anxiety; when Joanne had held her close she felt safe and secure. Now the nervousness was tempered with a new feeling, a heightened emotional consciousness that coloured everything.

Alice turned. Joanne had woken up and kissed her tenderly on the shoulder, careful not to disturb her.

'I didn't want to wake you,' Joanne said, sitting up on her elbow. She was naked, her bare breasts patterned by the shafts of sunlight that crossed the room.

'It's OK,' said Alice, turning over. 'I wasn't really sleeping. I just felt so happy I wanted to make the moment last forever.'

Joanne smiled and leaned forward, letting her breasts brush gently over Alice's arm, and kissed her lovingly on the lips. Very softly she moved her hand up and down Alice's thigh, pressing delicately against the smooth flawless skin.

Alice responded. Her breath came faster, she lifted herself up and opened her mouth fully to Joanne. She felt lost in the swell of sensation, drawn by the sweetness of the kiss and the electric feel of Joanne's fingers. The intense feeling of happiness returned, a powerful joyous rush of emotion pulsing through her body.

Disturbed by the sound of a key in the lock, they both turned suddenly to the door. The door opened wide and a chambermaid entered, dressed in a simple uniform of blue skirt and blouse and carrying a clean set of towels. She stepped into the room without looking, closed the door behind her, then stopped. She looked up, realising that she was not alone. 'I'm so sorry,' she said quickly, her voice heavily accented. 'I thought the room was empty.'

Alice looked away, grabbing at a thin cotton sheet to cover her nakedness. Her face flushed red hot with shame, and she felt a little nauseous. She knew what the chambermaid was thinking; she could see the scene through her eyes. Alice would have felt disgust and contempt if she had been in her place. And the worst of it was that all the conclusions the chambermaid would draw were true.

'That's perfectly understandable,' Joanne said, turning to face the girl completely. She looked to be about Alice's age, with dark olive skin and jet-black hair. If she felt any embarrassment she hid it well; there was no blushing or looking away.

'I'll come back later,' she said, backing towards the door.

'No, you're here now, you may as well finish the job,'

Joanne told her.

Alice buried her face in the pillow, unable to believe what she had just heard. It was a horrible idea. She wanted to get the girl out of the room as quickly as possible. She didn't want to meet her gaze, to see the disgust on her pretty face.

'Are you sure?' the girl asked incredulously. She looked at Joanne wide-eyed, then at Alice hiding herself away. That she thought it an odd situation was clear from her face. Her dark skin reddened, her eyes were darting around the room nervously.

'Yes, I'm sure,' Joanne assured her, smiling confidently. 'I want you to carry on as if we weren't here.'

The girl shrugged, turned and went into the bathroom to clear up.

'Why did you ask her to stay?' Alice asked, looking up to make sure that the girl really had gone into the other room.

'Why not?' Joanne shrugged nonchalantly.

'Because it makes me feel funny,' Alice said, straightening the sheet so that she was properly covered. It made her feel ashamed, knowing that what she and Joanne were doing was wrong. When they were alone they were in their own private world, where nothing else mattered. But the girl was a reminder of the real world outside, where everything did matter.

Joanne smoothed the cover with her hand, feeling Alice's naked body underneath. She massaged Alice's breasts, palming each fleshy peak in turn, delighted when the nipples hardened and pressed visibly against the snow-white cotton.

The girl emerged from the bathroom and walked straight to the door to drop the used towels into a basket outside. She turned back and saw the two women touching. For a second she hesitated, then walked back into the room.

45

Joanne touched her lips against Alice's, kissing her very gently on the mouth.

Alice turned away, a wave of pure nausea rising up from her stomach. 'Please,' she whispered hotly. 'Please . . . stop it.'

'Stop what?' Joanne whispered, kissing Alice on the cheek, massaging her body over the sheet.

'Stop it . . .' Alice pleaded, her dark eyes clouded with guilt and shame.

'But I want to,' Joanne said softly, her voice at once both gentle and yet firm.

Alice looked at her for a second. She closed her eyes and parted her lips, knowing that she couldn't resist. She was trembling, her whole body racked by a nervous excitement. When Joanne kissed her it felt as if her mouth was on fire.

She was aware of the chambermaid, a distant intrusive presence that had spurred Joanne on. The thought made her head spin. She wanted the girl out, away. But Joanne had wanted her to be there, had insisted in her own oblique way. Now the girl was a witness, and Alice hated it.

She tried to put the maid out of her mind. She was kissing Joanne furiously, sucking at her breath, opening her mouth to Joanne's tongue. Her breasts were aflame, the nipples hard buttons of flesh under the sheet. Her hands held Joanne's face, touching the soft skin of her cheeks, drawing her closer.

Joanne twisted her head a little, straining to catch sight of the chambermaid. She saw her, standing by the desk, wiping the surface aimlessly. She was staring at them wide-eyed, her face crimson with embarrassment and her mouth parted in amazement.

Joanne sat up on her knees, pulling away from Alice's hands and mouth. She tugged at the white sheet and exposed Alice's naked breasts, the dark nipples caught in the bright yellow sunlight. Alice closed her eyes, a look of horror on her face, her lips tender from all the kissing.

'Take my nipples into your mouth,' Joanne said, leaning forward so that her breasts hung close to Alice's mouth.

Silently Alice did as she was told. She opened her mouth and planted a long loving kiss on Joanne's left breast. The crimson flush of shame had spread down from her face and on to the soft skin of her neck. But married to that was the intense feeling of joy that surged through her. Her belly was aflame, the space between her thighs was hot and wet.

Joanne gasped once, then sighed a long slow sigh of pleasure. She closed her eyes, giving herself fully to the moment, letting Alice suck hard at her nipple. She took the other nipple in her hand and squeezed it, stimulating herself further.

Alice was vaguely aware of the door slamming. But that was in the distance, another dimension, somewhere that didn't matter any more. She had yielded to Joanne and now her pleasure was so much more potent. She sucked hard at the delightful knob of flesh in her mouth, biting it and then soothing with her tongue. Joanne's sighs of pleasure were an echo of her own desire. She knew that Joanne was near to climax, ready to reach the peak of ecstasy.

She tucked her hand down between Joanne's thighs and pressed her fingers deep into the raging furnace. Joanne caught her breath and then arched her back, crying out with little gasps of elation. She climaxed at once, the force of penetration too much for her.

Alice cried out at the same time. Her own climax took her by surprise, a sudden surge of exhilaration that carried her out of herself. Her pussy exploded, burning with a thick lava of pleasure. She hadn't touched herself, nor had Joanne touched her. But this was a new world, where all

47

emotion was amplified, where every act resonated with an unseen power.

Joanne sat at the poolside bar, facing the pool where Alice swam serenely in the silvery water. It was late afternoon; the sun had passed its highest point and was slowly heading down towards the horizon.

Joanne saw Amanda Trevelyan walking towards the bar, her tall elegant figure casting a long sticklike shadow that skimmed the surface of the water. Joanne recognised her at once: the famously long legs, the pale face that was strangely untouched by the sun despite her many travels. She wore heavy black sunglasses, the square lenses lending an angular quality to her oval face. Her lips were naturally slightly parted and glossed a striking scarlet shade that contrasted with the whiteness of her skin.

Amanda came around and sat at the bar, casually ignoring the eyes that followed her every movement. She turned her back to the pool and ordered a drink, the barman jumping to attention, eager to serve her.

Joanne couldn't help admiring her. Amanda wore a fashionable button-down dress, the upper half like a smart Italian jacket with sharply padded shoulders and ribbed darts down the back. The bottom half of the dress was cut to look like a short skirt, moulded tightly to her body and slit just an inch at the back.

'Hi,' Joanne said, turning to face her. 'Are you working, or here for a break?'

Amanda turned round. Her face was impassive, the full blood-red lips sculpted from the white alabaster of her face. She paused for a moment then relaxed, smiling slightly. 'Both. It started out as a holiday but now it's turning itself into work.'

'Is that good or bad?'

'Both,' she repeated, laughing lightly. 'It's turning into

48

'work because I like Frixos.'

'But if you hated Frixos it would probably turn into work again,' Joanne said, shifting to the seat next to Amanda.

'Absolutely,' Amanda agreed. 'You've been there, right?'

Joanne nodded. 'Work and play, it's hard to say which is which sometimes.'

'Would we want it any other way?'

'No, not really,' Joanne admitted, glad that she and Amanda were hitting it off so well. 'So what do you think of this place?' she asked, looking round across the pool to Alice, who saw her and smiled.

'It's good. Very good. If anyone had sat down to invent the perfect Greek island then they would have come up with this. Which is what they did, I guess.'

'What do you mean?' Joanne asked, intrigued.

'That's not how it was done!' Amanda laughed again, a relaxed kind of laugh that was rarely seen when she appeared on television. 'The reason this place is so good is that there are hardly any tourists here. And the reason there are no tourists is that there are no developments. There are no developments because transport to the island is difficult, and that's because the harbour is silted up.'

'But what's so strange about that?'

'How do you think the harbour got silted up?'

'Mud washed down from the rivers . . . No, that can't be right. An island this size couldn't have any rivers big enough . . .'

Amanda nodded meaningfully. 'The harbour was deliberately sabotaged during the second world war. God only knows how, but the British navy managed to clog up the harbour before the island fell into German hands. After the war things were so difficult, with the Greek civil war and so on, that nothing was done to clear it. Now it's just accepted as an act of nature and not a forgotten fact of history.'

'Is that true?' Joanne looked unconvinced, she couldn't tell whether Amanda was joking or not.

'Absolutely,' Amanda said. 'Though the government has never admitted responsibility. But the old men in the village will tell you, and so will certain retired Royal Marines.'

'That's amazing,' Joanne said, delighted by the strange story.

'That's what turned this from a holiday into an assignment. I couldn't let a story like that slip through my fingers.'

'Apart from the island, what do you think of this place?'

'Paradise Bay? Well run, very good layout, excellent staff, fantastic location. Considering it has an absolute monopoly, I'd say it was pretty damned amazing.'

'Are you going to say that?'

'Not in those words of course, but that's what I think.'

'On television or in the press?' Joanne edged closer still, breathing Amanda's subtle perfume.

'In writing,' she smiled. 'My readers are much more discriminating than my viewers. If I mention this place on TV then within a month you'll have yobs being sick in the village street, burger bars sprouting every ten yards and environmentalists forming a lynch mob to get me.'

'What it is to have power,' Joanne said, grinning.

'You seem very interested in all this. Idle curiosity, or is there something else?'

'Let's just say that I'm on very good terms with the owner,' Joanne said coyly.

'With Andreas?' Amanda asked, looking a little surprised.

'No, not him. Andreas is part owner, he has a partner in London. But I'd rather you didn't mention that to Andreas.'

50

Amanda sat back in her seat, smiling knowingly. 'Mixing work and pleasure yourself, I see.'

'I'm actually meant to be on holiday. I run a design studio in Covent Garden in my other life. I needed a break and this place sounded great, so here I am. I'm not going to do any real work. I've had a little sniff around and everything looks fine. You've only confirmed it for me.'

'Glad to be of help.' Amanda finished her drink quickly and stood up.

'Would you like another?' Joanne offered.

Amanda shook her head. 'There's no rest for the wicked, I'm afraid. I've got to arrange an interview with M. Jean-Pierre Giradot, he of the famous talent and infamous temperament.'

'Is he staying here too?'

'Jean-Pierre happens to be the most famous resident of Frixos, in fact the only famous resident on Frixos.' She laughed again, her long red-brown hair catching the sunlight and dancing like fire. 'He lives in one of the big houses up in the mountains. Not the easiest man in the world to meet.'

'Good luck with him,' Joanne said. 'Maybe we can have a drink some other time.'

'Absolutely. Well, see you.'

Joanne watched her go. She wore flat sandals laced with thin bands of leather pulled tightly into her ankles and snaking up the calves of her legs. Even though her shoes were flat there was no hiding the perfect roundness of her bottom or the ideal proportions of her lithe thighs.

It was impossible to hide the dagger of desire that shot through Joanne. Her heart beat faster and she felt the familiar stab of excitement in her belly. At that moment Alice emerged from the pool, her body glistening with myriad points of light reflected in the tiny beads of water on her smooth skin. She smiled, her face clear and

51

attractive, her eyes alert with a natural excitement.

Joanne smiled back, aroused by the sudden intersection of her desires for Alice and Amanda.

Alice emerged from the bathroom wearing a long baggy tee-shirt that reached down to her knees, the feminine contours of her body lost in the looseness of the oversize garment. Her long bedraggled hair was wet and shiny.

'Why didn't you come over to meet Amanda Trevelyan?' Joanne asked, sitting in the cane chair by the door.

'The water was so lovely and cool that I didn't feel like getting out,' Alice said, walking across to the centre of the room to comb her hair in front of the mirror.

'She seemed like a really nice person,' Joanne said. She came up behind Alice, stood directly behind her and brushed a hand through the thick dark hair that was cool to the touch.

'What did she think of Paradise Bay?'

'She loved it. You can see why her work's so good, she's done so much background research on the place. She told me some fantastic stories about the island. What was the real reason you didn't come up to meet her?'

'I told you, I didn't feel like it,' Alice lied unconvincingly.

Joanne slipped her hands under the tee-shirt and pulled it up, gathering the baggy garment in one hand and holding it high above Alice's chest. Underneath Alice was naked except for a pair of pink bikini briefs, the dark mound of her pussy discernible in outline.

'Did Amanda make you nervous?' Joanne asked, cupping Alice's heavy breast with her right hand, weighing the globe in her palm.

'Yes, sort of ...' Alice admitted. She leant back a little, feeling Joanne's hot breath on her shoulder.

There was a loud knock at the door, a single tap that startled Alice and made Joanne smile. 'Yes!' Joanne snapped loudly and the door opened.

'Your champagne, madam,' a waiter announced, entering the room with an ice bucket under one arm. He stopped only for a second, his lips touched by a fleeting smile, then continued into the room.

Joanne pulled the tee-shirt up over the shoulders and let it hang loose there. She crossed her hands over Alice's chest, taking hold of each breast and squeezing gently. She kissed Alice on the neck, soft loving kisses under the ear and down across the shoulder.

Alice closed her eyes, unable to face the waiter with his greedy eyes and a face kept impassive by sheer force of will. She felt her face hot with shame, her eyes were shut tight but still they filled with tears. Joanne's fingers were teasing her, playing with the nipples, rousing them so that they stood to attention.

'Would madam like me to open the champagne?' Alice heard the waiter ask, his voice quivering.

'Yes please.' Joanne looked up, smiled at the waiter and then continued kissing Alice. She pressed her lips firmly against the silky skin at the base of the neck and shoulder, and then drew in her breath, sucking hard, drawing the flesh into her mouth.

Alice opened her mouth, moaned quietly, Joanne was biting harder, pressing her teeth into the delicate flesh. She twisted her neck to one side, but Joanne nuzzled closer, at the same time squeezing the erect nipples tightly between thumb and fingers, crushing the tender berries. Alice squealed, cried out in agony at the same moment that the champagne popped. She opened her eyes wide, saw herself in the mirror, her breasts exposed, her face flaming red. She was wet between the thighs, but hoped that the wet patch in her briefs was not visible.

The waiter dawdled for a moment but finally turned and left, unable to hide the excitement in his eyes. Alice knew that the story would be all around the hotel, it would spread like wildfire. It was possible that the maid had kept quiet, but the waiter was sure to tell all his friends. Their eyes would follow her, their duplicitous smiles hiding their true thoughts and feelings. She felt sick.

Joanne finally stepped away, releasing Alice after brushing her hand down over the panties, lingering deliciously in the little circle of wetness where the pussy lips parted.

'Why do you do that?' Alice asked quietly, letting the tee-shirt cover her once more. She looked at Joanne standing by the ice bucket, smiling.

'Do what?'

'Touch me like that, in front of other people.'

'Is that why you stayed away from Amanda Trevelyan? Because you thought I was going to touch you in front of her?'

'You were, weren't you?' Alice said, her eyes dark and heavy with sadness, though her voice carried no trace of bitterness.

'Yes,' Joanne admitted. 'I was going to kiss you on the lips, or rub my hand up and down your legs.'

'Why do you do it?'

'I could make up a reason if you wanted one,' Joanne said. 'But why do any of us do anything? We come up with reasons, sometimes very good ones, but that's what people are good at. We pretend we have reasons, we rationalise everything. But who knows what really drives us? Who knows what goes on behind other people's eyes, or in your own head.'

'But you know that it embarrasses me,' said Alice, sitting on the edge of the bed.

'That's why I do it,' Joanne said. 'I can see the look

in your eyes, on that lovely face of yours. I can see when I've pushed you right to the very edge. I can see that your whole being is screaming out no more! Then I push you over the edge. I want to see you submit, to go beyond the edge just because I want you to. And you do it. Because the same devil that's inside me is inside you. When you do it your body comes alive. Jesus, yesterday you climaxed without me touching you. You get pleasure out of it, don't you?'

'But I don't want to. I don't want to be like this. I don't pretend not to want to do things, it's real. But then something funny goes off inside me.'

'Take that thing off,' Joanne ordered. She turned to her side and retrieved the bottle of Krug from the ice bucket.

Alice pulled the tee-shirt over her head and threw it in the corner.

Joanne strode back across the room, the icy bottle trailing water along the floor, an intense look on her face. She stood over Alice, who was leaning back on the edge of the bed, her naked body bathed in the warm sunlight. Very slowly she turned the bottle over, aiming the narrow mouth between Alice's breasts. The champagne fizzed noisily when it poured on to her, splashing down to her belly.

Alice cried out noisily, jumping up suddenly, but Joanne pressed her down again. The champagne was freezing, it bubbled and fizzed as it poured on to her belly. It trickled down her sides, soaking the bed, drops of it flicked over her breasts. It seemed to bubble into her belly button like a fountain. Joanne continued to pour, moving the fountain down further and further.

Alice closed her eyes and parted her thighs fully. Suddenly the trickle of sparkling liquid became a torrent, pouring down over her belly and cascading between her thighs and into her sex. Her pussy was filled with a cool tingling sensation, the sparkling champagne effervescing deep inside her. It poured from her sex and down along her arse crack to form little pools of excitement under her anal hole.

'Is it good?' Joanne asked, halting the flow momentarily, checking to see how much was left in the bottle.

'It feels delicious,' Alice admitted softly, her eyes still half closed. Her pussy seemed to be alive with the fizzing drink. It poured suggestively from her pussy, foaming white. It was cold and hot at the same time, icy cold but creating a deep sexual warmth inside her, sending tiny packets of excitement vibrating through her.

'Does this feel delicious too?' Joanne asked. She knelt on the floor and parted Alice's cunny lips with her fingers.

'No! Please!' Alice cried out in alarm, suddenly aware of what Joanne was planning. It was too late, she had no time to squirm away. Joanne pressed the cold mouth of the bottle between the parted cunny lips and into the sex. Alice caught her breath, too afraid to move. The bottle pressed deep into her, violating her, forcing her cunny lips further apart.

She shifted nervously, forcing her thighs further apart, pulling her knees up. The bottle was pressed in and out, each stroke sending a thrill of pleasure passing through her. The neck of the bottle was forcing her pussy lips apart, the force of penetration made easier by the fizzing drink pouring deep into her and dribbling out with the downward stroke.

Joanne lifted the bottle high so that the bubbling drink cascaded deep into Alice's pussy, fizzing and hissing all around the aroused pink bud. Alice closed her eyes, her breath escaping from her open mouth in a wordless ecstatic sigh.

Joanne withdrew the emptied bottle and let it fall to one side. She got down on her hands and knees and began to kiss Alice between the thighs. Alice's sex was still full of frothy liquid and Joanne lapped at it with her tongue, drawing it into her mouth. It tasted of champagne and sex cream, a magical cocktail of heady flavours. She pressed her tongue deep into Alice, pressing the walls of her vagina, swallowing the creamy sex honey along with the fizzy champagne.

Alice began to buck and writhe, opening herself fully, twisting ecstatically as Joanne's mouth worked expertly. Her breath was hot now, in contrast to the coolness imparted by the icy drink. Droplets of golden liquid still trickled between her arse cheeks, tracing cold outlines along her most sensitive places, driving her to a greater intensity of pleasure.

She began to fall and rise with the rhythm of Joanne's mouth, lifting herself high to meet the spearing tongue. She was wet and could feel Joanne drawing the juices deep into her mouth. Joanne seemed to focus on the prominent pink bud, attacking it with a special intensity that made Alice cry out and thrash her head back and forth wildly. She cried out once more and froze into position, her body seemed consumed by a single flame that burned deep in her cunt and on the red tips of her breasts.

Alice lay on her side, her body still tingling, her thighs still wet with a glistening trail of champagne and the creamy emissions from her sex. She had screamed at the moment of bliss, an involuntary cry of affirmation and desire. It was proof of all that Joanne had said, if proof were needed.

The empty champagne bottle, the instrument that had pushed Alice over the edge, lay between her and Joanne. She tried not to think about it, frightened by the thought of the inanimate object pressed deep into her body. It had been frightening, but at the same time exhilarating, forcing her to confront the fear and guilt. She had submitted to the violation, had allowed herself to be dominated and had found pleasure in the experience.

It had been an ecstatic experience, but she didn't want it to happen again. Her fear was real, and too much a part of her to be discarded easily.

She moved to pick up the bottle, wanting to put it out of view, when she became aware of a darkness by the balcony door. It was only when the vague form moved that she realised what it was. Her sharp cry shattered the silence of the room.

'What is it?' demanded Joanne, sitting bolt upright.

'By the door, someone's there,' Alice pointed to the shadow that moved.

Joanne stood up, naked. 'Who's there? Come on, who is it?'

The shadow moved again, there was a rustle of clothing and then a thin male figure emerged. The bright light caught his face and the two women recognised him as the strange man who had disturbed them in the restaurant.

'What do you want?' Joanne demanded furiously. She made no attempt to cover herself, but stood with hands on hips, defiantly naked. Behind her Alice covered herself with the discarded tee-shirt.

'I'm sorry ...' Martin stuttered. He looked at the ground, unwilling to look directly either at Joanne or Alice, rubbing his hands nervously together.

'How long have you been standing there?'

'Not long ... I ... Not long.'

'You've been spying on us haven't you? Well, were we good for you?'

'I ... I ... haven't...' Martin said falteringly. The accusation made his already pale face go a deathly white. He was shaking, his lower lip trembling visibly. 'I wasn't peeping. I wasn't,' he managed to say in a miserable whining tone.

'What do you want? Or do I have to get the manager?'

'No, not that.' Martin straightened up and looked at Joanne directly for the first time. It was as if the threat of the manager had given him back his confidence. 'I came to talk to you. About him actually.'

'What's wrong with the front door?' Joanne asked sarcastically.

'I have my reasons,' he said, trying to buy time.

Alice realised that he had got over the initial shock of being caught. His discomfort was receding and he was becoming altogether more confident. Furtively she hid the bottle, burying it under the thin white sheet on the bed.

'I didn't want that Karaplis man to see me talking to you,' he said. 'It's him I want to talk to you about.'

'Say what you have to say and get out,' Joanne told him angrily.

Martin stepped into the room, his voice had totally lost its earlier embarrassed and nervous tone. 'I have to apologise first. I couldn't help overhearing part of your conversation at lunch the other day. It was not intentional, I assure you.'

Alice looked at Joanne quizzically, things had taken an unexpected turn. Joanne turned and retreated back into the room. She sat back on the bed, her anger had disappeared, she listened with growing interest. 'Go on,' she said.

'I heard you say that your husband owns part of the hotel with Karaplis.'

'You didn't tell him that?' Alice whispered, a look of horror on her face.

'I didn't,' Martin said. 'But you might like to know that Karaplis is in some sort of financial mess. He came to me with an offer of a deal to buy land, quite an attractive deal at that. I turned it down flat,' he added quickly. 'I suggested that he contact his partner, your husband, but

59

he refused.'

'Did he give a reason?' Joanne asked.

'None. But I wouldn't trust him if I were your husband. Karaplis is in some sort of trouble, perhaps your husband ought to know about it.'

'He didn't say anything else?'

Martin shook his head emphatically. 'I'm sorry if I alarmed you,' he said, taking a step backwards. 'But I thought you ought to know.'

'Thank you for the information.' Joanne stood up again. 'You could use the door if you want. It's probably much safer than scaling balcony walls.'

'Yes ... No, I wouldn't want Karaplis to see me. And there's no need to worry, I won't mention that your husband's his partner.'

'Thanks again. But in future if you have anything to say to me then I would rather you chose some other means of communication.'

Martin smiled sheepishly, Joanne's admonishing tone chipped away at his cocky self-confidence. He turned without a word and disappeared.

'Do you think he was telling the truth?' Alice asked, as soon as she was certain that he had gone.

'He was telling the truth all right. But that was only accidental. He'd been spying on us, probably saw everything that we did. I guess that's what turns him on.'

'That's horrible,' Alice shivered. 'I don't like him. There's something nasty about him.'

'But I think he was telling the truth. He was stuck there for a bit. If he didn't have that little bit of a story he would have been in an awful lot of trouble.'

'So what do we do?'

'We find out what's going on,' Joanne said.

four

Amanda pulled up in front of the large white house, switched off the engine and jumped out of the jeep. She stood for a moment, facing the distant sea, enjoying the fresh breeze on her face. The whole of Frixos was spread out before her. The mountain track leading up to the house meandered down the rocky incline, carving its way through the dry rocky land. Further up on the steep mountainsides the trees became quite dense, but down below they were sparse, offering little in the way of shelter and doing nothing to retain the moisture in the soil. It was a hard landscape; the weatherbeaten old farmers who lived precariously in isolated shacks on the mountainside had to struggle to make the soil yield anything. Here and there small terraces had been sculpted out of the rock, cleared and tended by the old men and their wives, misshapen old women with dark red faces, clad from head to foot in black.

The further one got from the sea the harder life became. There was nothing bounteous or fertile about the mountains, nothing but the simple struggle for survival.

From her place Amanda could see Paradise Bay, a geometric complex of white buildings by the edge of the sea. She turned slightly to look at the village around the dead harbour. The few fishing boats had returned and were moored together by the mouth of the harbour, bobbing gently in the calm water, relics of a time when Frixos was alive with the coming and going of seafaring craft. Now they hardly ventured out into the sea, content instead with bringing their small catches to sell at the quayside early in the morning. The fishing families were dwindling, their arts and skills already forgotten.

Amanda turned to face the house, trying to put the thoughts out of her mind. Like all Greek tragedy, the tragedy of Frixos was double edged. The loss of the harbour meant that Frixos was spared that other death, death by tourism. Amanda was glad for that. She knew it was selfish, but it meant the island was an ideal resort for those rich enough to afford the serenity it offered. It also gave her a damned good story.

The house was by far the most impressive of the big houses on the island. It seemed to rise up from the rock, a white extrusion from the depths of the soil. It was long and low, the walls smooth and white, untouched by the ravages of the sun. The style was unobtrusively modern; Jean-Pierre had avoided the temptation to go for Ionic columns and grand classical motifs.

Amanda stepped up to the entrance and out of the searing heat. She took her sunglasses off and put them in her bag. She wore a short white skirt with a matching white backless blouse. It had been difficult to know how to dress for Jean-Pierre. He was notoriously temperamental and had agreed to meet her only because they had a friend in common. It was too late now, she thought; she brushed her skirt quickly then rang the bell.

She was made to wait a couple of minutes, but that was an old trick and didn't unsettle her. When the door was opened she recognised Jean-Pierre at once. He was much better-looking than he had appeared in his surly publicity pictures. He was of average height but big build; he had broad shoulders like a labourer and his stomach was perhaps a little too full. His face was round, unshaven with a large mouth and a flat nose. His eyes seemed to light up at once, dark fiery eyes that swept over her in an instant.

'I'm Amanda Trevelyan,' she said, stepping into the coolness of the house. She offered her hand and he took it, his mouth twisting into a smile that changed the shape of his whole face.

'You are beautiful,' he said, his deep voice carrying a slight trace of a French accent. He kissed Amanda's hand, pulling it up to his mouth while keeping his eyes fixed on her.

'This isn't the Jean-Pierre I expected,' Amanda said, smiling.

'Please, walk this way,' he said, taking her hand and leading her through the grand lobby of the house. 'Which Jean-Pierre did you expect?'

'I'm not sure. Probably the ''I hate journalists and critics'' Jean-Pierre, or the ''world doesn't understand me'' Jean-Pierre,' she said, hoping to play on his good mood.

'Oh that Jean-Pierre!' he laughed, a loud hearty laugh that filled the silence of the house. 'That Jean-Pierre doesn't exist for beautiful women like you. He only exists for tired old men who are too jealous to recognise true creativity when they see it. But you, my dear, you recognise creativity do you not?'

She winced. It had been a long time since she had been addressed as 'my dear' and the patronising tone jarred considerably. He led her into a vast open room, one end leading out to a balcony. At the other end, by the door, there was a well-stocked bar. The walls were bare apart from a number of abstract paintings, strange landscapes, the colours running into each other yet remaining distinct. The room was sparsely furnished: there were no books,

63

no alcoves containing sculpture, no decorative *objets d'art*.

'This is my thinking room,' Jean-Pierre said, noticing the way Amanda was looking around.

'Then you need lots of room to think,' she said.

'Yes, lots of room and lots of alcohol,' he laughed again. 'You want a drink? Pernod and ice?'

'Lots of ice, thank you.'

She walked up and studied the paintings on the wall, fascinated by the vivid cerise and black mixtures, the turbulent flow of paint on the canvas. 'These have never been exhibited, have they?'

'No, and they never shall. I will not allow it.'

'But they are so good, the combination works so well. Why ever not?'

Jean-Pierre took Amanda by the elbow, tugging her away from the paintings and directing her to one of the armchairs in the centre of the room. She sat down, taking her drink from him.

'A man can reveal too much of himself, the public demands too much,' he said. His expression was no longer so jovial, his smile had gone and he seemed tired. There were deep lines in his face, around the eyes.

'But that by definition is the job of the artist, to reveal, to expose.'

'No!' Jean-Pierre snapped loudly. 'These works are mine, a private exploration of my inner world. The world can go screw itself. These paintings are for me and me alone.'

'I'm sorry. I didn't mean to upset you,' Amanda said, surprised by the vehemence of his reaction, and a little afraid that she had destroyed the good humour that augured so well for her interview.

'The matter is closed. You have three things in your favour. First you are not a critic. Second you are not a dealer. Third you are totally beautiful.'

'Is the order significant? If I had been a beautiful dealer and critic would I have found you so charming?'

Jean-Pierre laughed, tickled by her remark. 'So clever, yet so naïve. How is it possible to be beautiful and be a critic? The two are mutually exclusive, are they not?'

'Perhaps,' Amanda said non-committally. She put her drink down beside her and searched through her bag. She found the small tape recorder and took it out, placing it on the drinks table, between her and Jean-Pierre.

'No,' Jean-Pierre said, pointing a thick finger at the tape recorder. 'No tape recorders.'

'But how will I record your words? Surely you don't expect me to write it all down? It'll completely destroy any sense of atmosphere or rapport.'

'Then you don't record what I say at all. You can be impressionistic in your work. Nuance and feeling is more important than verbatim reporting.'

'But I wouldn't want to be open to the accusation that I have misquoted you,' Amanda pointed out. Despite his charming exterior he was proving to be as difficult and stubborn as she had been led to believe.

'How can you misquote when there are no quotes? No tape recorders.'

'As you wish,' she agreed reluctantly, returning the tape recorder to her bag.

'You wish to discuss this lovely island, do you not? This island paradise that has accepted me as one of its sons.'

'Has it?'

'A wayward and disobedient son perhaps, but still a son and not a stranger. I have many friends on the island, the people of the hills regard me as one of theirs. They are a hardy people, proud and tough, burnt in the sun and crushed by the work.'

'And they accept you as one of them? A man who lives in a luxurious house like this, who no longer needs to work

65

in order to survive?' Amanda couldn't conceal the scepticism in her voice.

He looked at her for a moment, fixed his fierce gaze on her. 'I have worked this soil with them, breaking my back fourteen hours a day to gather the dark grapes before the winter comes. I have cleared the mud and rock that slides from the higher slopes in the winter and spring. These hands have been cut and callused, marked by the soil of this land. My people too spring from the land, my forefathers lived the same pitiful existence. It's in my blood just as it is in theirs. I haven't had the education to forget that, and these simple people recognise that. They have understanding.'

'But why Frixos? Why not France or the mainland?'

Jean-Pierre stood up, his bearlike body seeming to fill the room with a powerful, intimidating presence. 'Here. Follow me.' He took Amanda by the hand and escorted her out onto the balcony.

She heard the sound of splashing water, and the sound of voices and laughter. He put his finger to her lips to silence her. Together they ventured to the edge of the balcony. They looked down on to a large rectangular pool below. Two young men were playing in the water, their wiry young bodies naked in the sunlight. They were struggling, wrestling with each other in and out of the water.

Amanda saw how relaxed they were, how unself-conscious about their nakedness. They seemed completely at ease. Their young bodies were muscular and sinewy, glistening in the bright sunlight. They held each other close, struggling, their arms and legs locked tightly together. She could see their strong thighs, muscular buttocks, the dark hair between their thighs. It was an arousing sight and she found herself peering closer at the two male bodies bathed in sweat and water. She noticed

66

too that the two men were both aroused, their hard cocks pressing urgently against each other. But it was strange that they seemed unaware of it: their movements were still playful and not in the least bit sexual.

Laughing breathlessly, they emerged from the water and began wrestling by the poolside. They slipped round until one of them was on top of the other. He held the other's arms, forcing him to struggle furiously. Amanda could see the top one's back rippling with muscle, his boyish backside pressing the other young man down. He let out a cry of triumph, but that only goaded the other. Soon they were moving again, a fluid tangle of arms and legs. They fell into the water, laughing and yelping loudly.

Jean-Pierre took Amanda by the elbow and led her back to the room, out of the heat. Amanda went reluctantly. She had been transfixed by the sight, fascinated by the unconsciously sexual nature of their play and aroused also by the sexy male bodies.

'That, my dear,' Jean-Pierre said, 'is why I chose to live on Frixos. That was innocence. Innocence.'

'Absolutely,' Amanda agreed, nodding. That was exactly the word to describe what she had just seen. The two boys knew no shame, they were comfortable with their bodies because they still had an essentially innocent view of life.

'I know of nowhere else where that state of nature still exists. The world has been corrupted. But here man has yet to fall. Which is why I have a confession to make.'

'Yes?'

'I'm not sure that I want you here.'

'In this house? You mean on the island? I see. You think I might be the harbinger of all that's bad. The corrupter of the innocent.' Amanda lost her smile. The thought was disturbing because it carried an element of truth, a truth that she had been aware of for a long time.

67

'You understand that, do you not? I can see from your eyes that the thought does not strike you as fantastic.'

'I'll be frank with you, Jean-Pierre,' she said sadly. 'I have sinned in the past. But they were sins of innocence, if you like. I didn't know the effect that my words would have. I found places of interest, fantastic, beautiful places. And I wanted to share, to let others see things as I saw them, to enjoy as I enjoyed. I didn't understand that those places were beautiful because they were unknown and untouched. I didn't know that they would wither away as soon as they became known.'

'But now you know, and yet you carry on. Is that what you have in mind for Frixos?'

'I'm ...' Amanda was interrupted by a shout from outside.

Jean-Pierre went to the door just as the two young men entered the room. They were dressed in rough denim trousers and cotton shirts, their hair was wet and glossy black. One of them said something in Greek and then kissed Jean-Pierre on the mouth. They were chaste kisses, the simple touching of lips on lips. The other young man turned and saw Amanda seated alone in the room. Quickly he nudged his friend who pulled away from Jean-Pierre. The two young men looked embarrassed; they muttered something quickly and left.

'You see!' Jean-Pierre thundered angrily, turning to glare at Amanda. 'They only had to look at you and you made them conscious of themselves.'

'They would have acted the same way in front of any stranger!' Amanda retorted. 'If I had been someone from the village they would have acted the same way. How could one glance at me change them forever?'

'All the same, you are all the same!' he bellowed, snorting angrily, his eyes livid with anger.

'Is this why you stay here? So that you can have a stream

of young village boys to play with? Is that what you do?'

'You disgust me!' he cried aggressively. 'You come here with your filth. Corruption! That is what you bring with you.'

'Rubbish!' Amanda stood up. 'No wonder you didn't want me to tape you. I'm not the one who's corrupt, it's you! And to think I believed all that rubbish about working the soil, and tending the crops. That was rich. Jean-Pierre Giradot the peasant.'

'You wound me!' Jean-Pierre cried, clutching melodramatically at his chest. 'I work with these people. I have their trust and their respect. Do you really think that I would do all that for the sake of a few young boys? If I wanted that then I could buy all the men I wanted in Paris or London. It is I who have been mistaken. I thought that you could be trusted, that your beauty was spiritual as well as physical.'

Amanda sat down again and downed her drink. 'I'm sorry we've got all this out of proportion. Can we start again?'

'No, we don't start again,' Jean-Pierre muttered morosely. 'But we let it pass. Let us say that we have a better understanding of each other now. You can see, I love this island. I love it more passionately than you can ever know.'

'I can see that. And I don't want to destroy Frixos, honestly I don't. I assure you that I will do everything I possibly can to avoid Frixos turning into just another Greek holiday resort.'

'You can only do that by remaining silent,' Jean-Pierre said calmly, looking her straight in the eye, a clear note of challenge in his voice.

'No!' Amanda replied forcefully. 'My work is as important to me as yours is to you. Don't make the mistake of believing that only you are creative, or that creativity

69

doesn't matter to the rest of us. Sooner or later someone will discover Frixos. It can either be someone like me, someone who cares and understands, or someone who has no scruples or understanding. Who do you prefer?'

'I like passion,' Jean-Pierre said disarmingly. 'You are a very passionate woman. That's very attractive, very sexy. You have modelled have you not?'

'Briefly,' Amanda admitted, taking the change of subject to mean that he had made his choice. 'I did a season in Paris and Milan.'

'No, I mean real modelling, not that ephemeral stuff on the catwalk. Would you sit for me?'

'Christ, you really are the most infuriating man to deal with,' she sighed.

'Is this the Jean-Pierre that you expected?'

'Yes, difficult, stubborn, rude, temperamental . . .'

'But interesting, always interesting!' he interjected, raising a finger to emphasise the point.

'And charming,' she relented, happy to see his good humour returning.

'Let me show you something,' he said, standing up and stretching out his arm, waiting for her to take his hand.

They walked out of the room and through the sparsely furnished house. The house was built on a bank, the front entrance was actually on the first floor of the house, with the lower storey down a wide flight of stone steps. The house opened out on to the pool and a bar. The lower storey also contained the kitchen and a couple of large bedrooms. But the entire building had been designed around the studio. This too opened out on to the pool on one side. It was a large cavernous room, with glass on two sides. On one side the glass door opened on to the pool; the other side looked out across a wooded valley.

Amanda looked out across the valley. The house must have been built on the edge of a cliff, because there was

70

a sheer drop beneath the window. She stepped away for a second, startled by the apparent drop, dizzy with a feeling of vertigo. But the view was stunning. The valley was spectacular, thickly wooded, deeply scored through thick volcanic rock. In the distance the peaks of the mountains paled in the rippling haze, and behind them the sea shimmered like gold.

'It's fantastic. How can you ever work here?'

Jean-Pierre shrugged. 'I spend hours studying this landscape, the way the rock seems to change in texture with the movement of the sun overhead. The way landslides reveal new features, new shades of rock and earth. It's magical, forever shifting yet remaining the same.'

'Have you painted this?' She turned away from the view, back to face Jean-Pierre, who was standing close to her.

'Never,' he said simply. He stepped closer to Amanda then reached out his hand and touched her gently on the thigh.

She fell silent, made no move to step away from him. His finger pressed up and down the inside of her thigh, probing her soft skin. He had stopped smiling, his eyes were suddenly serious. He moved his hand further up, feeling her smooth skin just under her sex. She caught her breath, the arousal that she felt earlier returned at once. There was something sensual about Jean-Pierre that she had noticed as soon as she set eyes on him. He was a powerful man, his rough hands had indeed been smoothed by hard physical labour, but they were sensitive, touching her as if she were a goddess.

'So beautiful,' he murmured, his voice soft and low. 'Would you model for me?'

'If you want,' Amanda said without thinking, touched by the pleading tone of voice and the look in his eyes. His hand moved to her other thigh, tracing the shape of her curves, pressing firmly against her silky flesh.

'I have something to show you,' he said, taking his hand away and walking to the other end of the studio.

Amanda followed, distracted by the force of her arousal, aware of the heat building between her thighs.

Jean-Pierre waited by a large object, covered in a filthy white sheet, until she stood next to him. 'You are the first person to see this,' he said, pulling the cover away dramatically.

Amanda gasped. 'It's stunning. Absolutely stunning,' she whispered. She stood before a life-size statue of a man, reclining naked, holding his erect penis in his hand. A look of pleasure, eyes half closed, mouth half open, was sculpted on his delicate and sensitive face. Every muscle in the body stood out, clearly defined, flexed powerfully. The thighs were slightly parted, the thick muscles tensed. He lay back on one elbow, head bent back slightly, the other hand grasping the base of his enormous prick. The model had been caught in the instant before ejaculation, the expression of unbridled bliss captured forever in pure white marble.

'It was a struggle to get the marble up here. The purest, finest stone from Carrara. It could never have been done without my neighbours.'

'I'm stunned. To be honest, Jean-Pierre, I didn't even know that you worked with stone.'

'I have done from time to time. It is the subject that dictates the material, not the material the subject. Oils and water, iron and steel, and occasionally pure flawless marble. I had planned on a classical work, to form from the stone the idealised image of a young male. To shape the contours of bone and muscle with my bare hands. And then to use the subtlest of pigments to bring the flesh to life, to show the dark skin scored deep by the sun, to paint those heavy lidded eyes. But when I had finished carving the body from the unformed rock, I fell in love with it.

72

He is beautiful, is he not?'

Amanda made no reply. She felt drawn to the statue, attracted by the life force that seemed to emanate from the hard white stone. She could imagine the faint flow of breath from the half-open mouth, the dying sigh as he plunged into orgasm.

'Touch it, feel the muscle and bone that I have created,' Jean-Pierre said quietly. He took her hand and placed it on one of the statue's thighs, spreading her fingers so that her palm was flat against the curving object.

The statue was cold and smooth, gently contoured, with the long muscles of the thighs etched sensuously on the surface. She could imagine the power in those thighs, in the vigorously male body reclining before her. Every detail had been brilliantly sculpted, the large round nipples, the layers of muscle through which the ribs could be distinguished, the tautness of his stomach.

Amanda rubbed her hand up and down the smooth marble, thrilling to the perfection of the body, to the cold hardness beneath her fingers. She reached out and touched her finger against the base of the upstanding prick. Jean-Pierre had left no detail undone. The thick prick was ribbed along the underside, the thick vein running along its length clearly discernible. The prick tapered slightly just under the large dome, and the glans seemed swollen, ready to spurt thick wads of cream.

'A magnificent specimen,' Jean-Pierre said wistfully.

Amanda nodded, enthralled by the feel of the hardness in her hand. It felt fantastic, so incredibly hard. She rubbed her hand up and down the length, all the time becoming more and more excited. She knelt down before the statue, between the parted thighs, so that her face was close to the marble erection. It looked so much bigger, so much more promising, so attractive. She closed her eyes and brushed her cheek against it, feeling the marble fingers touch her on the chin and the smooth hardness against her face.

'Take it in your mouth,' Jean-Pierre urged her. 'Worship this divine object, just as I have done.'

Amanda needed no other bidding. She opened her mouth and closed her lips around the cold round dome. She brushed her lips against the underside, tracing the curve of the flesh, letting her tongue rest for a second in the eye at the top of the prick, an eye that was slightly parted by the pull of the hand. She took it further in her mouth, surprised at how lifelike it felt, despite the impossible stiffness and the coolness. In her mind she saw the man sigh, pressing himself deeper in her mouth as a thin trail of fluid was sucked on to her tongue.

Jean-Pierre stepped away, his blazing eyes catching every shade of meaning and movement.

Amanda began to rise and fall on the hard prick, working her mouth urgently on the marble prick, revelling in the sensations in her mouth. She knew that there would be no sudden gasp, her mouth would not fill with his pumping seed, but that made the experience even better. She had no need to think about her partner; all that mattered was the feel in her mouth and the pleasure she felt. Her belly was aflame, she was wet between the thighs, a raging heat that drove her faster and faster.

She stood up, unclipped her skirt and let it fall to the floor. Her panties were wet, a dark wet patch visible in the snow-white material. She slipped the panties off and stepped towards the statue, aware of the whiteness of her own skin and the fire in her belly. Swivelling round she saw Jean-Pierre, standing a few feet away, feasting his eyes on her and his creation. She sat back, carefully guiding herself between the marble thighs stretched out before her. She sat gingerly over the glans, pressing it between her pussy lips, which were puffy with desire.

She screamed once, a cry of pure bliss as she sat forcefully onto the hardness. The pleasure of penetration was complete. The prick filled her, forcing her pussy lips apart and working deep into her vagina. She rested for a moment, dizzy with the sensation of it inside her, then she began to move. She rocked her hips back and forth, up and down. She rose and fell on the hardness, driving herself to the edge of delirium. The base of the prick had been gripped tightly by the original model, the marble hands did likewise. As she moved with her own rhythm she felt the marble fingers beneath her, the thumb slightly raised, brushing gently under her anal crease.

She could hardly contain herself any more. She was moving with greater force, lifting herself to the very tip of the prick and then forcing herself down. The ripple of pleasure caused her to lose her breath, her head to spin. Her mind was blank, there was nothing but the pleasure, nothing but the feel of the statue deep inside her womanhood. She arched her back, a look of agonised pleasure on her face. She whispered some strange incantation, cried out with the force of climax. She forced herself down, the stone prick wedged deep in her cunt, the marble thumb forced into her behind.

Jean-Pierre took her in his hands and helped her off the statue. Her face was damp with sweat and she had a beatific look in her eyes. He kissed her gently on the lips, on the neck and throat.

She regained her breath at last. She stood on her own, moving away from Jean-Pierre's arms. 'That was good,' she said quietly, bending down to retrieve her skirt and panties.

'Now I know that you are beautiful,' he said rapturously. 'I know that I can trust you. You are an artist, I was wrong to doubt that.'

'This is a fantastic work, Jean-Pierre. Absolutely. You

must display this, it ranks beside any other work in the world. Surely you cannot keep this from the world?'

Jean-Pierre hestitated. He watched her get dressed, pulling on her soiled undergarment and then the short skirt. 'I don't know,' he said. 'I think this is a great work, one of my best. But there is so much of me here, so much of this beautiful young man too. Do you think that you are the first to have worshipped this figure in this way? I have paid homage too.'

He turned to the statue, rubbed his big hairy hand up and down the smooth leg. Without a word he moved closer, bending down over it.

'You see how your feminine body has marked this marble flesh. Do you see how your box has perfumed it?' He bent down and flicked his tongue against the hard prick, glistening in the light, wet from Amanda's pussy cream. His pink tongue lapped at the juices, taking them into his mouth. He turned to face her and swallowed her emissions, smiling with satisfaction and gratification. He turned back and this time took all of the marble prick deep into his mouth.

Amanda watched, fascinated by this display. His unshaven face was shaped around the prick, she could see it clearly impressed on his cheek. His eyes were closed and his lips worked up and down. The white marble contrasted with his own swarthy skin, his thick hairy arms against the slender musculature of the statue. His hands were everywhere, caressing the thighs and chest, moving over the body with unconcealed delight.

Amanda realised that he had been telling the truth. He was in love with his work, with this heavenly sculpture that he had made with his hands. He had made love to it too, had used it to find his pleasure just as she had. The thought was disturbing in a way, but exciting too.

Jean-Pierre finished, he looked up, smiled. He had

cleaned the statue with his mouth, had tasted woman on the cold hard cock. And it had tasted good.

The sun was sinking down below the horizon, disappearing into the golden sea far in the distance. Amanda had kicked her sandals off and was sitting with her legs folded beneath her. The room was light and airy; she could see why Jean-Pierre called it his thinking room. The four walls did not seem to intrude, to close things in. Rather the room gave the impression of vast open space, of the world beyond, beyond reality even.

Jean-Pierre returned with a silver platter full of fruit. Watermelon and honeydew melon, dark purple grapes, oranges as big as his fist, pomegranates split open to reveal the rosy crystalline flesh within.

'Tell me,' Amanda said, unable to contain her ardent curiosity, 'the model for the statue. Well, was he really that size?'

'I made no exaggerations. It is competely lifelike, and that includes his beautiful prize.'

'And how did you get him to pose like that?'

'I didn't exactly,' Jean-Pierre laughed, as he picked up an orange and sliced it with a small sharp knife. 'I saw him on many occasions playing with the other young men by the pool, or working in the fields. I watched him with an artist's eyes, so that his image was burned indelibly into my imagination. And then I produced my work.'

'Fantastic. The expression on the face, it's so real,' she smiled again. 'Have you ever made love with him?'

'Never,' Jean-Pierre said. 'You must remember these people are different. There is much about Frixos to remind one of the ancients. Here there is no shame if two men make love, none at all. It is considered as natural as drinking from the clear crystal streams that flow from the mountains. But this young man and I have never even touched each other.'

'But you must be tempted,' Amanda persisted, knowing her own desire was strong.

'I haven't even shown him the statue. I am afraid of his reaction. Perhaps he will hate it, and me. It is a strange position to be in, is it not?'

'Very strange,' Amanda agreed.

They ate in silence, enjoying the setting of the sun, the serenity, the stillness. The interview had not turned out the way that Amanda had expected or planned. Indeed she had little material that she could use directly. Even worse he had called into question her entire task.

'I must get back,' Amanda finally said. It was dark now and she and Jean-Pierre sat without light in the silent house. She could see his face, cast in shadows, the dark eyes brooding. He was a powerful man, sure of himself and aware of his own presence.

'Before you go there is one thing I must tell you,' he said. He leaned forward in the darkness so that his face was caught by the pale moonlight.

'Sure, go ahead.'

'I fear for the future of this island. I fear for Frixos.'

'I had hoped that you could trust me now,' Amanda said, disappointed by his words.

'But I do trust you, my dear,' he said, sounding hurt. 'It's not you that I worry about. I have been told by some of the older men that someone is buying up all the land by the sea.'

'Who's been buying it up?'

'You see, on this island the land is passed from father to son, it remains within the family for generations. But now this is changing.'

'Yes, but who has been buying up the land?' Amanda repeated eagerly.

'Andreas Karaplis, your host,' Jean-Pierre almost spat

the words out. He leaned back in his seat, an invisible presence looming in the darkness.

'Do you know why? Or how much land?'

'I don't know. All I know is that it can be for no good.'

'You can't be sure of that. But I think we ought to find out, don't you?'

'What can you do?'

'I don't know. It depends on what's going on. Will you help me?'

'What do you want me to do?'

Amanda sat up straight, drawing closer to Jean-Pierre. 'I want you to find out exactly how much land he has bought. How much he paid for it. Where the land is. And whether he had any help in buying the land.'

'I can do that. Give me a few days, I will have all of that. But you, what will you do?'

'I'll try to find things out as well, and try to figure out what I'm going to do about this place. After everything that we've said and done today I can hardly put any of it down on paper.'

She stood up and walked towards the door. She stopped by Jean-Pierre and bent down in the darkness. They kissed once, a long fervent embrace, and then she left, disappearing into the night.

five

Joanne was wide awake, sitting naked on the bed, scribbling notes untidily in a large notepad. Beside her Alice was asleep, the steady rhythm of her breath the only sound in the room. Joanne had tried to sleep, but she had merely tossed and turned, her mind returning again and again to thoughts about Andreas Karaplis and the hotel.

Though she had only spoken to Andreas briefly, she found it hard to believe that he was up to no good. There was something charming about him: it could have been his cool efficient manner, or perhaps his confident attractive smile. The fact that he was so charming made Joanne immediately suspicious, but at the same time she didn't want to believe that he was a crook.

Crook or not, she had to find out the whole truth about Paradise Bay and Andreas Karaplis. It was one of the reasons for the trip out, though she realised it had originally been nothing more than a convenient excuse. Only now the excuse had suddenly become real; there really did seem to be something that needed investigating. Joanne had considered calling Philip and telling him the news directly, warning him that something might be wrong. But such an action would interfere directly with her relationship with Alice.

She turned and looked at her, at the sleeping beauty

beside her. Alice's face looked angelic in the pale light of the reading lamp. Her lips were pursed slightly, waiting for an invisible kiss. The paleness of the light seemed to soften even further the curves of her delightful body. She was half covered by a thin cotton sheet, as if even in her sleep her natural modesty was at work.

Very gently, so as not to wake her, Joanne carefully pulled back the cover. She pulled it away and then flicked it on to the floor, completely exposing Alice's nakedness. She slept on her side, her hands tucked under her head, one knee pulled higher than the other. In the indistinct light it was impossible to make out the nest of dark pubic hair, or even to clearly distinguish the aureoles around her large nipples.

Joanne put her notepad down; she had written nothing of value, hoping that the simple act of putting pen to paper would cause ideas to come flooding into her head. Things were never that simple. She snuggled down closer to Alice, kissing her gently on the cheek, breathing her breath, sharing her warmth. It was so late, only hours before the break of dawn, yet she didn't feel at all tired. She felt more keyed up than ever.

She touched Alice idly with her fingers, playing back and forth over the silky smooth skin, tracing the curves of waist and chest. It would have been easy to wake Alice, to rouse her till consciousness came in a flash of orgasmic pleasure. She toyed with the idea of making love to her as she still slept, kissing her between the full heavy breasts, or flicking her tongue between the gently parted thighs. The thought didn't appeal to her; it lacked the frisson of excitement that she derived from watching Alice struggle with her reactions. To make love to her while she slept was altogether too simple, and Joanne knew that nothing that was good could be simple.

She sat up restlessly on one elbow, exhaling angrily.

If there was one thing that she could not abide it was not knowing what to do next. Some people seemed to thrive on indecision, but not Joanne.

On impulse she sat up and picked up the phone. She listened for a second to the low purring of the tone and then dialled nine. It rang, the tone changed to a steady pulsing ring at the other end. She waited impatiently for reception to pick it up. Room service was always one of the things that distinguished a very good hotel from merely a good hotel, and the time had come to make the decision where Paradise Bay stood on the scale. There was no answer. She put the phone down, annoyed that there was nobody on call, feeling somewhat disappointed that Paradise Bay had failed to live up to her high expectations.

Alice shifted in her sleep, turned over on to her belly. Her breathing pattern changed; for a second she seemed to hold her breath and then sighed gently. In her new position her breasts were squashed flat against the mattress, the nipples buried away. But her bottom was raised, one knee brought high, as if she were climbing up the bed.

Joanne leaned over her, rubbing her hand flat against the smooth flawless back. Desire suddenly flared up, she found herself studying Alice's bare behind with interest. She massaged the pert round backside, smoothing her hand over the fleshy arse-cheeks. Her hand traced every inch of the backside, pressing firmly against the firm flesh, tracing a finger around the join of the thighs and buttocks.

She wondered what it would be like to raise her hand and bring it down hard against the soft delicate flesh. The image aroused her intensely, causing a knot of excitement to form in the pit of her belly. She imagined Alice squealing with horror and shame, struggling fitfully, her backside tingling. She saw herself spanking Alice harder and harder, turning the perfectly formed backside pink and then red, her fingermarks etched firmly on each buttock.

Joanne stood up suddenly. She turned on her heel and marched impetuously towards the door. At the last moment she remembered that she was naked and burst out laughing. She looked at herself in the mirror and shook her head. Things were getting silly, too silly to be taken seriously. The idea of spanking Alice was ludicrous, ridiculous. They were both grown women, mature adults beyond such stupid games. She walked back into the room and found a robe in the wardrobe, slipping into a pair of sandals at the same time.

Outside it was much cooler than she imagined. The sky was as dark as pitch, the stars brilliantly sharp. The night was alive with the distant song of the sea, much louder than it was during the day, and the constant hiss of thousands of insects. She pulled the robe tight around her and headed for the main complex. Now that she had something to do, something clear and well defined, she felt better, in control again.

The hotel lobby was in semi-darkness and deserted. The doors swung open easily and she walked into the quiet enveloping warmth. All the lights were down apart from a thin strip light above the reception desk. The bar was empty, the counter neatly polished, the glasses reflecting back tiny squares of dim orange light.

'Hello?' Joanne said quietly, advancing up to the reception desk. She leaned over the counter and peered into the office at the back, searching for signs of life. There was nobody there. The door was open, the light in the office was blazing but there was no sign of anybody. She called again, this time raising her voice a notch higher, hoping that there would still be no reply.

Was somebody sleeping on the job? She strained across the counter, trying to catch a glimpse of a pair of legs stretched up on a desk, or of a body curled up in a corner somewhere. Nothing. She looked behind the counter, noting a half-empty packet of cigarettes and a lighter. To one side of the counter there was a kind of computerised till machine. Its fan whirred noisily, an orange LCD display flashing a message asking for input. It had a normal numeric pad like any other till, but also a special keyboard had been plugged in alongside, like a small computer keyboard except that the letter keys were in Greek. Beside the keyboard there were two boxes of small black diskettes. Each box was labelled in Greek. The diskettes had coloured stickers on them, blue for one box and red for the other, and a mixture of diskettes was scattered untidily by the keyboard, as if someone had abandoned a job half way.

Joanne called out one last time, almost whispering this time, waited for a few seconds then ducked under the counter. She stood for a second behind the counter, holding her breath, waiting for someone to appear. In a way it was exciting, like a mischievous little game, and the risk of getting caught only made it more exciting.

There really wasn't very much to look at behind the counter. Some pads full of incomprehensible notes, a diary full of room numbers and times, for early morning wake-up calls she guessed. There were lists and documents of various sorts in a drawer, but they were mostly in Greek, and looked unimportant. Joanne picked up a couple of the disks, looked at them blankly then put them down again. Whoever had been working the computer had no sense of order, the disks were scattered at random.

The office was in a similar state of untidiness. Papers were scattered all over the desk, rough notes covered in scribble. A Greek newspaper was open, a crossword half finished, notes scrawled in the margins in the same untidy hand as the notes on the desk. In the corner there was an empty bottle of Coke, still cool to the touch, drops of condensation on the outside. Whoever had been at the reception desk had only just gone.

Joanne opened the desk drawers, not sure what to look for, but certain that she had to make the effort. Again there was nothing that looked important, only the mundane documentation that littered every office. If she ignored the language Joanne was sure that she could guess what each document was for just by looking at the layout. Abandoning the desk she walked over to a grey filing cabinet. It was locked, but the small silver key was still in the lock. She pulled the top drawer open, cringing when it screeched loudly. She caught her breath and waited for someone to appear, but there was only silence.

This time she found that many of the documents were in English as well as Greek. But there was nothing of interest: page proofs for holiday brochures, promotional literature, letters to and from prospective corporate clients. It all looked so incredibly tedious. What Joanne wanted was something that would stand out, some document marked 'Personal' or 'Private and Confidential', anything that looked as if it was meant to be hidden. But if it was meant to be hidden it was not going to be in a filing cabinet where any of the reception staff could have access to it. She slammed the drawer shut, cursing herself when it complained again with an unoiled screech.

She looked around the office again quickly, checking that she hadn't missed anything obvious. The next step was to delve deeper into the building. She tried the door that led out of the office and into the back of the building. It had been closed but unlocked, opening on to a short corridor with other doors on the left and right, and a flight of stairs leading down on the right hand side.

This time she kept her mouth shut, certain that any call she made would be answered instantly. The first door she tried was unlocked. Inside the room was dark, illuminated only by the light from the corridor. It was a small office, two single desks, both with typewriters on them, the walls decorated with glossy posters of Frixos at its idyllic best. The typewriters were enough. There could be nothing worth knowing stashed in the room.

The second door was locked. Joanne translated the sign on the door: it was the most important room of all, Andreas's office. She felt let down, things had been going so smoothly, for a moment she had even imagined that it would be possible to find out once and for all if there was anything going on at Paradise Bay. But without access to Andreas's office things were going to be a bit more tricky.

The other doors were either locked or else the rooms they opened into looked thoroughly uninteresting. It was late, the childish excitement had died down, and now at last she had begun to feel tired and sleepy. She tried Andreas's door one more time, as if it were going to unlock itself miraculously. She turned to go back into the reception office when the flight of stairs caught her attention. Where everything else was either in darkness or dimly lit, the stairs were bathed in brilliant white light.

She listened out for a second at the top of the concrete steps, holding on to the cold steel handrail and twisting her head to catch even the faintest of sounds. There was nothing but the dull hum of a fridge or freezer, echoing up. The kitchens. Suddenly she remembered that she was really hungry; it was no longer just the glib excuse she had prepared in case of capture.

Almost without thinking she skipped down the stairs, planning a sumptuous meal of cooked meats and feta cheese, and whatever else the fridge would yield. At the bottom of the steps there was a further corridor with another concrete flight of stairs leading down into the depths. The warning signs required no translation: the steps led down into the machine room.

The entrance to the kitchen was through two big double doors, and she was about to barge in when she stopped. Perhaps it was the fact the lights were on, or else she remembered the missing receptionist, but something made her pause for a second. Very gently she pushed the door open an inch and looked inside. Her caution was justified. Someone was definitely in the kitchen. Her excitement came flooding back in a sudden rush of adrenalin. The game was on again.

She couldn't see anyone directly. But a large steel door from one of the half-dozen fridges in the kitchen was open. The fridges were massive, easily taller than a man, and split in different-sized compartments. She couldn't see anyone directly, but she could see a pair of bare legs poking out from under the door. Whoever the legs belonged to was rummaging through the fridge, obviously leaning deep into the cool compartment.

It was a man; the legs, visible from the ground up to a few inches below the knee, were too hairy to belong to a woman. A youngish man, Joanne guessed, and quite thin. She almost cried out with shock when the fridge door was suddenly slammed shut. She had been correct, it was a young man, not more than about twenty years old, tall and wiry. What she hadn't guessed was that he was naked.

The young man was carrying a large watermelon, a massive beast of an object that he had to hold with both arms. He staggered across the kitchen and plonked it down on one of the tables, balancing it right on the edge of a chopping board.

He stepped back from the table and looked at the melon, brushing his hand through his hair. His body was tanned a dark golden brown, except for his buttocks which were lighter, but only just. Joanne smiled; his thin wiry frame rippling with well defined muscle, was deeply attractive to her.

When he turned she caught sight of his face, long and thin, with a sharp nose and dark black eyes, the eyebrows joined at the centre. His prick was limp, hanging loosely in a dark brush of hair. He searched through a couple of drawers, opening and closing them again quickly, his eyes scanning intently. He found what he was looking for, a sharp knife, and then padded back to the watermelon, his prick swinging gently as he walked.

He examined the melon carefully, turning it over so that it rested more evenly on the flat surface. He wiped the waxy exterior of the massive fruit with his hand, then carefully made an incision with the knife. Joanne waited for him to slice through the green skin to reveal the dark red flesh inside, but instead he carefully worked the knife into the flesh, cutting out a small circle of the rind. He used the knife to extract the circle he had cut out, bringing out a sliver of juicy red flesh with it. He put the knife down and threw the extracted part of the melon across the kitchen into a sink.

Joanne was bemused, unable to work out what the man was up to. She watched him examining the hole that he had made, gingerly poking a finger into the sweetness and then tasting it. He padded across the tiled floor to the other side of the room, so that Joanne couldn't see him, then returned a few seconds later carrying a magazine. He flicked through the pages quickly, found the page he was looking for and laid it out next to the melon. He had his back turned to Joanne once more, he seemed to be studying the magazine intently, running his hands over the pages, turning to the next page once or twice.

He turned quickly, looked over his shoulder nervously, then returned to the magazine. In that instant Joanne was sure that he had seen her, but the fear of capture was nothing compared to the surprise she felt when she spotted his erection. In that single moment she had seen his thick hard prick standing to attention, thrusting proudly out from the dense jungle of dark hair.

He suddenly moved right up close to the table, almost pressing directly on to it. He wiggled from side to side then plunged forward, gasping audibly.

Joanne slipped into the kitchen immediately, unable to believe what was happening. She slid into a dark corner, hiding in the shadow, holding her breath. From her new vantage point she had a much better view of the man. And she was right, incredible as it had seemed, the man was pressing his prick in and out of the hole in the melon. She could see that the watery juice of the fruit was already smeared over him, dripping down his thighs, daubed on to his belly. His prick was gliding in and out, glistening with the red pulpy flesh of the melon. He was holding on to the fruit with both hands, pulling himself deep into it, his backside thrusting powerfully. His eyes were closed and he was moaning quietly, catching his breath with every thrust into the fruit.

She thought about creeping up behind him, tapping him lightly on the shoulder and saying hello. It was sure to frighten the life out of him, and give her a good laugh. But she waited, wanting to see if he was going to go the full way. Was there a word for having sex with food? If there was she couldn't remember it. The only stories she had ever heard of were about women using various phallic shaped fruit or vegetables to masturbate with. And those were all stories told by men. But this was new, and strange.

His strokes were getting faster, more frenzied, his knuckles had turned white. He sighed once, thrust himself deep into the object and stopped. She saw his backside twitching as he pumped his seed into the sweetness of the fruit.

'Hello,' Joanne said quietly, stepping out of the shadows. It was absurd, but she couldn't think of anything else to say. It was such an odd situation to be in.

The man swung round, totally aghast. His jaw dropped and his eyes were wide with pure shock. He whispered something in Greek, shook his head to wake himself up. Belatedly he tried to cover himself up. His prick was still glistening with an odd mixture of sperm and sticky fruit juices, but his erection was gone.

'Do you speak English?' Joanne said, taking a step towards him.

'Yes. I speak English. Please, you not say something,' he said tremulously.

'Do you always do that?'

'No. I try today for first time,' he lied unconvincingly. 'Please, you not say to manager. Mr Karaplis he tell me finish my job, if you tell him.'

'Don't worry,' Joanne smiled to him. 'Your secret is safe with me.' She reached out and touched him, running her hand across his smooth hairless chest, her fingers tracing a path up over his dark masculine nipples and along his shoulder. He relaxed, smiled at last, as if noticing for the first time that she was a woman. She looked up to him, opened her mouth and took his kiss, tasting the warm, moist lips.

They kissed only for an instant before she broke loose, stepping away from him. He looked at her with bewilderment written all over him, his darting eyes trying to glean an ounce of understanding from the inscrutable expression on her face. She knelt down before him, letting her robe fall slightly open so that he could see the slope of her breasts and know that she was naked underneath.

His prick was limp, nestling in the tussled prickly hair flecked with the crystal sugars of the watermelon. It was smeared liberally with watery juices and bits of red melon, all mixed in with his own semen, the whole glistening mixture dribbling down to the end of his cock and then

90

dripping on to the floor.

She took his prick in her hand, cradling it tenderly in her palm. He looked down at her excitedly, a massive grin on his face. Joanne saw that he couldn't believe his luck and was tickled by it. 'I'm hungry,' she explained, smothering her laughter.

His prick had started to respond to the warmth of her fingers, twitching back to life majestically. She opened her mouth and took it in at once, keen to feel it growing hard and strong in her mouth. The sweetness of the melon contrasted to the salty taste of his come, she could feel the different textures of the mixture on her tongue. She swallowed it all, sucking it clean, rubbing her tongue up and down the entire length.

He took her head in his hands, guiding her gently so that she could take it all into her mouth. The thick purple dome tickled the back of her throat, thick drops of fluid still seeping from the tip. He began to move his hips up and down slowly, enjoying the rub of her lips on his smooth prick.

Joanne rose and fell on his prick, moving up till the thick dome was on the tip of her tongue then plunging down to take him all, sucking her cheeks around his hardness. Her hands explored his thighs and buttocks, massaging his body, running her fingers through the thick hairy legs and over the smooth flesh of his backside. His movements became more urgent, he was thrusting harder and faster, his thighs were taut with exertion. As he exploded into her mouth he tried to move away, giving her room to free herself, but she took his seed deep into her throat, ingesting his creamy load completely.

She stood up and kissed him, falling into his grateful arms. She could feel his heart still racing, his breath was hot on her face.

'You're the receptionist, aren't you?' she said, closing

her eyes and relaxing in his arms.

'Night auditor,' he corrected. 'I work at night, not in day.'

'Night auditor then. How well do you know Andreas Karaplis?'

'Very well. He is second cousin with my father,' the young man explained proudly.

'Do you know anything about his plans?'

'Plans?'

'Yes,' Joanne looked up. 'What he has planned for Paradise Bay? Is he going to make it bigger? Smaller? What is he going to do in the future?'

'You mean about the boat?' he asked, looking blank.

'What about the boat?' Joanne asked suspiciously.

'I don't know about the boat,' he shrugged.

'Then why mention it?' she said crossly. 'Do you know anything at all?'

The young man shrugged again. 'I know there is a boat,' he said. 'But I don't know what about the boat. But my friend he knows about the boat. He knows good English.'

'Where is he?' Joanne asked, hoping that she could make some headway at last.

'He is waiter in hotel. But he is not here in the night, only in the day. You want me to tell him what about the boat?'

'Why don't you tell him to come and see me,' she suggested. 'In my room tomorrow.'

'No,' he said, smiling. 'I bring him to your room, together me and him. Yes?'

Joanne laughed. 'Yes, together you and him. Hey, you know I really am hungry,' she remembered.

'When I bring him tomorrow, you not say about this,' he pointed to the melon, smiling sheepishly.

Joanne laughed again. She took the knife and sliced into the fruit, the thick waxy rind split down the middle and the two halves of the melon rolled apart. She took one of the halves, rocking gently on the table, and cut off a slice. The shape of his prick had been burrowed into the flesh and it was full of creamy spunk glistening thickly. She brought it up to her mouth and took a bite, her eyes fixed on him. She swallowed a mouthful of sweetness and tasted his emissions sliding smoothly down her throat, enjoying the look of sick fascination displayed on his face.

Alice opened her eyes, slowly. Her whole body seemed to be suffused with a warm orange glow. She was naked, her body fully exposed to the sun flooding into the room. She turned to find Joanne lying next to her, smiling warmly.

'Good morning,' Alice whispered, drawing closer to Joanne. She wanted to snuggle up close, to feel Joanne's arms around her, to breathe with the same rhythm as her, to close her eyes and enjoy the feel of Joanne's skin against her own.

'I've been admiring your lovely backside,' Joanne purred. She opened her arms and let Alice shift closer. She kissed her on the shoulder and on the neck, tender loving caresses.

'Shall we go down to the village today?' Alice asked, her eyes closed dreamily.

'A lovely backside,' Joanne repeated, ignoring Alice's question. She stretched out her hand and tenderly rubbed her palm down Alice's smooth back. 'Have you ever been smacked on the bottom before?'

'No, never!' said Alice vehemently, sounding shocked.

'Not by your parents? Not even when you were small?' Joanne teased, massaging Alice's backside insistently, pressing her fingers firmly into the silky flesh.

'No, not even when I was small. And not by my teachers at school,' Alice said, knowing that that would be Joanne's next question. She snuggled up closer, burying her face under Joanne's arm. The feel of Joanne's fingers on her backside made her feel almost sleepy, it was a kind of soothing pleasant sensation, very sexy in an indistinct kind of way.

'A boyfriend perhaps? Did he put you over his knee and pull down your knickers before spanking you?' Joanne whispered, leaning right over to pass a finger down between Alice's bottom cheeks.

'Never. I would never let anybody treat me like that,' Alice affirmed, then regretted it. It was just the sort of remark that Joanne wanted to hear, it set up a limit, a fixed point to aim for.

'What about a girlfriend?'

'I've never had a girlfriend, you know that.'

'What am I?' Joanne challenged, resting a finger on Alice's tightly puckered arsehole.

'A girlfriend I suppose,' Alice conceded quietly. She didn't want to talk about it. Talking about it made her feel funny, sort of guilty and confused. It was better not to think, to just let things happen, to enjoy every moment as it happened.

'Am I? Am I a nice sort of girlfriend? The sort of girlfriend who would put you over her knee and spank your bare bottom?'

Alice hesitated, appalled at the thought, the image clear in her mind. 'Yes,' she admitted reluctantly. 'You could spank me like that if you wanted to.'

'And would you let me?'

'I don't know . . . Yes . . . If you wanted to.'

'But you said that you'd never let anyone treat you like that. That is what you said isn't it?'

'Yes. I wouldn't let anyone treat me like that. Except you.'

'Except me? What if I wanted to let someone else spank

you?' Joanne said. She suddenly pressed her finger into Alice's anal hole, eager to explore her there.

'That hurts . . .' Alice complained. She tensed up, frightened by the painful intrusion.

'When we get back to the office,' Joanne said, pressing her finger in a little deeper, 'I think I'm going to have to spank you quite regularly.'

'Please no . . .' Alice whined, wriggling her backside, trying to escape Joanne's probing finger. 'Why do you have to do this?'

'I'm going to have to put you over my knee and spank your perfect little bottom. I'll use my hand, or maybe a ruler, until you're begging for me to stop. Sometimes I'll bend you over my desk and punish you there.'

Alice caught her breath. The pain had subsided, and she was left now with the feel of Joanne's finger pressed deep into her arsehole. She could feel the muscles in her backside clutching tightly at the intruding object. Joanne's words were frightening and sinister. She couldn't tell whether they were an idle fantasy or something else. They had never discussed the future, certainly not what was going to happen when they returned home. She had assumed that Frixos was going to last forever, that there would be no return to home, and no return to normality.

'I'll call the other girls into the office to watch,' Joanne continued, excited by her story. 'I want them to see what happens to you when you're a naughty girl. I'll get Carmel to spank you for me sometimes. I'd like to see you over her knee, being spanked by her. Would you like that?'

'No, I don't want any of it. I don't want to be spanked by anyone. Not her and not you.'

'Then what do you want?' Joanne asked, removing her finger from Alice's arse-cheeks. She sat up and smiled sweetly, her eyes glittering with excitement.

'I want you to hold me close. I want you to kiss me

95

and for us to make love,' Alice said quietly, a serious look on her face. There was no gaiety to her voice, no sign even of hope. Her forlorn words matched her feelings exactly.

'I want that too,' Joanne said. 'But I want much more. I want every moment to be intense, for every second to be worth a hundred.' She scooped down and kissed Alice on the mouth, inserting her tongue between the moist pursed lips.

Alice felt the fear and discomfort drain instantly from her body. The same suffusing orange glow returned, a dreamy feeling that was like floating on air. Her hands touched Joanne's thighs, and she thrilled to the touch of the smooth lithe flesh.

'You see, just talking about spanking you has made me wet,' Joanne explained, parting her thighs to show Alice. 'You do that to me. You excite me. Suck me in my pussy,' she whispered, parting her thighs, and kissing Alice once more on the lips.

Alice knelt down, moved in closer. She could see that Joanne was aroused, her pussy lips were slightly parted, puffy. The pink flesh within seemed to be oozing drops of sex honey. She parted the pussy lips with her fingers, breathed deeply of the delicate feminine bouquet of desire. This was what Alice wanted, to give and receive pleasure, to share unselfishly. She opened her mouth and slipped her tongue into Joanne, knowing that both of them would soon be brought to climax.

six

The sharp knock at the door brought Joanne back to her senses. She had spent the morning alone, trying to piece together every scrap of information that she had about Paradise Bay and Andreas Karaplis. The most frustrating thing was that none of it seemed to make any sense. Worse still her mind kept wandering, her thoughts returning again and again to Alice.

'Yes?' she called out loudly, turning to check her face in the mirror. She was seated in the cane armchair she had moved to the side of the desk.

The door opened and the young night auditor slipped into the room, followed furtively by another young man dressed in the dark trousers and jacket of a waiter.

'I bring my friend,' the auditor explained quietly.

'My name is Nicholas,' the waiter said, stepping forward nervously. 'But English people call me Nicky.'

'I'm sorry,' Joanne smiled at the night auditor, 'but I don't seem to have your name.'

The waiter snorted derisively, spat something in Greek to the night auditor, something mocking because the night auditor coloured, looked angry.

'I am called Petros,' he said gravely, frowning.

'I forgot to ask you the other evening,' she told him. It was obviously the right thing to say: his smile returned, triumphant. He shoved the waiter under the ribs, hissed something incomprehensible. Whatever he had told his friend had been vindicated.

'You wanted to see me, miss?' the waiter said, giving Petros a dirty look. He looked a few years younger than Petros, smaller in build, his features still boyish. But his English was better, he spoke clearly and with only the faintest trace of an accent.

'Yes, please sit down,' she said, pointing the two young men to the bed. They sat down together, right on the very edge of the bed, hunched down, with legs parted and arms resting on their knees. 'I understand from Petros that you are very close to Andreas.'

'Yes, we are relatives. His father and my father are cousins,' Nicky explained, eyeing Joanne suspiciously.

'And you are close?'

Nicky shrugged. 'On Frixos everybody is related to everybody else. It is a small island.'

'Do you know anything of his plans for the future of this place?'

Nicky muttered something under his breath, something to Petros who replied in the same low tone. He looked down at his feet then mumbled, 'Why do you want to know?'

Stupidly Joanne had failed to anticipate the question. She had assumed that the waiter would tell her everything, without asking questions of his own or getting in the least bit suspicious. Damn, she hadn't realised what a patronising attitude she had to the locals. It had been so entirely unintentional. She felt guilty, and in a fix.

'You talk to journalist? To Amanda?' Petros suggested, noticing Joanne's hesitation.

'Yes, that's right,' Joanne jumped at the excuse, relieved. 'I'm doing some extra research work for her, she's too busy to do everything herself.'

98

'Then why not ask Andreas yourself?'

There was no pause this time. 'Amanda has already spoken to him. But I just wanted to get the views of some other people. People who aren't so closely connected to the running of the hotel.'

'You talk to people in village too?' Petros asked, leaning forward.

'Yes, soon. But I imagine Andreas has given you all instructions to help Amanda Trevelyan as much as possible,' Joanne guessed.

'Yes, before she arrived,' Nicky confirmed, a note of hesitation still in his voice. 'But I have spoken to Amanda before, she never mentioned you, or any extra research.'

'Why should she?' Joanne said. She smiled at Nicky, gazing into his dark intelligent eyes directly.

Petros muttered something again, nudging Nicky with his elbow.

'What you want to know?' he said gruffly.

'Just what kind of plans there are for the future,' Joanne said, relaxing a little, certain that she was about to make some progress. 'Is Andreas going to build a golf course? An extension to the hotel? Anything of that sort.'

'I thought you wanted to know about the boat!' Nicky laughed, amused by his misunderstanding.

'What boat? Is he going to buy a boat?'

'You said you didn't want to know about the boat,' Nicky complained.

'I said I want to know about the future,' Joanne said, frustrated by the feeling of going round in circles. 'Is he going to buy a boat for the guests here?'

'No golf course. No extension,' Nicky said coldly. He stood suddenly, as if to walk out. Petros grabbed hold of him, glaring angrily.

'Look it's getting rather hot in here,' Joanne said, also standing. 'Would you like a drink? A beer? Petros?'

'Beer please,' Petros smiled. He pulled Nicky back down.

'Nicky?'

'Beer for me also please,' he sighed.

Joanne walked across the room, her high heels cracking on the pine floor. She was buying time, hoping to put Nicky into a more relaxed sort of mood. Whatever the young man knew it had to be something of value. She bent down to look in the mini-bar and saw them both looking at her intently. Her skirt was stretched tightly over her thighs, the slit at the back revealing a good length of bare flesh. Her high heels accentuated the long curve of her legs and the roundness of her rear. She bent lower, keeping her legs straight so that the skirt was stretched ever tighter.

She unbuttoned the first few buttons of her blouse before turning back to the young men. They had been speaking quietly, whispering sharply at each other but they fell silent when she turned round. She carried a tray with two tins of icy cold beer and a scotch and Coke for herself. Again she was aware of their eyes on her, following every movement of her body. She bent down to offer them the drinks and her blouse fell open at the top, revealing the valley between her breasts.

'You were saying,' Joanne purred seductively, standing between the two men, smiling at Nicky.

'I don't know about any plans for the hotel,' he said quietly, cradling the ice cold beer in his hands.

'You look very hot,' Joanne said. 'Why don't you relax a little?' She put her hand on his shoulder, felt him tense up. Very softly she traced her finger back and forth across his shoulder, waiting for him to make some move.

'You are very beautiful,' Petros said, placing his hand on her leg, resting it just behind her knee, waiting to see how she would react.

Joanne turned to Petros and smiled, shifting round so

that she was more evenly placed between them. Petros smiled back, gaining in confidence. He rubbed his palm further up her leg, making slow movements up and down, working gradually higher. She turned back to Nicky, but he was looking resolutely away, sipping from his beer, eyes fixed firmly on the ground. He was shy, and she knew that the only way to get over that was for her to make the moves.

She bent down low and brushed her hand through his wavy hair, bleached by the sun. He looked up, with dark intense eyes, his lips trembling slightly. Had he never been with a woman? It was hard to believe, he was certainly an attractive young lad. But living on a small island where everyone knew everyone else, and where strict morals still applied, she imagined that it could well be difficult for a young man to find a first partner.

She kissed him softly on the mouth, pressing her lips on his, pushing her tongue between his teeth. He responded at once, moving round, opening his mouth and pushing his tongue into hers. His breath was hot, but his mouth was cool and tasted of the beer he had just been drinking. She felt his hand seek out her thigh, brushing up and down her leg, eager to explore.

Petros stood up behind her, his hand high up her skirt, touching her just below her pussy, tracing the outline of her backside with his finger. He stopped for a second and found the catch of the skirt, unclipped it and pulled down the zip at the side. He pulled the skirt down an inch and then let it drop to the floor.

Joanne straightened up and smiled at the two young men in turn, feeling a well of excitement stirring deep inside her. The feel of their hands touching her, gently exploring her, was arousing. She had never made love to two men at the same time before, and the idea of it was immensely exciting. She unbuttoned her blouse quickly and let it slip off her shoulders and cascade down to the floor on to her skirt.

'Lovely,' murmured Nicky, his blazing eyes drinking in her image. He reached out and touched her right breast, two fingers brushing her nipple. Petros stepped right up against her from behind. She could feel his thick prick pressing against her, padded by his trousers but still hard enough to be arousing. He slipped his arm over her shoulder and crossed her body, cupping her right breast with his left hand.

Nicky could control himself no longer. He sat up on the edge of the bed, on his knees, and began to kiss and suck her nipple. Feverishly he licked and kissed, his hot lips rousing her nipple to erection. He held her by the waist, pulling her close, balancing himself against her body.

Joanne sighed with pleasure, throwing her head back and closing her eyes. Both her breasts were being stimulated, Nicky was sucking the nipple into his mouth, lapping at it with his tongue, playfully sucking hard. More expertly Petros was massaging her nipple between his thumb and fingers, pulling the tight node of flesh till it was hard and sensitive. Her pussy was wet, burning already with a fiery juice of expectation.

She could feel Petros's hard prick wedged between her bottom cheeks, moving up and down slowly, moving her panties with the same motion. Blindly she sought Nicky's prick, her hands touched him, feeling the outside of his trousers. Nicky stopped, let go of her breasts for an instant, and undressed quickly. He threw his jacket and shirt off, dropping them into an untidy bundle behind him. He unzipped his trousers and rolled them down, pulling down his boxer shorts at the same time. He took her hand and placed it round his hard prick, sighing with relief when she squeezed him there.

Petros took this as a signal. He too stepped back and undressed completely. Joanne turned and saw his prick, long and hard, just as she remembered it. His body was tough and masculine, his wiry frame glistening with a thin layer of sweat. When Joanne turned she found that Nicky had finished stripping off too, pulling his trousers off completely. His body was thinner, not so muscular, but his prick was large and thick, and his body hairless apart from a dense pubic bush.

Joanne pulled her panties down, aware that they were visibly wet, with a telltale smear of her oozing cream sliding down her thigh. She moved on to the bed, sliding gracefully past Nicky. Her body was aflame with desire, she wanted them both, inside her, fucking her together.

She knelt on all fours, her backside raised high, buttocks slightly parted. Petros muttered something, his voice low and indistinct. She felt something brush between her thighs, then cried out. One of them had mounted her, suddenly forcing his huge hard prick deep into her well of joy. The force of penetration sent a spasm of delight pulsing through her body, an electrifying sensation of pure pleasure.

He began to fuck her, slicing long slow strokes into her, pressing his prick into her wet warmth. She had her eyes closed, sighing softly, overwhelmed by the ecstatic rhythm of his movement. She felt something in front of her, felt a shadow blot out the sun falling on her face. It was Nicky, kneeling in front of her, holding his prick in his hand. She stretched forward and kissed it softly, pressing her lips on the very tip of the purple-headed dome. He sighed, a look of pleasure and delight etched on his face.

Joanne was pressing her backside out, wanting Petros to fuck her deeper, to enter her further. He was moving faster, driving forward with all his strength. She wanted to cry out with pleasure, to scream with sheer blissful joy. She smothered her cries by taking Nicky's prick into her mouth, closing her lips over the engorged tool. He reciprocated by making sharp rotating movements with his pelvis, seeking his own rhythm. She rose and fell on his prick, letting him fuck her, as if her mouth were a warm tight feminine sex. She could taste the salty fluid dripping from his glans, knowing that he was nearing the end.

Petros suddenly went wild. He thrashed forward several times, forcing himself deep inside Joanne's soaking pussy, pulling her arse-cheeks apart with his hands. He froze, cried out incoherently. She cried out at the same time, driven to climax by the wild uncontrolled passion. She felt lost in a white plateau of pleasure, her body aflame, accepting the thick wads of seed he was pumping into her.

Seconds later, her body tingling with a pleasurable orgasmic afterglow, Nicky forced his prick high into her mouth. He held her head in his arms, his body jerking time and time again. She swallowed his come, taking the thick sap deep into her mouth and letting it float smoothly down her throat.

Petros stood up first, a smear of golden sweat glistening on his broad chest, his prick still hard, a glob of thick spunk dribbling down its length. Joanne stood up as well, feeling a little dazed, her body still tingling, the taste of come strong in her mouth. The two of them stood and looked down at Nicky, who was lying flat on his back, breathing deeply.

'His first time,' Petros whispered, finding it rather amusing. He turned and picked his clothes up off the floor lazily, smiling to himself all the while.

Joanne walked into the bathroom, drops of come seeping from her sex and sliding down her thighs. Quickly she towelled herself, rubbing her thighs clean, wiping the beads of perspiration from under her arms. There was nothing to wear in the bathroom so she returned to the room naked, ignoring the admiring looks from the young men. She found her robe and put it on loosely, not bothering to tie the cord around the waist. She padded back to her seat and sat down heavily, feeling tired and sated, but happy and excited.

'What about the boat?'

Nicky sat up on the edge of the bed, and smiled weakly. 'I don't know very much about it,' he said quietly.

'You must know something,' Joanne said sceptically. She had given him more than he had imagined possible, she had given him his first taste of woman. Now he had to pay for it. It wasn't blackmail exactly, nor an out-and-out business proposition. More like a favour for a favour.

'It's not a boat for people. I don't know the English word for it. It's a flat kind of boat,' Nicky explained.

'So it's not a ferry, like the one that brought me from the mainland?'

'No, not for people, no passengers.'

'Is it some sort of cruise boat? For quick tours around the island,' Joanne suggested, unclear what kind of boat Nicky was trying to describe. She silently cursed the fact that his excellent grasp of English failed him at this point.

'No,' he said emphatically. 'Not for people at all. It's a long flat ship. From Pireaus.'

'Is he buying this ship?'

'No, it's too big for that. He is renting the boat from an agent in Pireaus.'

'What's he going to use it for?'

Nicky shrugged. 'I don't know. It's a secret, none of us are supposed to know about it at all. Even his own family don't know about it.'

'Then how do you know about it?'

'I have a cousin who works for a shipping agency on the mainland, they own the ferry. He put Mr Karaplis in touch with the agent in Pireaus.'

'I see,' Joanne said, though she didn't. None of it made any sense. Least of all the description of a long flat ship. 'Does your cousin know anything else?'

'No,' Nicky said simply.

'Tell me more about this flat ship. Does it carry things? Like a cargo ship?'

'Cargo ship?' Nicky repeated, scratching his head.

'Cargo ship?' Petros echoed, looking at Nicky and then Petros and then back again.

'Like an oil tanker?' Joanne tried hopefully.

'Not exactly. This ship doesn't carry oil. Or things like fruit or vegetables. I think it is for stones and dirt.'

'Stones and dirt?'

Petros said something in Greek, something disbelieving. Nicky snapped back, hurt, angry.

'I have to go now,' he said, turning from Petros to Joanne. 'I am supposed to be working. If Mr Karaplis catches me he'll throw me out.'

'Please, just a few more questions.' Joanne stood up, realising that she had made no real progress. The mysterious boat meant nothing. If anything she was farther from the truth than when she had started.

'I'm sorry, I have to go,' Nicky said, hurriedly pulling his clothes on.

'We come back another time?' Petros offered, smiling broadly.

'Perhaps,' Joanne said glumly, sitting back down. 'A boat for stone and dirt?'

'A flat boat,' Nicky tried to explain once more. 'Not a big ship like the ones that carry the food and the things. Goodbye, I have to go now. And . . . and . . . thank you.'

He smiled shyly then slipped out of the room, checking first to see that there was no one outside. Petros smiled again then followed, carefully shutting the door behind him.

Joanne was alone in the room. The thoughts kept going round in circles, never connecting. A boat, a flat boat for stones and dirt. Not a passenger craft of any sort. A big flat boat.

She walked over to the bar, poured herself another drink. The balcony door was open and she stepped outside into the bright direct light. Her robe was loose and the sun beat down on her bare skin, warming her all over. She held her hand up to shield her eyes from the golden light. Down below was the sea, rising and falling tirelessly, washing up against the golden sand then ebbing away again. It was quiet, the sound of the surf soothing in its rhythm, like a special form of silence.

She looked out on the horizon, trying to picture a long flat boat resting on the glittering blue waters. Nicky's words were lifeless, they formed no picture in her mind, stirred no images. She didn't know about ships and boats, and evidently neither did he. Yet he had a special form of craft in mind, had tried to find the words to describe it.

The bay was empty, the open waters an empty expanse of gold and blue. What sort of craft could glide into those shallow waters? Water so shallow that even the ferry had to anchor outside the bay. A flat boat. Not a tanker, not a cargo ship, or container craft. Flat. Flat-bottomed.

'Got it!' she cried out excitedly. She almost jumped into the air with excitement. It seemed so obvious. A flat craft. For stones and dirt. A dredger!

She returned to the room, certain now that she had cracked the mystery. It all fitted so well. Amanda's story about the artificial silting up of the bay. Martin's story about buying up land around the island. Nicky's story about the flat boat. The devious bastard! Andreas was planning on dredging the bay, opening it up again. And when the tourists came flooding in he was going to have the land for development already in his hands, He couldn't lose. It was a brilliant scheme, utterly brilliant. She couldn't help admiring him for that.

A dredger! She rubbed her hands with excitement. What next? Should she call Philip or wait until she knew more? It could wait. It had to wait. She thought of Alice, alone in her room. No, it had to wait. The two of them would carry on investigating. The story needed confirmation of some sort. They had to find out the name of the dredger, some times and dates. And then, when everything was ready, they would call Philip. Until then of course, she and Alice would remain alone, totally alone.

Jean-Pierre welcomed Amanda heartily, opening his arms wide and kissing her gently on the cheek. He was smiling and laughing, his mood open and lighthearted.

'Well?' Amanda asked eagerly, following him into his 'thinking' room. The day was already hot, the thermometer gradually climbing the scale, higher and higher. All the windows and doors to the room were opened, but hardly a breeze disturbed the thick hot air. She was dressed in a simple white skirt and blouse, loosely fitting clothes that didn't stick uncomfortably.

'I've been very busy!' Jean-Pierre announced grandly. He poured two drinks and passed one to Amanda. 'I have talked to many people, friends from all over the island. And you?'

'Not good news, I'm afraid,' she said. 'I tried ringing at the development office, to see if any plans had been filed with the authorities, but it was a waste of time.'

'Of course it was,' Jean-Pierre said, as if it were plainly obvious. 'Karaplis has a brother there, that's how he managed to get permission for Paradise Bay. That is what you found, is it not?'

'I should have asked you first,' Amanda sighed. 'I didn't

know until it was too late, by then I was speaking to his brother. And he knew all about me.'

'Your fame precedes you,' Jean-Pierre laughed.

'More like Andreas has got his family well briefed. I just made up an excuse about collecting background material on the island. He didn't sound suspicious by the time I put the phone down.'

'Perhaps. But the story will still get back to Karaplis. That is the way things are on Frixos. Any bit of news gets passed on, especially anything to do with someone as beautiful and as glamorous as you my dear.'

'Please, Jean-Pierre,' Amanda said sweetly, 'do not call me "my dear".'

'I have offended you?' Jean-Pierre looked hurt. 'I'm sorry, I don't mean to offend, but for me you are a beautiful and desirable woman. I can't put that out of my mind.'

'It's not that,' Amanda said, taking his massive hand in hers. 'It's being called "my dear". It makes me feel I'm being talked down to ...'

'I don't mean to talk that way. Perhaps it sounds different in French. Will you forgive me?'

'Yes, of course.'

'Thank you, my dear!'

She looked at him sideways, not sure whether it had been unintentional or not. He smiled back, shrugged his shoulders and they burst out laughing.

'OK, I also came to one important decision,' she said, becoming more serious. She had spent most of the night wrestling with her conscience, trying to weigh up all the factors. Now that she had made a decision she wanted Jean-Pierre to know.

'Yes?'

'After that guilt trip you laid on me I've decided not to do a piece on Frixos in front of the cameras.'

'No TV?'

'No TV. Also I'll only write a very short piece for a travel journal. It'll be a good piece, I can't paint the island black just to keep people away. Also I won't mention how the harbour came to be silted up. You won't know how difficult that is for me. It's a good piece for writing, a nice little story. But I guess once it becomes known someone somewhere will want to reverse the process. And if the harbour is opened then the island will finish.'

'Thank you,' Jean-Pierre said quietly. He leaned forward in his seat, his eyes were suddenly misted, he looked genuinely moved. He reached out and kissed Amanda once on the lips, his rough face and thick lips rubbing against her smooth skin and delicate petalled lips.

'It was the least I could do,' Amanda mumbled, a little embarrassed by the unexpected show of emotion. Jean-Pierre was a monster to deal with, but his emotions were plain to see.

'I am grateful, honestly I am,' he said once more.

'Your turn,' she said, sitting upright again. 'What did you find out?'

'Very much! Look over here,' he said, standing up. He went over to the far end of the room and knelt down by a low glass-topped coffee table. Amanda knelt down beside him excitedly, wondering what he was going to produce.

Beside the table there was a large rolled-up tube, bound by delicate pink ribbon. Ceremoniously he undid the bow and rolled out the stiff canvas. He unfurled the object and laid it out flat on the coffee table. It was a map of the island, drawn by hand and roughly shaded using thick pastel strokes.

'Your own map!' Amanda squealed, recognising the delicate work and the subtle use of colour.

'I would make a good cartographer, would I not?'

'Well, I don't know,' Amanda teased him. 'I think you

have the directions all wrong.'

'Directions? Directions are for people who don't know where they are going. Jean-Pierre knows exactly where he is going.'

Amanda looked at the map. From an angle the island looked like a foetus curled up on itself, the inlet around Paradise Bay the first inkling of a face, its arms curving around the harbour. It was a strangely disconcerting thought, and she shook it from her head. 'What does this tell me?' she asked.

'Karaplis has bought land in those places I have left unshaded,' he said, pointing out a number of uncoloured patches on the map. 'Those places are dead, I ought to shade them darkest black.'

'All of it land around the coast. Do you know any of the places?'

'Not all of them. Most are very nice places, sandy beaches, quiet inlets and bays, beautiful land. I shall weep if they are destroyed, weep like a parent who has lost a child. My heart is heavy just thinking about it.'

'Don't think about it,' Amanda told him sharply. Her mind was racing, trying to see if a pattern would emerge from the oddly discoloured patches on the map. 'This place,' she pointed to a largish patch in the centre of the island. 'What is it?'

'Useless. It's mostly dry land, no good for crops. Not even good for building houses, there are no wells in the area. Useless.'

'So why buy it?'

'Because it's cheap?' Jean-Pierre suggested.

'No, there's got to be some other reason. He doesn't sound like the sort of man that would buy land just because it's cheap. Is it wooded?'

'A little, not like it is higher up. You think he bought it for the wood?'

'Does that sound unreasonable?'

'Yes.'

'Do you know who owned the land before?'

'Sadly, no. But I can tell you that he has bought twelve separate plots of land. From ten different people.'

'And how much did he pay?'

Jean-Pierre smiled. 'The island people never speak of such things,' he said. 'But I believe he paid good prices for it all. The people I spoke to all complained that they had been robbed, that they had been tricked out of their lands. But that's all for show, it is the way of the people. If they had been tricked the whole island would have been up in arms.'

Amanda sat back on her heels, she kept looking at the map, trying to piece it all together. Karaplis had bought coastal plots of land all around the island, on every side. And one piece inland, away from everything. Why?

'Where is the airfield on this map?' Amanda suddenly asked.

Jean-Pierre looked at her and then jabbed with a thick round finger at a point towards the centre of the island. Near to the large discoloured plot.

'This land is fairly flat isn't it?'

'An airport?' Jean-Pierre mumbled, half to himself.

'That's it!' Amanda said excitedly. 'He's going to expand the airfield, or build a new one. And open up new resorts to take the increased capacity.'

'He has it all planned...'

'Absolutely,' Amanda said, standing up. It all made perfect sense. It would be stupid to build new resorts if you couldn't get the people to fill them. And you couldn't get people to fill new resorts without the means to transport them in and out. One required the other. And Andreas Karaplis was ensuring that he had an interest in both sides of the equation.

'What do we do now?' Jean-Pierre staggered up from his knees, the laughter gone from his eyes. He looked worried, tired.

'We stop him, of course,' Amanda said without thinking. She had no idea how yet, but it was her honest first reaction.

'What do I do?'

'I'm not sure what you do. But I think it's time Andreas and I had a nice long talk.'

Alice moped about the room dejectedly, listening for a time to the radio, flicking through a magazine, trying to read a book. It was a sweltering morning, the hottest so far. She had ventured out on to the balcony for a time, sitting under the sunshade, looking out at the sea, reading and rereading the same pages of a paperback. But the heat and the boredom soon forced her back into the cooler silence of the room.

She couldn't concentrate. Maybe it was the heat. Or the fact that Joanne had sent her away soon after they had made love, first thing that same morning. Joanne had made some excuse, mumbling something about business and doing some work. But Alice recognised an excuse when she heard one.

She didn't say anything to her at the time, but felt certain that her feeling of rejection was plain to see. It was a horrible feeling, she felt cold and alone. Horrible. She had wanted to cry, her eyes had filled with tears and her heart felt heavy. But she didn't succumb to the self-pity, she returned to her room, feeling rotten but with her face dry.

Things had changed so much, and so quickly. Where had it all come from? Alice was certain that sex and desire weren't things that you learned. Sex and desire, the things that secretly drive a person, they were all things that you were born with. Except that most people didn't know what went on inside them, they had no idea. And she had been like that, not knowing, not caring, thinking that she was someone else altogether. And then Joanne had changed things.

Suddenly there were all these things seeping out, strange needs and emotions, alien reactions. But they weren't alien, not really. They were things that had been inside her all along. And what else was in there? What else was there to discover about herself?'

Things were easier before, Alice knew that for sure. Her life had been simple and uncomplicated. She did things like everyone else, without thinking and without bothering. But that was all gone. It was gone and she regretted it, sort of. It was the simplicity that she missed, that pure uncomplicated way of looking at the world.

Joanne had told a story that morning, repeating out loud her fantasy. Alice had been shocked by it. She had listened while Joanne had described spanking her, beating her on the naked backside, in the office, in front of the other women. Her reaction had been one of absolute amazement, and shock. But by the end of the story she had felt the first pangs of desire, felt the heat growing inside her. And then they had made love, sucking and kissing, touching and exploring. The story still in their minds, sharing the fantasy and the excitement.

And if it came to real life? Alice didn't want to think about it. Because she was afraid of her reaction, afraid that she would willingly submit to the punishment and humiliation. Afraid that she would find pleasure in it above all else.

She got up from the bed where she had been lying for an hour, her eyes closed, hoping to fall into a deep relaxing sleep so that the thoughts in her head could be stilled, the shrill disturbing clamour silenced. But it had been a vain hope. She couldn't sleep, just as she couldn't concentrate on anything but her and Joanne.

Her skin felt clammy, her clothes sticky and uncomfortable. It was time for a shower.

In a moment she was naked, standing under the showerhead, letting the cool water wash over her. The sharp jets of water washing away the sweat and the irritation. It felt good, refreshing. The water flowed over her smooth dark skin, flowing down her face like a thousand tears, dripping rivulets down between her breasts.

She didn't bother to soap herself, but stood for several minutes, just enjoying the feel of the water on her body. In the back of her mind she hoped that Joanne would come in, walk through the door and join her. But most of all she just stood under the water and let it pour.

She felt much better by the time she turned the water off. The gushing jet slowed to a trickle then stopped. Tiny ripples of water still fell over her body, dripping down through her glossy black hair and coursing over her breasts. Her nipples were hard and the drops of water fell from them on to the tiled floor.

She got out of the shower cubicle to dry herself, towelling her body vigorously with a thick hotel towel. Her skin felt cool again. The towel slipped from her grasp and she bent down to pick it up, as she did so she caught sight of herself in the mirror. She was bent down low, her backside sticking out, feet together, knees slightly bent. She stopped and looked at herself for a minute, studying the contours of her body in the mirror. Her arse-cheeks were slightly parted, the dark crease curving round between her thighs, a tiny hint of pink flesh visible between her pussy lips.

It was the sort of position that Joanne had described, bent low ready for a spanking. Alice felt a sudden thrill of excitement and her heart raced. She imagined Joanne standing over her, scolding her, tormenting her with a few well-chosen words. She imagined Carmel and Belinda and the others, all standing by the door to Joanne's office, watching in wide-eyed silence.

She left the towel on the floor and straightened up her knees, trying to bend lower, eager to see herself displayed. Her arse-cheeks had become rounder, more parted; she could see the faint darkness around her anus, her pussy mound now visible from the back.

She raised her hand high behind her and brought it down hard on her backside. The sudden jolt of pain surprised her; it hurt more than she had anticipated. Her backside immediately flared red, the imprint of her fingers clear to see. The pain throbbed, sending dark daggers of sensation pulsing through her. She caught her breath, suddenly feeling dizzy.

Without waiting she raised her hand again and brought it down, smacking herself on the other buttock. And then again, and again. She beat herself hard on the rear, smacking herself evenly on both bottom cheeks. Each smack made her burn, turning the flesh a deep fleshy scarlet, the imprint of her fingers criss-crossed on her skin.

She stopped just as suddenly as she had begun. Her arse seemed to be aflame, the skin dark and red. The excitement she had felt had been transformed into a raging heat in the pit of her belly. She stood up and staggered out of the bathroom, aware of the fire on her behind, the sharp stinging spreading deeper into her, working tendrils of sensation into her pussy.

She collapsed on to the bed, lying on her belly to avoid sitting on the tender arse flesh. The space between her thighs was damp, burning with the aftereffect of the self-inflicted spanking.

There had been no choice, it had to be done. Joanne had set the idea in her mind, planted the seed of doubt,

Alice had merely acted on the doubt. She knew the answer now. If it came to it she would willingly submit herself to punishment. And she would find pleasure in the chastisement. It was a strange pleasure, pulsing through her veins, inflamed by the smarting of her arse-cheeks. She moved her hand under her belly, nestling a finger in the warm entrance to her sex.

Spanking herself had been strange, but all the time she had been thinking of Joanne, imagining that it was her hand coming down so hard. And now, lying naked on the bed, she imagined that it was Joanne who was snaking a finger into the moistness of her sex. She closed her eyes and thought only of Joanne.

seven

The bar was almost empty. A single female guest was seated in one corner, reading a magazine and drinking from a long cool drink. There was only one barman on duty, the poolside bar being much busier. Amanda stepped into the air-conditioned coolness and saw Andreas leaning against the bar, chatting quietly to the barman. She took a deep breath then strode confidently through the bar towards Andreas, the loud staccato beat of her high heels signalling her arrival.

Andreas turned and smiled, then stood up straight and indicated to the barman that their conversation was over. 'You wish to speak with me?' he said to Amanda when she was close to him.

'Yes,' she said, feeling a little deflated by his charming smile.

'You have been talking to my brother, also,' he said, taking her by the arm and leading her to a seat. They sat opposite each other. He looked relaxed and happy, not in the least bit apprehensive.

'Yes. And other people too,' she said, hoping to wipe the confident smile from his face. She had psyched herself up for a confrontation with him, certain that he would deny all her accusations.

'Of course, of course. You have been speaking to that

118

strange Frenchman who lives in the mountains.'

'He is not strange,' Amanda said defensively. 'He is a fine artist, and a very nice man.'

'I know,' Andreas laughed. 'He is what you English people like to call eccentric.'

'Yes, a little eccentric perhaps,' Amanda admitted reluctantly.

'But I always thought that eccentric was a polite way of calling someone strange,' Andreas said slyly, and then laughed.

Amanda laughed too, the edge of her anger having been blunted. Andreas was a smart operator, he had turned the situation around very quickly, not even giving her a chance to express her anger. 'OK, Jean-Pierre might be a little strange, but he is rightly worried about the future of this island. And, to be honest, so am I.'

'What is there to be worried about?'

'You,' she said bluntly.

'Me?' Andreas asked, sounding shocked and confused.

'Yes, you,' Amanda repeated, not taken in by his exaggerated expression of surprise.

'I don't know what you mean. I love this island more than anybody. I have the future of this island close to my heart.'

'Yes, next to your wallet. We know that you've been buying up land all over the place.'

'I know you do,' Andreas countered. 'The Frenchman was not very discreet in asking questions. This is a small island, nothing goes on without everybody knowing about it.'

'So it's true then?'

Andreas called across to the barman for two drinks. 'Of course it's true. I don't deny that I've bought some land, it's not a great secret.'

'But what you plan on doing with it is a secret,' Amanda

said, fixing him with a cold stare.

'Not a bit of it. What do we Greeks do with our land? We pass it down to our sons. That is the way we are. We are still peasants at heart, still bound to the soil.'

'God,' Amanda shook her head with disbelief. 'You sound like you've been talking to Jean-Pierre yourself.'

'Sorry?'

'Nothing.' Amanda took her icy drink from the barman. 'So all this land is to pass on to your sons. How many sons do you have, Andreas?'

'None, of course,' he said, smiling. 'But I will have, when I have found myself a wife. And my sons will have the land that I have bought.'

'It's so rare to find a man as forward-looking as you. This land that you have bought, it's all good farming land is it?'

'Of course not,' Andreas looked genuinely affronted. 'I don't want my sons to be farmers. I haven't escaped that fate to send my own sons back to it. No, this is good land for building homes on. My sons will be lawyers and accountants, teachers and scientists. Not farmers.'

'What about your daughters?'

'My daughters as well, they will be doctors or teachers also. All my children will do well.'

'I see,' Amanda said. 'You have the soul of a Greek peasant, an indissolvable and sacred link to the soil, but you don't want anything to do with working the land. Very strange.'

'Strange enough to be considered eccentric?' Andreas smiled.

'No.' She refused to be drawn by his easy manner. 'I think you're lying. I know you're lying, I can feel it in my bones.'

'And very nice bones they are too,' Andreas said slickly.

'Don't annoy me,' Amanda said coldly. 'You've bought

that land to build on. You're planning to develop more resorts. That's why you've bought those beachside plots. Paradise Bay is only the first, isn't it?'

'I see you too are branching out,' he said sourly, his smile gone now. 'You have moved from second-rate travel writing to third-rate fiction.'

'That's good, very bitchy. Can I take that as implicit agreement that I am right?'

'I don't know what you are talking about. I asked you to Paradise Bay as a personal guest. I thought that you would write about the things that you saw here, not about the rumours dreamt up by some crazy Frenchman.'

'So Jean-Pierre has gone from eccentric to strange to crazy, what next?'

'He is also a sick man who likes to watch young men playing naked in the water. I am sure that if I search hard enough, I could also find young men who will tell me that he has done more than just watch. Do you think the police are interested in art?'

'I thought you were quite a nice man, Andreas,' Amanda said quietly, a note of sadness in her voice. 'I really didn't imagine that you'd be such a bastard.'

'Perhaps you have been naïve. Let me assure you that I am indeed a very nice man. I have no intention of building up a vast empire, it is a story that jealous people have made up about me. These are island people we are dealing with, not very clever, not sophisticated, and very jealous of my success. I apologise, I am sorry for speaking the way I have. How can I convince you that you are mistaken?'

'You can't. You've blown it, Andreas. For a time I wasn't sure, but just then I got to see the real you, didn't I? It wasn't a very pretty sight.'

Andreas got up, his face was as white as a mask. 'You are wrong, but I see that you've made your mind up. Well, never mind. You can neither prove nor disprove your fantasy, and I would suggest that you speak to a very good lawyer before you commit a single word to paper.' He turned on his heel and stormed out of the bar.

'And what about building an airfield?' Amanda cried after him. 'Is that a fantasy too?'

Amanda slumped back in her seat, her heart racing, suddenly aware of just how keyed up she felt. It had worked out badly; she had blown her chances completely. She felt angry with herself, she had screwed up. Andreas had given nothing away; rather he had been prepared for her, knowing in advance that she was going to question him.

She stood up, anxious to call Jean-Pierre to let him know what had happened. Damn it, what were they going to do next?

'You'll never guess what I've just heard,' Liza said excitedly, crashing into Martin's room. She stopped in her tracks immediately, surprised to find Martin had company. One of the young waiters was already in the room, sitting sullenly in a chair, legs outstretched, an expression of pure boredom on his swarthy face.

'This is my wife,' Martin said, walking across the room to take Liza by the hand. 'Isn't she lovely?'

'Yes sir,' the waiter replied, sitting up. He shifted uneasily in his seat, glancing nervously at Liza and Martin with dark soulful eyes.

'What's going on?' Liza whispered to Martin, keeping her voice low in front of the younger man.

Martin led Liza to the bed and made her sit down on the edge. His hands were damp with sweat and he was almost shaking with unconcealed excitement. Liza had never seen him so voluble before, he was smiling jocularly and looked to be completely at ease.

'This is Marios,' Martin told her, sitting for a moment

beside her.

'Hello, Marios,' she smiled, getting a momentary wary smile from the young man. He looked uncomfortable, glancing at his watch several times.

'Marios, I want you to make love to my wife,' Martin said quickly, not sounding in the least bit embarrassed.

'What?' Marios sat up in his seat.

'I'll pay you of course,' Martin added soberly. He stood up and crossed the room, drawing a bundle of notes from his wallet.

Liza said nothing. She sat on the edge of the bed looking at the waiter, amused by the look of shock on his young face.

'You want me to make love to your wife, for money?' Marios said finally, not quite sure that he had understood what Martin was suggesting.

'That's right,' Martin agreed, smiling genially. 'You want more money?'

'I don't understand,' Marios admitted, shaking his head sadly.

'Wouldn't you want to make love to me?' Liza asked him, realising that neither of them had any real choice in the matter. The waiter was honour bound to accept; to refuse would be to cast doubt on his virility.

'I would like to make love to you very much, madam,' Marios said stiffly. 'But I don't understand how a man would allow someone else to make love to his beautiful young wife.'

'Look,' Martin snapped irritably, 'it's not your job to understand.' He paused then continued more evenly. 'It's very simple, you make love to my wife and I pay you in return. Will you do it?'

'Yes sir,' Marios stood up and began to strip off, removing his jacket and then unbuttoning his plain white shirt.

'What about you?' Liza said, turning to Martin.

'I'll be next door, having a shower,' he lied unconvincingly.

'But ... I ... I thought you were going to leave, sir,' Marios stuttered.

'I'll be next door,' Martin repeated. 'I'll leave you two in peace, don't worry.'

'It's all right,' Liza said reassuringly. 'We'll have complete privacy.'

Martin left the money in a neat pile on the coffee table. He smiled to Liza then disappeared into the bathroom. Moments later the room was filled with the sound of running water and the faint hiss of the shower.

Liza stood up and undressed slowly, making sure that Marios was watching her. She wore a loose silk blouson and loose cotton trousers. The blouson slipped from her shoulders and fell on to the bed. Her breasts were naked, beautiful white globes centred with large red nipples. She pulled down her cotton trousers to reveal that she wore no panties underneath. Marios smiled, his eyes glittering greedily.

He was naked in a second, his long dark prick upright at once. It jogged lightly as he padded across the room towards her. He took her in his arms nervously, pressing his hardness against her thigh. She opened her mouth and they kissed once, a single exploratory embrace.

'Your husband is crazy,' he whispered in her ear, running his powerful hands down the smooth flawless skin of her back.

'Aren't you glad he's crazy?' Liza responded, reaching a hand down to touch his hardness.

'If you were my wife I would spend all day and night making love to you, I would kill any man who even looked at you.'

'Forget that,' Liza whispered. 'Make love to me now,

124

I want you inside me.'

'Not so quickly,' Marios cautioned. 'Is that what he does? I want you to have your pleasure also. Do you want sex or love?'

'Sex and love,' Liza said.

They sat on the edge of the bed, kissing and touching, feeling each other's body for the first time. Liza massaged her hand over his muscular body, over his flat muscular stomach, feeling the ridged muscle rippling under his fingers. His prick was long and hard, the ribbed underside capped by the bulbous purple glans. She traced a finger along the length of his prick, delighting in the feel of his stiff flesh.

Marios was kissing her slowly, sucking at her mouth and neck with his full red lips. His hands were big and rough, but they moved over her body sensitively, touching her, exciting her all the time. Liza parted her thighs, inviting him to touch her there, anxious to feel his fingers inside her.

He cupped her breasts with his hands, squeezing the firm flesh, massaging gently, exciting her nipples with the briefest of caresses. Her breath was coming faster, the fire in her belly growing in intensity, her blood pulsing with excitement. She took his hardness in her hand and stroked it urgently, closing her hand over the stiff pole. She moved her hand up and down, feeling him catch his breath, responding to her movement by pressing himself against her even more. He swooped down and lunged at her nipples, his hands pulling at her breasts and feeding both nipples into his mouth. He sucked hard, catching the erect berries between his teeth, flicking his tongue over them at the same time.

Liza cried out. He was biting at her nipples, hurting her and yet sending glowing spasms of pleasure pulsing through her. She cradled his head in her arms, frightened by the ferocity of his attack, her eyes closed, her head swimming. He slipped out of her grasp and fell to his knees, he began to kiss her thighs, sliding along from her knees towards her opening. He planted soft gentle kisses on the smooth glassy flesh of her thighs, his hands sliding along in the wake of his lips. She stretched her thighs further, opening herself in anticipation.

Marios paused, looked up at Liza and smiled. She smiled back and then parted the lips of her pussy with her fingers, exposing the soft recesses of her cunt. Marios bent lower and kissed her there, pressing his lips against the soft skin of her labia, shooting his tongue deep into her warmth. She sighed loudly, stretched her head back, lost in the flurry of dreamy sensations. His hot tongue pressed against the walls of her sex, lapping at the thick creamy emissions from deep inside. He sought and found the engorged rosebud of her sex, flicked his tongue over it, then pressed his mouth closer, clamped tight over her vagina.

Liza was sighing, singing softly, head thrown back and eyes closed. Marios was proving to be an expert lover, considerate, skilled, full of surprises. His hands were massaging the insides of her thighs, adding another layer to the multi-tiered edifice of her pleasure. He slid one hand under her thigh and began to explore the underside of her sex, probing with his finger. Liza moved forward instinctively, lifting herself a little higher. He passed a stubby finger back and forth along the crease between the arse-cheeks, wetting his finger at the mouth of her sex with the creamy honey seeping from her pussy.

Liza cried out, her strangled voice filling the room. She clutched Marios closely, digging her fingers into his muscular shoulders. The feel of his mouth on her rosebud, sweeping waves of pleasure into her cunt, had driven her to the edge. At the final moment he had pressed his lubricated finger into her anus, slipping it deep into her tight rear hole. It had been the final element that pushed her over the edge, making her cry out with the unbridled pleasure of orgasm.

Liza was flat on her back, still dizzy from the intensity of her joyous climax. She felt so good, so clean again. She moved further up the bed, making room for Marios beside her. They kissed once more, slow lazy kisses. She could taste herself still on his lips and deep in his cool soft mouth. She ran her hands up over his chest, through the forest of dark black hair. He turned and lay on his back, pulling her over so that she rested on his chest, her breasts flattened on him. She reached down and caressed his cock once more, touching it softly, letting him press himself urgently against her fingers.

'Suck me, take me in your mouth,' he whispered softly, kissing her on the neck, his breath hot on her skin.

Liza moved down his body, brushing her nipples down his sweaty muscular body. He smelt of sweat and work, a deeply attractive masculine smell. She touched her lips tenderly on the very tip of his glans, resting her mouth for a second on the tiny opening, wet with a golden jewel of fluid. He flexed his prick impatiently, eager to enter her warm inviting mouth.

She smothered the length of his hardness with slow lingering kisses, pressing her lips flat on his smooth prick, tasting his salty taste on her tongue. She opened her mouth and closed her lips around the purple dome, smothering it with her tongue, sucking hard. The silver jewel of prick fluid was drawn into her mouth, sticky, sexy. She moved down suddenly, closing her mouth around his prick, like a warm exciting sex, her tongue sliding along the thick underside. She took him all, deep into the back of her throat, the base of his prick wedged between her rosy lips.

Marios began to move up and down, guiding himself in and out of her mouth, sighing with the feel of her lips

127

rushing up and down his hardness. He took her hair in his hand, brushing it back so that he could watch her sensitive mouth playing over his prick. She sucked and licked, flicking her tongue over the sensitive spot just under his glans, making him catch his breath and tense his entire body. The taste of his prick filled her mouth, the sticky fluid drawn from his prick into the moist recess of her mouth.

He was bucking, making hard thrusts deep into her mouth, his prick throbbing and twitching. Liza knew that he was on the verge of exploding into her mouth. She wanted to feel him in her pussy, to fill her completely, to force apart the walls of her sex with his massive prick. She tried to withdraw but he held her fast, thrusting rhythmically. His prick seemed to grow bigger and harder in her mouth. Quickly she stretched her mouth open a little more, took him in as deep as she could without gagging. He froze, his body suddenly rigid, and then her mouth was flooded with spurt after spurt of thick warm come.

Marios collapsed back on the bed, his breathing slow and relaxed once more. Liza crawled back up the bed, sliding her body alongside his. They kissed slowly and she passed the thick wads of come floating on her tongue deep into the warmth of his mouth. She felt him stiffen, surprised by her kiss, but it was only a momentary hesitation. He opened his mouth fully, pressing his tongue between her lips, sucking his sperm into his mouth. Her mouth was suffused with his taste, with the drops of come smeared on to her tongue, mixed with her spit, sliding down the back of her throat.

He sat up on his knees, pulling her up into the same position. He cupped her breasts with his hands, pinching her nipples between thumb and fingers. Liza sat up, pulled her shoulders back and pressed her chest forward, arching her back, offering him her breasts. Marios smiled then

128

knelt down in front of her, as he cupped her breasts and then opened his mouth, letting the glistening mixture of spit and come fall onto her breasts. The viscous mixture slid down the incline of her breasts, leaving a glistening wet smear, the thicker drops of come sliding down in fits and starts. It slid down on to her nipples, the thick drops clinging momentarily, stretching down like glittering icicles before falling down to her belly.

Liza pressed her fingers over her nipples, smearing and spreading the cream like silver haloes around the cherry red of her nipples. She cupped her breasts together, forcing the last drops of come down to her hardened nipples. She felt incredibly sexy, excited by the way he had marked her, smearing his essence on her in an almost animal way. The smell of his semen was faintly discernible, rising from her breasts as the stains began to dry out in the heat.

Marios watched Liza smearing herself, spreading his juices over her skin, rubbing it deep into her flesh. He scooped down and caught her glistening nipples in his mouth, lapping at them, licking off his come and swallowing it. His prick was still hard, still strong.

Liza lay on her back, opening her thighs, sliding her fingers down into her burning vagina. She was hot, her pussy raging with an unquenched fire. Her fingers pressed deep into her moist quim, flicking directly at the inflamed clitoris. She cried out at once, the fire from her belly was strong, aching for satisfaction.

Marios pulled Liza's hands from her pussy, threw them back. He moved in between her thighs, forcced them apart with his knees. Liza cried out, shuddering with pleasure when he plunged his hardness deep into her. His strong hard prick wedged deep between the slippery walls of her cunt, forcing far into her, riding roughly across her rosebud. He began to pump back and forth, a long slow rhythm, pulling his prick out and then plunging back fully.

Every stroke caused Liza to moan ecstatically, bucking her hips up to meet his strong downward thrust.

She cried out, moaning with wordless pleasure, reaching climax once, twice. He had come already, there was no hurry or urgency in his motion. Her pleasure was complete. Driven over the edge, she orgasmed once then came round to find him thrusting still. At last he came. He made no sound, just jerked deep inside her and stayed still. His prick spilled its load inside her, throbbing violently. They rolled apart.

Liza looked up when Martin emerged from the bathroom. Marios had rested for a moment then disappeared without a word, slipping the bundle of notes into his pocket, shaking his head with silent bewilderment. Martin had waited a few moments before emerging. His face was drained of its earlier colour, but his smile was still there.

'Brilliant,' he said enthusiastically. 'What a brilliant performance.'

'Look, we ought to talk,' Liza said wearily, sitting up and leaning on one elbow. She was still naked; the semen stains had dried on her, flaking in places like peeling skin.

'There's nothing to talk about,' Martin snapped rudely.

'You know there is,' Liza insisted.

'What's wrong?' Martin sneered. 'Wasn't he good enough? You certainly looked like you enjoyed it, letting him spunk over you like that.'

'That's not the point, we're here...'

'What's wrong, you slut?' Martin shouted angrily, his face turning red, his eyes bulging. He stepped forward, edging towards her, his fists clenched menacingly.

'Don't you dare call me that!' Liza stood up and faced him, her green eyes blazing with indignation. 'Take that back! Apologise now, go on!'

Martin stood and faced her for a moment, staring at her

nakedness, looking straight at her. Finally he relented, he seemed to shrivel up, his anger melted and he looked away guiltily. 'I'm sorry,' he muttered. He turned and slumped into an empty chair, drained of all anger and emotion.

'You really need to pull yourself together,' Liza said coolly. She sat back on the bed, no longer angry with him, her anger replaced with a feeling of disappointment and hopelessness. The room was filled with a brilliant light, but somehow it failed to touch him. She noticed that even when he sat down, he sat away from the light, sitting down in the only patch of darkness and shade in the room. He was hopeless, carrying his foul mood with him like a shadow.

'I just need some time,' he mumbled in a dull monotone.

'Just how much time do you need?'

'I don't know,' he shrugged. 'You started to say something earlier, when you came into the room.'

'Oh that,' Liza said heavily. 'It was nothing important. It was about Andreas, that's all.'

'What about him?'

'Forget him,' Liza sighed. 'He's the least of our worries.'

Alice lay on her front, stretched out on a sunbed, eyes closed, basking in the heat of the sun. It was late afternoon and the fierce heat had already started to die down a little. She wore a black wet-look swimsuit with the straps undone; she had carefully rolled down the garment to expose her bare back to the scorching sun.

She was half asleep, feeling relaxed and dreamy, floating in the soft unfocused glow of the sun. The poolside was quiet and the pool itself was empty, many of the guests preferring to doze in the languid heat of the day. Joanne lay on her back on the adjacent sunbed, wearing fashionably dark sunglasses and reading through a pile of papers.

She sipped occasionally from a tall milky cocktail at her side, peering over the edge of her glasses at the people wandering lazily to and fro.

Even sound seemed to be dulled by the heat, as if a shallow torpid calm had fallen over the hotel so that even the distant roar of the sea was muted.

'I've just had an idea,' Joanne said suddenly, sitting up and looking over at Alice.

'Yes?' Alice said sleepily, not moving, keeping her eyes closed. It was too hot to have ideas; she knew it was better just to let the heat wash over her, carrying her along.

'Amanda Trevelyan might know what Andreas is up to,' Joanne said, looking around the pool to see if Amanda was one of the bodies lying in the sun.

'Ask her,' Alice remarked listlessly.

'I'll have to find out what her room number is, or leave a message for her with the reception desk.'

Alice lapsed back into listless silence. She didn't want to think about Andreas or Amanda or anything else. She felt happy, resting in the glorious sunshine, Joanne at her side. When a dark shadow fell across her face, obscuring the direct play of the sun, she knew that it was Joanne.

'I've been neglecting you, haven't I?' Joanne said tenderly, a note of guilt in her softly spoken words.

'No, I'm OK,' Alice said, opening her eyes. Joanne had shifted round and was sitting on the edge of her sunbed. She also wore a single-piece swimsuit, but the thin silky material was slit right down the front, exposing the slope of her breasts and the deep valley between them.

'I have.' Joanne smiled. 'I've been so busy thinking about Andreas and Philip that I've forgotten all about you today. I didn't mean to, I'm sorry.'

'I don't mind, honestly I don't.'

'Look, tomorrow we can go down to the village, I promise,' Joanne said, as she swung her long legs round and slipped off the sunbed, kneeling down in front of Alice. She kissed her tenderly on the cheek, just brushing her lips on the soft skin of Alice's face.

'What did you do this morning?' Alice asked, finally plucking up the courage to ask the question that had played on her mind so much earlier.

Joanne paused momentarily, a look of hesitation clouding her clear blue eyes. 'I was just finding out about Andreas and his plans,' she said, choosing her words carefully.

'Is that all?' Alice sighed, visibly relieved. She seemed to relax once more, the tension clearing from her face. She closed her eyes once more, giving herself to the glorious rays of the sun.

'Here let me do your back,' Joanne suggested, sitting herself on the edge of Alice's sunbed and reaching for the bottle of sun oil underneath it. She squirted some on to the palm of her hand and then began to rub it into Alice's dark soft skin.

'That feels good,' Alice sighed dreamily. Joanne's fingers were massaging the cool creamy oil over her back, gliding slowly over the flawless skin. It felt good, soft and relaxing, the slow circular motion of her hands causing a gentle rippling of pleasure.

Joanne began to work lower, pausing to apply some more lotion directly on to Alice's lower back, then continued the slow sensual massage. Her hands were flowing over the smooth skin, pressing firmly the warm supple flesh. She reached the rolled down swimsuit, the garment carefully folded back just below Alice's hips, where the slope of her back finished and the curve of her bottom began. The skin was lighter there, softer too.

Joanne looked around; everyone else seemed to be asleep or dozing in the sunshine, not a soul was stirring. Very carefully she began to pull Alice's swimsuit lower,

133

exposing the tops of her bottom cheeks and the start of the rear cleft.

'Don't do that,' Alice whispered plaintively, suddenly awake again.

'I just wanted to do your back, ' Joanne said, smiling wickedly. She pulled the garment down a little lower then stopped. The bottle of sun oil was almost empty, and she squirted the last drops between the tops of Alice's bottom cheeks. She began to massage once more, with a slower more sensual rhythm.

Alice lay back down with her eyes tightly shut, hoping that if she couldn't see anyone else, they couldn't see her. She felt hot and bothered, and not a little excited by the gentle back-and-forth play of Joanne's fingers. There was also the fear that her bottom was still marked by her earlier self-inflicted spanking. The thought of trying to explain away the fingermarks made her shiver with horror.

'You've got a lovely backside,' Joanne whispered, pulling the arse-cheeks gently apart.

Alice's excitement was growing. Joanne's fingers had ignited a fire burning in her belly. Her arse-cheeks were being massaged, pulled apart slowly then pressed together again in a long slow oval motion. It felt as if she were being fully exposed then hidden once more, and each time the dampness between her thighs seemed to increase a shade more.

Joanne pulled the swimsuit down completely, letting it rest down around Alice's knees. She didn't even bother to look to see if they were being watched; her eyes were fixed firmly on Alice's beautiful bared backside.

Alice knew resistance was useless. She was exposed now, naked in front of both staff and guests. Joanne's fingers were moving feverishly, massaging the buttocks and down over the tops of the thighs. She began to lift herself higher, lifting her backside and arching her back

134

in counterpoint to Joanne's fingers. Her body was now blazing with excitement, the heat in her pussy was raging. She wanted to resist the movement, to lie still and not draw attention to herself, but the flood of sensations was impossible to ignore.

Joanne slipped her hand down the inside of Alice's thigh, rubbing the expanse of smooth flesh and pressing into the warmth of the damp sex. Alice moaned and moved herself lower, parting her thighs to allow entry into her quim. The way she moved exposed the parting between her bottom cheeks, revealing the dark jewel set between the perfect roundness of the buttocks.

Alice cried out with a sudden wincing pain: unexpectedly Joanne had speared a finger into the exposed anus. It felt so strange; she pressed herself flat on her belly, but Joanne pressed deeper. The pain turned to pleasure, the pleasure to pain, in a whirl the two feelings were indistinguishable. Alice felt violated, invaded, but alive to the pulsing pleasure in her arsehole. She began to ride with Joanne's rhythm, moving up and down, lifting her backside up. The feel of the finger in her anal opening caused slivers of pure molten joy to spear through her pussy, making her moan with pleasure.

'Oh God,' Alice moaned, 'I think I'm going to scream ...'

'Scream my darling,' Joanne whispered, kissing her on the mouth. 'I want you to scream when you climax in front of all these people.'

Alice looked up suddenly, shocked to find herself the centre of attention, watched by any number of guests and staff. But any shame she felt was suddenly washed away. Joanne had slipped the fingers of her other hand into her soaking wet pussy. She buried her face in her arms, unable to face the crowd, but also unable to resist the pleasure of being fingered in the bumhole and in the pussy. Her body was racked with a powerful spasm of pleasure, and unable to smother her cries, Alice climaxed at once, lost in the sudden furious pleasure-pain.

eight

'I'll get it,' Joanne said, crossing the room to pick up the phone. She was still not dressed, clad only in silky black panties with matching lace bra, but felt in no great hurry. Alice was still dawdling in the shower, wasting time, not at all certain that she wanted to go out that evening.

'Hello, this is Nicky,' said the voice at the other end of the line in a hoarse whisper.

'Yes?' Joanne said uncertainly, unable for the moment to connect the name to a face.

'I have some more information for Amanda Trevelyan,' Nicky revealed, lowering his voice even more.

'Good,' Joanne said, remembering who Nicky was. 'Do you want to come round now?'

'Yes, just give me a few minutes,' Nicky said then put the phone down.

'Who was that?' Alice asked emerging from the bathroom, dressed in a very short silk bath-robe. Her long black hair was combed straight back, wet and glossy.

'Someone who might help us find out more about what Andreas is up to,' Joanne said. She crossed the room to Alice and took her in her arms. 'What's wrong?' she asked, looking Alice straight in the eye.

'You know what's wrong,' Alice said sullenly. 'How can I face anyone after what happened today? You've made sure that everyone knows about us. Not just the waiters and the staff, but even the other guests now.'

'But you enjoyed what I was doing, didn't you?'

'Yes,' Alice admitted. 'But that's not the point is it?'

'What is the point? Why all this guilt and secrecy? We enjoy having sex together, that should be enough.'

Alice pulled free from Joanne's grasp, taking a hesitant step back. 'It's not that simple,' she said tensely. 'It's more than just sex. You would never do anything with Philip so openly, in front of everybody.'

'That's real life, that's another planet. This is Frixos, this isn't real, no one knows us here, we can be who we want to be, do what we want to do.'

Alice's intended reply was interrupted by a sharp knock at the door. Joanne, still in her underwear, opened the door and let Nicky into the room. He took a step into the room and then stopped, waiting for Joanne, hardly glancing at Alice who was seated on the edge of the bed.

'It's OK, you can relax,' Joanne told Nicky, taking him by the arm and leading him into the room. She suddenly felt happy, almost lightheaded. 'This is Alice,' she said. 'Alice, this is Nicky.'

'Hello, Nicky,' Alice smiled nervously, turning away from the young man's dark, piercing eyes.

'Hello miss,' Nicky said, smiling, his eyes fixed on Alice's long, smooth thighs barely hidden by the short robe.

'Would you like a drink?' Joanne offered, letting go of Nicky and taking a step towards the fridge. She checked in the mirror and was pleased to see Nicky following her with his eyes, staring greedily at her half-clothed body.

'No, thank you,' Nicky said politely. 'Are you ...' he said, pausing to find the right words, 'like the man?'

'Pardon?' Joanne stopped and turned. She looked at Alice, who looked just as confused by the question, and

138

then at Nicky.

'Are you like the man? And your friend is like the woman. When you make love.' Nicky looked embarrassed to be asking the question. He turned away from Joanne's searching gaze, choosing to look at the floor like an errant schoolboy.

'Now look what you've done!' Alice cried petulantly and stormed off to the bathroom, brushing past Nicky who looked confused by the sudden outburst.

'I'm sorry, Nicky,' Joanne smiled apologetically. 'Can you just give me one moment with my friend?'

'Yes miss, I'm sorry if I upset her, I didn't think . . .'

'It's not your fault. Please help yourself to a drink, I'll only be a second.' She crossed towards the bathroom, brushing her chest softly against him along the way. 'What the hell are you doing!' Joanne snapped, once inside the cocoon of the bathroom. Her harsh words echoed tinily in the tiled room.

'What have I done? Look what you've done,' Alice complained bitterly. She stood against the closed door, her robe partly open, her body tense.

'I've done nothing that you haven't enjoyed,' Joanne said indignantly, raising her voice a notch. 'This is important to me. Nicky might have some information for me and I don't want to screw that up. So pull yourself together, girl, now.'

Alice looked up. Her face seemed to change, to lose the darkness of expression, the sullen sulk that had soured her serene good looks. Somehow Joanne's harsh words, the scolding reproach, had cleared her mood. She seemed to lose the tension, her body looked more relaxed, less hunched up for confrontation.

'Now, I want you to go back in there and do as you're told,' Joanne continued, recognising that her firm manner was exactly what Alice had desired. 'If I tell you to do something, you'll do it, without question. Understood?'

'Yes,' Alice said meekly. She smiled and stood up straight, arms awkwardly by her side.

'Good girl,' Joanne said, pleased that she had sorted Alice out. She stepped forward and slipped a hand into Alice's open robe, at the same time kissing her gently on the mouth. Alice's breasts felt soft and smooth, the skin was cool to the touch. 'We better go out,' she said, opening the bathroom door.

Nicky was standing nervously in the centre of the room. He looked up at Joanne and Alice emerging from the bathroom, arm in arm.

'I'm sorry about that,' Joanne purred blithely. 'You were asking about my relationship with Alice?'

'It's just that the other waiters were saying things about you,' Nicky explained, looking sheepishly at the two women. 'They say you were doing things by the pool. Sexy kind of things with each other.'

'Are they shocked by this? Are you shocked by it?' Joanne asked archly, smiling when she saw that Nicky seemed as embarrassed as Alice.

'I didn't believe the stories at first,' Nicky mumbled. 'One of the chambermaids had told us first, but none of us believed her. But so many different people saw you today that I had to believe it.'

'Are you shocked?' Joanne asked again, sitting by Alice on the bed, putting an arm around her shoulders protectively.

'I couldn't understand it,' Nicky admitted. 'Why would two women make love to each other when there are so many men here? What do you do to each other?'

'Have you never heard of Sappho? She was a famous poet from the island of Lesbos. The ancients adored her poetry. She was famous also for loving many women.'

'I have never heard of her,' Nicky shrugged.

'People can find pleasure in so many ways,' Joanne said, turning to kiss Alice gently on the face, smothering her with long slow kisses. She tugged at the cord tied tightly around Alice's robe. The knot came loose and the robe fell open at the shoulder.

Nicky stood and watched, enticed by the vision of the two women before him, half naked, arms entwined, mouths locked tightly. His eyes were wide, mouth open, his expression somewhere between shock and prurient excitement.

Joanne began to massage Alice's gorgeous breasts, palming the two round globes, pressing the flesh so that the nipples stood out like bright red cherries. She saw Alice close her eyes, throwing her head back in slow motion, opening her mouth wordlessly. 'You see,' she said, turning to look at Nicky, standing wide-eyed in the centre of the room, 'I can give and receive pleasure from another woman, as well as from a man.'

Nicky said nothing, he was aroused by the erotic display. His heart was racing with excitement, drops of sweat beading like glistening jewels on his dark skin. His tight trousers pressed painfully against his stiff prick, barely containing his erection.

Joanne stood up and unclipped her bra from behind, nonchalantly letting it fall to the floor. Nicky was watching her, his dark eyes focused on her bared breasts, the bulge in his trousers plain to see. She wondered how long it would take him to undress and join in, or whether his shock would turn to disgusted fascination.

'Undress me,' she said, looking over her shoulder at Alice, seated on the edge of the bed, her legs drawn up under her.

Alice slipped out of the robe, letting the silky garment slide smoothly down her back. She knelt down, on hands and knees, behind Joanne, looking up at her with dark eyes

141

blazing, her face carrying a look of rapt attention. She slipped her fingers under Joanne's black silk panties then drew them down slowly, feasting her eyes on Joanne's exquisite backside.

'I believe you had some information for me?' Joanne said to Nicky, stepping out of the panties that lay in a pretty bundle around her ankles.

'About the boat,' Nicky replied absently. 'I have spoken once more to my cousin at the shipping agent.'

'And what did he have to say?' Joanne asked. She stood with legs apart, chest held high, baring herself fully to the young man's view. She could see his obvious discomfort, the way he squirmed, the way his thick hard prick was etched in the tight black trousers of his uniform. His eyes kept shifting from Joanne's nakedness to Alice kneeling on the floor.

Alice leaned forward and began to kiss Joanne gently on the back of the legs, pressing her lips from the calves and working slowly up, kissing and sucking at the softly perfumed flesh. Her hands worked in unison, charting the route her lips would take, pressing gently, exploring the lithe thighs with infinite patience.

Nicky's eyes seemed to grow wider; his movements became more agitated. 'I said to my cousin the thing you said to me. But he laughed and said the boat is not a dredger.'

'Then what is it?' Joanne asked. She caught her breath, Alice was sliding her hands up and down her thighs, pausing for an infinitesimal moment to press her lips against the satin skin before continuing the slow movement. The effect was to heighten Joanne's sense of excitement, arousing her even more.

'He gave me the name of the ship, and...' Nicky's sentence trailed into silence. Alice had crawled around to Joanne's front, so that Nicky was presented with an

142

alluring display of Alice's rounded bottom jutting high in the air.

'Undress,' Joanne told him, unable to hold out any longer. The details of the ship could wait, now that she knew that Nicky had the information she had sought. She felt a shiver of pleasure, a sense of power, knowing that she could choreograph Alice and Nicky, binding them in a subtle dance of bodies.

Nicky stripped off quickly, eagerly shedding his clothes in a few moments. He could hardly keep his eyes off Alice on her hands and knees, kissing and sucking Joanne between the thighs.

'Join me here,' Joanne whispered, unable to keep an even tone to her voice. She parted her legs once more, opening herself to Alice's hot mouth. The fire in her belly was almost overwhelming; when Alice flicked her tongue over her cunt-bud she cried out with ecstasy, closing her eyes and giving herself fully to the pleasure.

Nicky stepped up close to Joanne, his thick prick standing hard. He reached out and touched her gently on the belly, then moved his hand up to her chest. With his other hand he carefully touched Alice's face, brushing away the dark hair that fell over her eyes.

Joanne turned to Nicky and kissed him on the mouth, sharing her breath with him, opening her mouth to his searching quicksilver tongue. His face was both hard and masculine and soft and feminine; there was something unformed about him, and he seemed to have an innocence Petros and the other men did not. It was precisely the same quality that drew her to Alice.

She took his hard prick in her hand, closing her fingers around his reassuring hardness. He turned towards her, pressing closer so that she could caress his throbbing prick.

Joanne cried out, arched her back, clawed wildly at the thick mane of Alice's jet black hair. She clung to Nicky for support, her body seized with a sudden white-hot climax. She cried out again, almost sobbing with the pure exquisite pleasure of it.

The waves of pleasure continued to burn in her pussy, ignited by Alice's mouth and tongue and lips. Joanne took Alice under the chin and lifted her head up, their eyes met. She bent down low and kissed Alice softly on the mouth, sucking at her full red lips, tasting herself on Alice's searching tongue.

Joanne knelt down beside Alice, their mouths locked in a long passionate embrace. With her hand she was massaging Nicky's stiff prick, wanking him up and down slowly. She drew her mouth away from Alice, prolonging the kiss for as long as possible then pulling away with a pure effort of will. Her face felt hot, flushed with excitement. She looked into Alice's eyes, saw the joy and elation reflected in the dark ovals — joy and a certain kind of indelible sadness.

Joanne took Nicky's prick and kissed it very delicately at the top of the glans, brushing her lips on the most sensitive point, with an airy touch of her butterfly lips like the softest breeze of the morning. He murmured softly, his voice low and breathless. Joanne kissed him again, parting her lips and sucking tenderly at the tiny mouth of his penis.

Alice watched for a second, then began to kiss Joanne on the neck and throat, her hands fluttering over Joanne's body, caressing the gentle curves of thigh and back.

'Kiss me,' Joanne whispered, her lips still playing on Nicky's thick erection, sliding up and down the hardness of his cock.

Alice responded at once, twisting her head, tilting to one side so that her long hair fell down over her shoulder. She leaned closer, opening her mouth over Nicky's purple glans so that her lips made contact with Joanne's. Her mouth slid over his glistening prick, her tongue sliding along his sensitive rod, touching Joanne's darting tongue.

Joanne sucked hard, she could taste Nicky's masculine taste, the taste of his prick and the fluid seeping from the glans. She could taste Alice's sweet mouth and lips. The different textures of prick and mouth, the tastes of male and female mingled in her mouth, a dizzying cascade of sensations. She closed her eyes, twisting her head round and round, breathing Alice's air, hearing Nicky's increasingly urgent murmuring of pleasure. She felt her own pleasure increasing, the dampness in her thighs seeping out. She sought and found Alice's sopping pussy, slipping her fingers into the warm damp heat.

Alice was bucking wildly, shifting herself so that Joanne's fingers were pressing in and out of her pussy. Her mouth was closed over Nicky's prick, sucking at it as if it was the sweetest of candies, her tongue also pressing into Joanne's hungry mouth. She sat up on her knees. She could hardly breathe; her frantic ecstatic moans of pleasure were smothered by the stiff prick or swallowed by Joanne.

Joanne could feel that the play of her mouth and Alice's were causing waves of ecstatic pleasure to wash over Nicky. He was standing tensely, his body rigid, panting for breath. He cried out, a strangled sigh of relief, then climaxed. Waves of thick creamy spunk flooded from his throbbing cock, spilling into their mouths. She swallowed his emissions, letting the thick cream slide down her throat like pure honey.

A moment later Alice cried out. She let go of Nicky and clung to Joanne, holding on to her for dear life. Her face was a mask of pure pleasure, her expression one of purest ecstasy. She climaxed, frozen into position, her eyes closed, a trail of Nicky's come sliding from the corner of her parted lips.

'What about this boat?' Joanne said, handing Nicky, slumped naked on the bed, a cold glass of beer.

Nicky leaned up on one elbow and took the glass shakily. His face lacked expression, as if their lovemaking had left him drained of all emotion. He took a sip of the beer, looking round the room for Alice.

'She's having a shower,' Joanne explained. She had wrapped herself in the robe Alice had abandoned, and stood now waiting for the information that Nicky had promised.

'The boat is not a dredger,' Nicky explained, between gulps of cold beer. 'He laughed when I told him you thought it was a dredger. It is a special kind of cargo ship, with a very flat kind of hull. It can easily get into our harbour.'

'Did your cousin say what the cargo was expected to be?'

'His office isn't handling the ship, he just put Andreas in contact with someone else.'

'But he must have spoken to this other contact since then,' Joanne said hopefully. 'Did he tell you more?'

'Yes,' Nicky paused and looked at Joanne coolly. 'Are you sure that this information is for Amanda Trevelyan?'

'Yes, who else would it be for?'

'I don't know,' Nicky shrugged. He finished off the glass of beer and set it down on the bedside cabinet. 'The cargo might be some special kind of equipment. Digging equipment.'

'Digging equipment?' Joanne looked perplexed. She had pinned her hopes on the boat being a dredger to clear the harbour. It had been a good theory, it seemed to fit the facts and to offer a plausible motive for Andreas's actions. But now that theory had been sunk by a boatload of digging equipment.

'Yes. Digging equipment for building work. Tractors and things.'

'Tractors? You mean farming equipment.'

'No, tractors with big spades to clear land. For building work.'

'Bulldozers?'

'Yes,' he laughed, 'that is exactly it. Bulldozers. And other things.'

Joanne watched him getting dressed, his body glistening with a thin layer of sweat. 'Do you know what this equipment is for?'

'No, I don't know.'

'Any ideas?' she said, hopefully.

'None,' he said simply, pulling on his trousers.

'Is it the sort of equipment they used to build this hotel?'

'No, I can remember when they were building this. They used only what is on Frixos, nothing from the mainland.'

'Not even the building equipment?'

'No, everything from Frixos, and built by our own people,' he said proudly.

Joanne opened the door for him, but stopped him as he left, taking him for a moment by the elbow. 'You've been really helpful today,' she said quietly. 'I appreciate it.'

'I enjoyed it,' he said with a wide grin.

'If you get any more information, let me know,' she said. She kissed him on the mouth softly, tasting his lips once more.

'I know,' he smiled wickedly. 'Background information for Amanda Trevelyan, but for you only.'

'Good boy,' she laughed and watched him go, walking out with a slight swagger.

'Did you learn anything useful?' Alice asked, emerging from the bathroom, wrapped in a white bath towel tucked under her arms.

'Bang goes my theory,' Joanne admitted. 'The mysterious boat isn't a dredger for opening up the harbour again. It's for carrying heavy plant and machinery, for

147

building work of some sort.'

'Does that mean Andreas is planning on putting up another few hotels?'

'That's what it sounds like,' Joanne agreed. She sat down in the cane armchair, trying to figure it all out once more.

'Maybe you ought to think about calling Philip,' Alice said sensibly.

'No,' Joanne replied instantly, 'not yet. This isn't as straightforward as it seems. If this place isn't generating the profits that it should, why would Andreas want to build more?'

'Are we going to go out tonight?' Alice asked quietly.

Joanne paused. There had been no trace of complaint in Alice's question, which only made her feel guilty. 'Of course we are,' she replied, forcing a note of enthusiasm into her voice. 'Get dressed. We're probably late but what the hell. We'll make a grand entrance when we arrive.'

'Yes, I don't doubt that we will,' Alice said, smiling weakly, a faraway look in her eyes.

Joanne was sitting at the bar staring into her drink, oblivious to all the early-morning coming and going around her. She had been turning the same thoughts over and over in her mind without conclusion. Something was missing, some vital fact that would put everything into focus. As it was there was nothing to hold on to, nothing to pin on to Andreas except a vague suspicion that he was up to no good.

She looked at her watch again, absently checking the time, waiting for Alice to arrive. They had planned on visiting the village for so long that now it was time neither of them could muster much enthusiasm for the trip. Alice was worried that all the villagers would point at them, singling them out as the two strange women from the hotel, certain that the story had spread around the entire island.

As far as Joanne was concerned that could only be the highlight of an otherwise dull journey down into the sleepy little village.

Joanne's thoughts were interrupted, and she looked up and smiled. The attractive blonde she and Alice had seen around the hotel had taken the seat next to her.

'Hello,' the young woman said, smiling back affably.

'Hi,' Joanne said, sitting up straight.

'That was quite a performance yesterday,' the woman said, smiling even more, her bright eyes like purest jade.

'Thank you, it seems we caused quite a stir,' Joanne said, relishing the attention. She felt an immediate intense attraction to the young woman. There was something very sexy about her, something deeper than her good looks alone.

'It was very, very sexy,' she said, lowering her voice slightly and leaning closer to Joanne.

'Maybe we ought to repeat the performance,' Joanne suggested, breathing in the young woman's subtly intoxicating perfume.

'Why not?' the young woman agreed. She put her hand on Joanne's knee, letting her fingers rest there for a moment.

'My name's Joanne. Why don't you come round to my room later for a drink?' Joanne said, regretting the terrible choice of words, but hoping that the young woman would agree in spite of them.

'I'm Liza, and sure, I'd like that.' She moved her hand further up Joanne's thigh, sliding her palm against the smooth satin skin.

'I'm going out soon, down to the village with Alice, my friend, how would you like to join us?' Joanne said, breathing deeply, aroused by the sure way that Liza was touching her. Desire had flared up so suddenly, unexpectedly, causing excitement to butterfly inside her.

'Sorry,' Liza shook her head sadly. 'I've got other things planned for this morning. But when you get back you can come round to my room for a drink, if you like. You and Alice.'

'What about your friend?' Joanne asked warily, remembering the strange discomforting man that Liza was staying with. She didn't fancy being in the same room as him, and she knew that Alice's reaction was bound to be even more negative.

'Don't worry about him,' Liza said dismissively. 'Even if he's around he'll only watch. He won't get in our way.'

Joanne smiled. She stood up, catching sight of Alice waiting for her in the reception area. 'I'll see you later then,' she said, lingering for a moment, unable to pull herself away.

'Yes, I'm looking forward to it,' Liza said, pursing her lips in a delectable smile.

Joanne pulled herself away at last, excited by the invitation, and hoping to get the tedious trip to the village out of the way as quickly as possible.

The trip to the village had been much more exhausting than Alice had imagined. They hadn't spent too long there, just a couple of hours wandering through the narrow streets and walking down by the harbour. There were no real tourist shops, though a few of the shop keepers by the harbour had started to keep souvenirs and local handicrafts. Everywhere they went Alice had felt uncomfortable, she had felt a sense of creeping paranoia, certain that she was being stared at.

They had bought a few presents, had lunch by a café near to the quay and then waited for the hotel bus to pick them up again. Though Alice felt nervous of all the attention, real or imagined, she saw how Joanne had positively revelled in it. It had been embarrassing. Joanne had touched her surreptitiously on the thighs, stroking her sexily. She had laughed and joked, flirting outrageously the way she would have with a male lover. The worst part of it for Alice was that it served only to increase her paranoia, at the same time as exciting her, making her feel hot and bothered, setting her body tingling with expectation.

By the time the hotel bus pulled up in front of the reception Alice just wanted to get out of the sun, out of people's way. She wanted to just wash away all the frustration, all the dirty guilt feelings in the back of her mind, under the cool splashing waters of a cold shower. A headache had been building up, a dull ache buzzing in her head, threatening to ruin the whole day.

'Don't look so glum,' Joanne said cheerfully, following Alice off the bus, stepping into the fierce dry heat.

'I'm just so tired,' Alice said wearily. Her arms and legs felt heavy, like she'd been doing hard labour under the cloudless blue-white sky.

'Well, I've got something to cheer you up,' Joanne said, cheerily taking Alice by the arm and leading her towards her room.

'Let's shower together first,' Alice said, cheering up a little at the thought.

'We're not going to our room, we're going to visit somebody first.'

'Who?' Alice asked suspiciously. That explained Joanne's jaunty agitated mood, she thought; she had been planning something all along. Alice didn't feel up to visiting; she wanted to get out of everyone's way, to be left alone with her thoughts for a while. But she knew that Joanne wouldn't take no for an answer.

'Just someone I met this morning,' Joanne said mysteriously, quickening her pace.

They walked into the room complex, through the glass

doors and along the corridor. Everything was quiet, and Alice could almost see the heavy weight of the still air. Her headache threatened to get worse, and she felt as if she were wading through space, walking on a thick carpet of air.

'But this is your room,' Alice said, and felt as if her words were swallowed by the silence.

'Not quite,' Joanne said. She walked a couple more steps and stopped outside the room next door. She smiled and knocked quietly on the door.

Alice didn't hear an answer, but she meekly followed Joanne into the room. It was only when she had stepped into the room that she remembered to whom the room belonged. Her first instinct was to back out, to make some polite excuse to escape, for an instant she wanted to just turn and run away. But already the good-looking young blonde was smiling at her, walking across the room to greet her and Joanne.

She heard Joanne making the introductions, smiling excitedly, hardly able to keep her eyes off the blonde. It was like watching a scene through thick fog, in slow motion, freeze-framing an inch at a time.

'Are you feeling all right?' the blonde was saying, her eyes flashing concern.

'Yes, I think so,' Alice said, but the moment she said it they all knew that it was wrong. She stepped forward, then seemed to stumble into the young blonde's arms.

The fog cleared suddenly, the low indistinct murmur became focused. Alice opened her eyes and looked up at the dull white ceiling.

'Are you OK?' Joanne asked, her soft voice edged with concern. She wiped Alice's brow with her hand, her fingers brushing away the cold dew drops of sweat.

'Do you want a drink? A glass of water?'

'No thank you,' Alice said, finding her voice again. She

sat up slowly, afraid that the world would spin away from her once more. When it didn't she smiled weakly at the young blonde. Liza, that was her name. It was the last thing she remembered hearing before blacking out.

'What happened?' Joanne asked, sitting closer to her on the bed.

'I don't know,' Alice said. 'Everything sort of got on top of me. I felt strange all day today and then this happened.'

'Has this happened before?' Liza asked, sitting on Alice's other side.

'No, never.'

'Maybe I've been pushing you too hard, poor darling,' Joanne said guiltily. 'I promise I'll stop.'

'No, I don't think it's that,' Alice said. She knew there was an element of truth in what Joanne was saying, but the thought of their relationship coming to a halt was too much to contemplate.

'It sounds like you don't want it to stop,' Liza observed wryly.

Alice bit her tongue, knowing that she couldn't deny it. The colour started to return to her cheeks, and she was feeling better already. She realised that she felt comfortable in Liza's presence, as if they had known each other for years and there could be no secrets between them.

Joanne put a hand on Alice's shoulder and Alice turned to her. They didn't have to say any more. They kissed tenderly, pressing their lips together softly. Liza moved closer, bridging an arm across Alice's body. Joanne pulled away and Liza looked at Alice face to face, their eyes meeting searchingly. Alice tilted her head slightly and opened her mouth to Liza, accepting her probing tongue and in turn exploring Liza's cool mouth with her own tongue. They breathed together, mouths locked together as a single unit. Then they swapped again, Alice watched

153

Joanne and Liza kissing passionately, her own excitement fired up.

They kissed and touched in turn, sharing, giving, exploring. Alice was lost in a giddy swirl of excitement that swept away all her dull misgivings and the memory of blacking out. They undressed each other gradually, touching each other in turn, mouth to mouth, mouth to breast, hand to thigh.

Alice closed her eyes and shivered with exhilaration. Her pussy was being fingered, skilful fingers pressing deep into her vagina, brushing deliciously against her cunt-bud. Her breasts were being mouthed, the nipples sucked hard and deep. She was massaging someone's nipples, delighting in pinching them and then soothing them with her thumbs. It was a delicious confusion of bodies, a shifting geometry of arms and legs.

Alice cried out, her voice rising with the tempo of the fingers frigging her in the pussy. She climaxed, her body convulsed with sheer waves of white-hot pleasure. It felt as if her whole body was aflame, the fire burning most intensely between her thighs and on the incandescent tips of her nipples.

Joanne and Liza continued to make love with Alice, taking her beyond orgasm. Alice moved her hand between Joanne's legs, sliding her palm up the soft silky thigh and then passing it over the exposed pussy flesh.

'Finger me,' Joanne whispered hotly, a look of pleading desperation in her eyes. She sighed blissfully, her body collapsing forwards when Alice pressed her fingers deep into the moist sex. She was panting forcefully, gasping for breath, her head thrown back in an aspect of purest elation. Her cries were smothered by Liza who took her by the face and pressed their mouths together, breathing her intoxicated air.

Alice slid her other hand down the flawless white skin

of Liza's back, revelling in the feel of the warm flesh. She lingered momentarily at the base of Liza's spine, tracing the curvature of her rounded bottom, eager to explore further. Liza shifted round, sitting flat on her bottom but opening her thighs and exposing the deep pink flesh of her sex to Alice, her mouth still sucking at Joanne's lips.

Liza turned to Alice with an expression of absolute desire. There was no smile, just a look of unspoken intensity. Her green eyes smouldered with intent. She parted her thighs further, drawing her knees up, sitting flat on her bottom, opening herself fully. She leant forward, her blonde hair falling over her shoulders in a dazzling cascade that caught the light streaming into the room.

Alice kissed Liza on the mouth, and at the same moment pressed two fingers of her upturned hand between her pussy lips. Liza drew a sharp breath, her eyes rolling, her body tensing with a sudden ripple of pleasure. Alice smiled. Her own excitement was at fever pitch, the pleasure in her pussy boiling up again. She was going to climax once more; she could feel the moment of release fast approaching. And she wanted to make Liza and Joanne scream in ecstasy at that precise moment, so that they could share in the primal blissful moment. She was frigging them at the same time, fingering them with deep slow thrusts of her hands, driving them to higher and higher peaks of sensation.

Alice cried out. Liza and Joanne had joined hands, together thrusting their fingers into her pussy, forcing her pussy lips apart and pressing swiftly to the heart of her sex. It happened just as she had wanted. The three women climaxed together, their bodies convulsed, stretched rigid, sharing the same feeling of pure bliss.

Alice lost herself, unable to differentiate herself from

Joanne and Liza, their bodies fused into one in the heat of orgasm. She sang out, her cry turning into a fitful sob of pleasure and pain.

Alice lay flat on her back, naked, warmed by the dying embers of the sun. She dozed fitfully, waking and then sleeping once more, unable to tell reality from the dream. It felt like the perfect day was coming to a close, disappearing with the falling sun.

It had started so badly. The trip to the village had been nothing but an ordeal, a painful reminder that life outside the four walls of Paradise Bay was anything but a dream. And then there had been the horrible feeling of dislocation, when the world collapsed into a thousand pieces.

And then it had changed once more. Alice felt safe and warm again, aware of Joanne and Liza sitting close by, talking quietly, swapping kisses, making love. It was a dream, far too good to be true. She turned over, sneaking a glance at Liza and Joanne, making sure they were still there. Sex had been fantastic, a total high, the memory of which made her body tingle with excitement. If only all sex could be that good, that intense, that special. She wished that it would never end, that the day would stretch on forever and ever.

'Are you awake?' Joanne said, looking around at Alice.

'Yes, I just woke up.'

'Are you feeling OK?' Liza asked, getting up from her seat and coming over to sit by her.

'Yes, I feel fine. I've just been thinking what a lovely day this has turned out to be.'

'You've got such lovely dark skin,' Liza said wistfully, brushing her hand softly over Alice's belly. 'You look like you've lived in the sun all your life.'

'I only look dark compared to you,' Alice smiled, placing her arm next to Liza's to show the contrast.

'I've got something that'll make your skin look as white as snow,' Liza said delightedly, jumping up off the bed and crossing to the wardrobe. She wore only a skimpy yellow top, a cut-down tee-shirt that barely covered her breasts, and as she moved the very tips of her nipples peeked out tantalisingly. Her long white thighs were taut, curving up deliciously to the pale symmetrical globes of her bottom.

'What are you two doing?' Joanne asked Alice, joining her on the bed. She looked radiant, her blue eyes sparkling like diamonds, a relaxed and happy smile on her face.

Liza bent down low, searching through a suitcase that lay flat on the wardrobe floor. Her long legs were stretched taut, every sinew and muscle extended, the pale bush between her slightly parted thighs giving an unguarded glimpse of the glistening pink flesh within. Alice sat up, unable to take her feasting eyes off Liza's behind. She and Joanne fell silent, their attention captivated by the glorious view. Liza's buttocks were slightly parted, and they could see the tight dark anal hole set deep in her rear cleavage.

'Turn round now,' Liza said, finding the object that she had been searching for. She straightened up but kept her back to the other two women.

Alice laughed excitedly, Liza's excitable mood was infectious, and she felt like a silly frivolous schoolgirl again. 'Come on, show us what it is,' she urged, sitting up on her knees right on the very edge of the bed.

'No, turn around,' Liza insisted, but this time she sounded less sure of herself.

'Yes, turn around,' Joanne said quietly, her words sounding a note of hesitation also. She was smiling, but her mood had also become more sombre, as if she knew what Liza had found.

Alice looked at Joanne for a second, tried to divine in

157

her clear blue eyes the nature of the secret that she shared with Liza. Joanne touched her gently on the face, caressing her softly with her fingers. Alice turned around, and fell silent, a pang of fear and excitement welling up from nowhere. She heard the muffled sound of Liza padding barefoot on the pine floor, felt the mattress rock slightly when she got on the bed, then felt Liza's breath hot on her shoulder.

Something touched Alice between the thighs, something cool and hard and frightening. Joanne took Alice by the shoulders, held her tightly, at once comforting and constraining.

'Just relax, darling,' Joanne whispered, unable to hide the edge of excitement in her voice.

'Please what is it?' Alice said. She tried to shift away, to get up from her knees.

'Don't worry, you'll enjoy it,' Liza promised. She slid her hand under Alice's bottom, pressing her fingers between the arse-cheeks, brushing casually against the tight anal bud. She palmed Alice between the thighs, pressing her fingers over the soft puffy labia, but not entering.

'Why are you doing this to me?' Alice cried, looking accusingly at Joanne.

'Because that's what you want, and what I want, and what Liza wants,' Joanne explained calmly. She held Alice tightly and began to kiss her, pressing her lips along her shoulder, kissing and biting.

Alice closed her eyes to stop the tears streaming down her face. It felt so bad, so absolutely awful. The day had switched mood with manic regularity. Just when she had decided that it was the perfect day it had changed again. And Joanne was the root cause of it all. It had been Joanne who had caused the paranoia, Joanne who had brought her to Liza's room, Joanne who had led the way when making love. And now Joanne was holding her down.

Liza continued to caress Alice's pussy, rubbing her hand against the sensitive pussy lips, always threatening to invade but never moving further. Alice began to sigh, the fear in her belly turning quickly into desire, hot and urgent. Joanne's kisses were becoming more passionate, arousing her still further. She tried to move, but Joanne held her tightly, forcing her in place. Strangely that only caused her to become more excited, causing nervous flutters in her stomach.

Alice cried out suddenly, almost freeing herself from Joanne's grip. The thing, the unseen hardness that Liza had found, was pressed deep into her. She climaxed at once, the force of penetration pushing her over the edge. Her body froze, she arched her back impossibly, spat her breath in a final cry of pleasure.

But it wasn't over. Liza began to slide the thing in and out, pressing it hard and deep. Alice was dizzy; it felt huge, pressing powerfully against the walls of her pussy. Liza was pumping it in and out rhythmically, wielding the thing expertly, pushing Alice out on to the edge of experience, halfway between pure blind ecstasy and hysteria.

Joanne loosened her grip. She seized Alice by the mouth and forced their lips together. Alice returned the kiss, letting Joanne press her tongue into her mouth. She felt confused by the stream of sensations. Her pussy was burning, she could feel her juices slipping out of her pussy and making her thighs wet. Joanne was kissing her passionately.

'On to your hands and knees,' Joanne said, pulling away.

Alice obeyed instantly. She sat up on all fours, her back arched so that her backside was round and tight, her legs slightly parted so that Liza could fuck her with the thing as deep as possible. Her breasts were loose, swinging in tight circles, her nipples erect points of flesh.

'Now suck me,' Joanne ordered curtly. She lay on her

belly, directly in front of Alice, her bottom raised up in expectation.

Alice scooped down and buried her face in the soft mound of hair between Joanne's thighs. She breathed the faint scent of Joanne's pussy, an intoxicating perfume that made her head spin. She kissed Joanne lightly on the tops of the thighs, preparing to press her tongue deep into the inviting pussy crack.

'I want you to suck me here,' Joanne said, lifting her backside even higher. She extended a finger and passed it slowly between her arse-cheeks, her long red fingernails in contrast to the pale tones of her skin. She stopped at her anal hole, tapped her finger over the rear opening. She looked over her shoulder and smiled sweetly, her eyes glittering with greedy desire.

Alice was horrified, her mouth fell open. But the shock was short-lived. Liza was fucking her faster and faster, driving her inexorably to orgasm once more. She bent down, excited now by the strange demand, glad to serve Joanne, finding pleasure in being forced to obey. She kissed Joanne tentatively on the anus, touching her ruby-red lips against the dark petals of the rear hole. And then she closed her eyes and forced her tongue into the opening, feeling the tight ring of muscle expand around her tongue.

She began to move up and down over Joanne's raised backside, pressing her tongue in and out of the anal hole, now fully lubricated by the spit on her tongue. She closed her eyes, giving herself to this one task, mouth fucking Joanne in the arse.

Joanne began to cry out with pleasure, bucking, pulling her buttocks apart with her hands. 'Deeper, suck me deeper,' she urged, her voice trailing into whimpers of pleasure.

Alice smothered her cries of orgasm in Joanne's arsehole, her body tingling with electric energy. Somewhere in the distance she felt Joanne orgasm, her body seized by the unstoppable climactic finish. They collapsed together on the bed, naked, drained, sated.

Alice realised later that evening that the day had been perfect, too perfect for words. She had experienced the full range of emotions, from black despair to purest pleasure, to finish in the strange erotic world where submission to Joanne was the highest principle she could aspire to.

nine

Alice woke up shivering, her heart pounding, bathed in a cold sweat. She opened her eyes suddenly, overcome with disorientation and the desire to open her mouth and scream. Her head was filled with the echoes of her dream, half nightmare and half bittersweet memory. She ached, and when she moved her joints creaked like an old woman's.

She sat up with an effort, saw that she was alone in the brightness of the room, and sank back to the bed. The memories were fresh and painful, etched indelibly into her mind.

Joanne and Liza had held her down to make love with her. Liza's toy had been a massive black vibrator, a sleek missile-shaped penis of monstrous proportions. Liza had been right. The blackness of the instument had contrasted strongly with Alice's skin, making her look virginally pale.

Alice touched herself softly between the thighs. The puffy lips to her sex were tender, and it stung slightly when she pressed a finger questioningly into herself. They had held her down and forced the black penis into her, time and time again, making her writhe with pain and pleasure. And then she had mouthed Joanne's anus, pressing her tongue down into the tight sheath of warm muscle, kissing it as if it were the sweetest of mouths. Joanne had climaxed; the sheer pleasure of having her arsehole tongued had taken her over the edge. And Alice had orgasmed too, from the double pleasure of arse-sucking Joanne and from the powerful penetrating thrusts of Liza's special implement.

But it hadn't ended there. Liza had swapped places with Joanne, demanding that she be brought to pleasure in the same way. A powerful feeling of rebellion had swelled up at that moment, Alice wanted to say no, this is enough; to define once more the limits of her submission. But it was a fantasy to imagine that there were limits beyond which she would not go. Joanne had commanded, had looked at her in that special way, had spoken in the strange tone of voice that made Alice go weak at the knees. She had submitted, had given in, and had been rewarded by a private thrill of pleasure that made her want to weep.

Alice shifted uncomfortably on the bed, her naked body lying in the sun but feeling as cold as ice. She didn't understand. What was wrong with her? It didn't make sense for her to act that way. She submitted, let herself be used. She had sucked Liza's arsehole, pressing her tongue far and deep into the tight arse-jewel, filling her mouth with the strangest cloying taste and sensation. And she had orgasmed when Liza did, sharing the pleasure, sharing the bliss. And at the same time Joanne had been using the black instrument, pressing it hard and deep, forcing her cunny lips apart painfully. But that too was part of the bizarre thrill. How was it that pleasure and pain and submission had become so confused, intertwined so that the three emotions had merged into one all-powerful motive force?

There were too many questions crowding her mind. Alice tossed and turned, haunted by the vivid images in her mind's eye. She touched herself again, forcing her fingers into her bruised sex. It hurt, but the pain was only an edge to the flood of pleasurable sensation that washed through her, a white blinding ecstasy that touched her at the very core of her being.

Before she knew it she was on her hands and knees, looking over her shoulder, at her bottom displayed in the golden light of the mirror across the room. She hardly recognised herself. Her hair was bedraggled, her eyes ringed with dark haloes, her face pale and lips scarlet.

The smack echoed around the room, she closed her eyes for a second, savoured the sharp pain on her backside, tensed momentarily then felt the warmth seeping from her bottom into her pussy. This was her new solitary vice, the game she played only with herself, afraid even to tell Joanne about it. She raised her hand and smacked herself again, aiming for the other arse-cheek.

Vaguely she wondered what new shocks the day would bring. Their time on Frixos was limited, but in some ways experience had expanded to fill the short time allowed, each day was more intense than the last. She closed her eyes again, forcing the questions from her mind, losing herself in the steady rhythm of self-correction.

Amanda let the phone ring for an age, hoping that it would die away and leave her to the contemplative silence of the morning. She was sitting out on the balcony of her room, staring out across the bay to the clear blue sea and the whiteness of the sky. But the phone rang and rang with an irritating consistency that jarred the senses. At last she got up and went back into the room crossly, catching a glimpse of herself in the mirror, her silk robe billowing behind her in a scarlet flurry.

'Jean-Pierre,' she said, recognising the familiar rumble of his voice at once.

'I was beginning to lose hope,' he said, the phone line unable to do justice to the full mellifluous power of his voice.

'I'm sorry,' she said guiltily. 'I just wanted time on my own to think.'

'How can you think there? Alone in an alien room, with nothing to call your own, nothing that resonates with your personality?'

'You mean why aren't I up at your place?' Amanda said dubiously.

His thick laughter crackled on the line. 'Just so,' he said. 'But I have called you to tell you something of great interest.'

'What, something about Andreas?'

'Precisely that. My questions have borne fruit at last, the doubts I cast lay buried in the soil only to germinate at this late stage.'

'Yes, yes,' Amanda said hurriedly, eager to find out the details.

'I have heard a rumour about how Mr Karaplis acquired his money. I have done well, have I not?'

'Absolutely,' Amanda said impatiently. 'Now what is it?'

'Andreas has been ... '

Jean-Pierre's excited voice was suddenly cut off and Amanda heard the dull whining of the dialling tone. She swore under her breath, angered both by the failure of the phone and by Jean-Pierre's inability to say something in two words when ten would do. She slammed the phone down in its cradle and glared at it, half hoping that it would ring back to life with Jean-Pierre at the other end.

She snatched it up again and listened for the dialling tone humming innocuously as if nothing had happened. Her purse was by the phone and she found Jean-Pierre's number quickly. But the moment she dialled for an external line the phone died. She tried a number of times and failed, each time her anger increasing. She swore again, louder this time, certain that her call had been deliberately cut off, and that her phone was being tampered with.

'Give me Andreas!' she demanded venomously, dialling through to the reception.

'I am sorry, madam, but he is not here,' the voice at the other end said coolly.

'Why was my phone call cut off?' she said accusingly.

'I'm sorry, madam?' the voice replied in an obsequious manner that only made her angrier.

'And why can't I get an external line?'

'I'm sorry, madam,' the voice continued. 'Are you saying that you have lost a phone call, or are you having trouble making a call?'

'Don't give me that bullshit,' Amanda exploded at the obvious note of sarcasm in the other's voice. 'Get Andreas Karaplis now or you'll regret the day you messed me around.'

There was a muffled silence, Amanda thought she heard lowered voices arguing, then Andreas took the line.

'How can I help you, Ms Trevelyan?' he enquired with exaggerated politeness.

'Why was my call disconnected?'

'I'm sorry, madam, but I was not aware that that had happened. I will make enquiries and take the appropriate action if any of my staff have acted improperly.'

'And why can't I make an outside call now?'

'Ah, I see,' Andreas said knowingly. 'It is a technical problem that we suffer occasionally. A by-product of our strict acquisition policy.'

'What are you talking about?'

'As we have previously discussed, the hotel was built using local materials and local craftsmen. That includes the telephone system. Unfortunately the local people are a little less technically competent than desirable, and so occasionally we have equipment malfunctions . . .'

'I don't believe you,' Amanda said. 'I don't take kindly

166

to being lied to, Andreas, not one little bit. And if you think that you can gag me by stopping my phone calls then you are very much mistaken.'

'I don't know what you are implying, Ms Trevelyan,' Andreas said, his voice cold and flat, its veneer of polished civility long since abandoned. 'If you would be happier leaving Paradise Bay then you only have to say so.'

'Are you asking me to leave?' Amanda sounded a little shocked by the suggestion. It had been a long career, but this was the first time she had been forced out of a hotel.

'I am not suggesting anything,' Andreas said coldly. 'In fact it seems to me that it is you who is doing all the suggesting.'

'Fine. I'll be out in an hour.'

'And your account will be settled in full I trust?'

'What account? I was invited here as a guest,' Amanda said.

'I am afraid that guests do not abuse their hosts as you have done. I will have a bill prepared, and if it is not settled in full I will have no choice but to call the police.'

'Well, fuck you too!' Amanda spat down the phone. She slammed it down heavily, almost smashing it. The room was plunged into silence once more. Andreas had gone further than she had expected. He was showing a real mean streak that she hadn't even suspected existed. The only conclusion could be that Jean-Pierre had really dug the dirt on him. Whatever it was, it sounded like dynamite.

Excitedly Amanda began to pack her bags, already composing the first sensational sentences of an account of her stay at Paradise Bay. It was turning out to be a brilliant story, much better than anything her agent had promised.

Alice looked drained when Joanne came to take her out to lunch. Her face was pale and her brown eyes looked even darker. Her mood was heavy too, Joanne noticed immediately, despite Alice's attempts to smile it all away. Joanne said nothing; she didn't want to push things, though she couldn't help wondering whether there was something that she was missing. It seemed odd for Alice's dark mood to last right through the morning, and even a kiss and a cuddle failed to cheer her up.

Joanne had hitched a lift for them with another couple driving into the village. Alice hardly said a word during the short journey, only bothering with a few monosyllables to avoid offending the middle-aged couple giving them the lift. Once or twice Joanne had gently nudged her into saying something in reply to a question, but for the most part she seemed to be far away, lost in her private thoughts.

'Are you feeling OK?' Joanne asked, finally cracking under the strain of trying to carry on a one-sided conversation over lunch in a quayside cafe.

'I don't know.' Alice shrugged, her voice a sullen monotone barely audible over the clamour of the quayside and the shrill keening of the gulls overhead.

'Is it about last night?'

'No, not really,' Alice said, picking unenthusiastically over her lunch.

'Then what is it? Still troubling over the meaning of it all?'

'Don't make it sound so stupid,' Alice said, a flash of anger in her eyes.

'I'm sorry, I didn't mean it to sound so dismissive. Is that it, though? Are you still worried about how it all makes sense?'

Alice shrugged, pursing her lips sulkily.

'Is there something that I can do? Do you want to talk about it?' Joanne offered helpfully, though in truth she didn't fancy it at all. The last thing she wanted was a long and heavy period of soul-searching that would get them

168

nowhere.

'No. Look, there's something I have to tell you, something about me . . .' She stopped and looked at Joanne, their eyes meeting.

'Yes, go on,' Joanne urged when Alice paused, holding her hands reassuringly.

'No, forget it,' Alice shook her head, turned away from Joanne's piercing blue eyes.

'Go on, you can tell me. What is it?'

'No it's all right. I'm just being silly. Forget I ever mentioned it,' Alice said hurriedly.

'This is very difficult,' Joanne sighed, half talking to herself. 'If it's about last night then I'm sorry, really I am. I thought that it was what you wanted, honestly I did. If I went too far, then I'm sorry. It's just that you didn't struggle very hard . . . I thought that you enjoyed it, if enjoy is the right word.'

'No, it's not that,' Alice said. She looked up and for the first time that day seemed to relax, the bitterness in her eyes fading to nothing. 'You're right, I'm not sure if enjoy is the right word for what I felt. I don't even think there are right words for what you make me feel. But it was what I wanted, sort of.'

'If things ever do go too far you only have to tell me to stop,' Joanne said quietly, smiling a little nervously. She felt a dagger of excitement in her belly, just thinking about all the things she wanted to do with Alice, of the multitude of perverse acts that she had dreamed of for so long. And she had dreamed so much, long before she had even thought of Frixos, when all she had had of Alice was vivid fantasy.

'You know I can never tell you to stop,' Alice said, and there was a note of genuine fear in her voice, as if she had no control over herself. 'If I tell you to stop then all this would finish, wouldn't it?'

It was Joanne's turn to shrug; she shivered, suddenly aware that time was running out. She touched Alice's hands again, anxious to feel the soft warmth of her skin. She felt a painful yearning inside, a wordless kind of need and desire. It was going to end. The brittle pink rose was going to flower and die, and there was nothing any of them could do about it. It made her want to love Alice more intensely, to savour every moment they had left together.

'Have you called Philip yet?' Alice asked, as if knowing what was in the back of Joanne's mind, knowing that he was the shadow that linked them to reality, the only connection between Frixos and the real world.

'No, though the time when I do call him is getting near,' Joanne said, snapping back to life.

'Why's that?'

'Because Liza told me something very interesting yesterday.'

'When was that? I didn't hear her say anything about the hotel.'

'It was while you were asleep.' Joanne smiled at the memory. 'We had a very long and interesting conversation. She's a very smart woman, very smart.'

'What did she tell you?'

'She overheard Amanda Trevelyan and Andreas have an argument in the bar.' Joanne leaned across the table, pushing her plate away. She smiled, recognising that Alice was slowly regaining her normal mood, leaving behind the black gloom of the morning.

'What was it about?'

'About buying up the land on the island. She also accused him of planning to build an airport on the island.'

'But that's good, isn't it?' Alice said, looking a mite confused.

'Is it? Amanda Trevelyan didn't seem to think so. She practically accused him of planning to rape the island. I

170

can't help thinking that she might be right.'

'But if Andreas builds an airport then more people can visit Paradise Bay, and that'll do Philip some good,' Alice persisted.

'But Andreas has bought up all this extra land. He's obviously going to build more hotels here, not just Paradise Bay.'

'But Andreas is hardly likely to kill Paradise Bay, is he? There'd be no point in undermining his own business would there?'

'No. But I bet you his plans for future expansion don't include his current partner.'

'In that case when do you call Philip?' Alice asked sadly.

'Not yet,' Joanne said, smiling fixedly. She knew she was taking a gamble, but she wanted to delay calling Philip for as long as possible. She simply had to have the extra time.

'What are you going to do then?'

'Talk to Amanda Trevelyan first, find out what else she knows. I need to have all the evidence before I call Philip.'

'Are you sure that's the only reason you're waiting?' Alice said, smiling slyly.

'No, and you know that's not,' Joanne said, feeling altogether happier. She felt the sudden pang of desire once more, stronger this time, like an electric current passing through her body. Alice looked so sexy, her dark eyes staring back, her face wearing an expression of flirtatious knowing and open innocent charm. Joanne wanted her there and then, to make love to her, to make those eyes flutter blissfully, to hear the breath escaping from her dark red lips in a whispered sigh.

The hotel bus picked them up after lunch, winding its way out of the narrow village streets and then up on to the open road back to the hotel. The sun beat down fiercely, making the stifling atmosphere in the bus uncomfortably tense. Alice noticed that Joanne kept glancing at her watch, becoming more and more agitated the closer they got to home.

When the bus finally came to a halt Joanne dived off first, pulling Alice along behind her.

'Why the hurry?' Alice asked plaintively, finding herself pulled headlong towards their room.

They stopped outside Liza's room, Joanne smiling when she saw Alice's knowing look. 'I said we'd meet her after lunch,' Joanne explained, half apologetically. She brushed a hand through her hair and then knocked once at the door.

Liza opened the door and stepped back to let them in. She wore a simple white tee-shirt that clung sensuously to her body, displaying the shape of her breasts, her nipples dark circles on the white fabric, and a pair of cut-down denim shorts.

They kissed affectionately, Joanne and Liza and then Liza and Alice. The feel of Liza's soft lips and the taste of her mouth brought back a flood of memories, making Alice secretly quiver with excitement.

'I'm sorry if we're a bit late,' Joanne said, standing by the door, still looking agitated.

'That's OK,' Liza said, smiling.

Alice thought she saw Liza and Joanne exchange a glance, their eyes meeting for a moment and then looking purposefully away.

'Oh, I'm sorry ...' Joanne said, turning to Alice. 'I ... I had promised to go and find Amanda Trevelyan, to find out more about the hotel. I ought to go now.'

'But I can come with you ...' Alice began to say. She looked between Liza and Joanne and recognised that the two of them had pre-arranged the meeting. She felt lost, unable to fathom the extent of the relationship that Joanne had established with Liza.

'No, I have to talk to her alone,' Joanne said, stepping back out of the room. She spoke confidently, but the feeling wasn't reflected in her eyes. Alice saw the look of hesitation, the doubt etched clearly on Joanne's face.

'It's OK, Alice can spend the afternoon with me,' Liza said innocently, taking Alice by the hand and pulling her into the room, away from Joanne.

'Yes, that's a good idea. I'll see you later,' Joanne agreed. She smiled then turned to leave, closing the door behind her.

Alice felt cold, abandoned. She turned to face Liza, tears welling in her eyes. She had been handed over for the afternoon, as if her feelings counted for nothing and Joanne and Liza had decided she had no say in the matter.

'Don't look so worried,' Liza said, taking her by the hand and leading her into the back of the room. The balcony door was open and a gentle breeze was flowing into the room, taking the edge off the heat.

'You had it planned, didn't you?' Alice said accusingly, though there was no anger in her voice, just a note of quiet resignation. She sat down on the seat next to the bed, a bright rectangle of light falling across her body.

'Joanne was busy this afternoon, that's all,' Liza said positively, her look telling Alice that the topic was closed for the moment. 'What would you like to drink?'

'Nothing for me, thanks,' Alice mumbled.

'Why are you so nervous?' Liza asked. She let go of Alice and walked over to the mini-bar. Her shorts were tight, pressing high into her flesh, her backside prominently displayed.

'I'm not,' Alice said defensively, then regretted it. She was nervous, and to deny it only proved the point. If only Joanne was with her, things would have been so much easier. It wasn't that she was afraid of Liza, or the things that Liza would do; rather it was much simpler. All she wanted, all that she desired, was to be with Joanne, to be with her all the time, close by, sharing everything.

'You are, you're nervous. Look at your arms.'

Alice looked at herself, her legs were crossed, arms folded tightly across her chest. She felt as if her whole body was hunched over, clenched tight, like a flesh of armour. She changed posture, aware of Liza's eyes on her, examining her closely.

'So why are you so negative? Are you afraid of me?' Liza took a cold drink and stood up straight, leaning up against the wall, one leg crossed casually over the other.

Alice looked at her and realised just how desirable Liza was. Her body was perfectly proportioned: long agile legs, gently curving thighs, a beautiful rear, wide hips and a narrow waist curving up to her pert breasts. The way she stood, relaxed, at ease with herself, made her seem even more beautiful, more sexy.

'Well?' Liza prompted, smiling indulgently.

Alice had momentarily forgotten the question, lost in her silent admiration of Liza's poised perfection. 'No, I'm not scared of you. I just thought I was going to spend the afternoon with Joanne that's all.'

'Does that mean that you don't fancy me?' Liza challenged, smiling again, her green eyes flashing mischievously.

'I . . . Well . . .' Alice was tongue-tied. There was something disturbing about Liza's manner. It came across as brutally straightforward but at the same time Alice suspected that there was something deeper to it.

'Just relax,' Liza laughed. She raised her drink and drank deeply, her head thrown back, her chest thrust forward provocatively. Her chest rose and fell, her nipples pressed tantalisingly against the thin cotton. 'How did you enjoy your last visit here?'

'You hurt me,' Alice whispered. She looked away, the

familiar flush of embarrassment burning her face.

'But you enjoyed it,' Liza said, sounding totally certain of herself.

'Yes,' Alice admitted after a pause. She felt guilty in the admission, feeling that it was better to lie and deny that the pain had become part of the pleasure.

'And are you afraid that it'll hurt again if we try it?'

'No, it's not that,' Alice replied slowly, trying hard to work out what her feelings really were.

'No, what you're scared of is that you'll enjoy it again.'

'Is that why Joanne brought me here? So that you could use that thing on me again?'

Liza laughed. 'That thing? You mean my vibrator? Say it.'

'Vibrator. Is that why I'm here?'

'I fucked you in the cunt with my vibrator while you were sucking your lesbian lover's bumhole, and you enjoyed every second of it. Now what shocks you, my saying that or you doing it?'

Alice got up, her face was bright red with anger and shame. 'I'm going to my room,' she said. 'I don't want this.'

'But I thought you wanted to talk about it. That's what Joanne told me.'

Alice sat down again. 'What else did Joanne say?'

'Just that. So, do you want to talk about what you feel?'

'Not with you, not with a stranger,' she said coldly.

'A stranger? But, darling, you sucked my arsehole just after you sucked Joanne's. Doesn't that make us just a bit closer than strangers?'

'Why are you doing this?'

'That's not the question,' Liza said, shaking her head. She walked across to Alice and bent down over her, taking her under the chin and kissing her on the mouth.

Alice closed her eyes. Instinctively she wanted to pull away, to recoil from the embrace. It felt wrong. And it

175

felt wrong because Joanne was missing.

'Look what I bought down in the village,' Liza said, dancing across the room before Alice knew what was happening. She shuffled through a drawer for a second and produced a leather handbag wrapped in a plastic bag. It was made from stiff brown leather, with a map of Frixos etched out on the top flap and a small compass below it. The work was crudely tooled, the wording on the map roughly cut out, the letters indistinct. Liza handed the bag to Alice.

'Yes, I saw one like this as well,' she said, wondering what it was she was missing. She handled the leather bag gingerly, turning it over, noting the thick stitching around the outside. A label hung from one side with the legend 'hand-made' printed in block capitals.

'It's not very nice,' Liza laughed. 'But we aren't exactly spoilt for choice on Frixos are we?'

'No, we're not,' Alice agreed, though it sounded more like a question. She felt like she had just missed the punchline of a joke, waiting for understanding to dawn suddenly, and then to feel stupid for having missed it the first time.

'What I liked about it was the strap,' Liza explained. She opened the flap and unbuckled the long leather strap. She threw the bag across the room, not even bothering to look where it landed. The strap was long and stiff, with a silver clip at either end.

'What about the strap?'

'I realised what a useful little thing it could turn out to be,' Liza said, advancing on Alice with the strap in her hand, smiling, her eyes blazing with excitement.

Alice let Liza come up to her and take her hands, allowing herself to be pulled to her feet. They stood face to face, Alice could feel Liza's hot breath on her face, their eyes met and she felt a dagger of excitement pierce

176

her. Her heart was racing, pumping wildly.

Liza pushed Alice towards the bed, turning her round at the same time, so that Alice faced the bed fully. She pushed her on to the bed. Alice fell unresistingly, landing on her belly, her hands out in front of her to stop her hurting herself. Quickly Liza straddled her, sitting herself on the small of Alice's back. She grabbed Alice's hands and pulled them back roughly, crossing them behind her back and tying them quickly with the stiff leather strap.

It happened quickly, every move was expertly executed, and Alice knew that Liza had done this before. The underside of the strap was rough against her skin, chafing the soft skin of her wrists. Liza turned her over and threaded the length of the strap round her waist, then clipped the two ends together using the silver catches.

Liza got up off the bed and stood back, looking down on Alice with an excited smile. Alice was on her back, her arms tied behind her, the strap tight around her waist as well as around her wrists. She tried to move but her hands were too tightly bound. She was breathless, partly from the exertion of trying to break free but also with an underlying excitement caused by the strange feeling of containment. She was bound, and there was the secret fear and exhilaration of knowing that she no longer had any control. To all intents and purposes she was at Liza's mercy. The thought struck a chord inside her, making her struggle even more, making her become damp between the thighs.

'Does that feel good?' Liza said, smiling, a wicked glint in her eye. 'As soon as I saw the strap I realised that it could turn out to be useful, and I was right.'

'Why are you doing this to me?' Alice said, ceasing the fruitless struggle to free her arms from the tight bonds.

'I haven't decided yet,' Liza teased. She bent down and began to unbutton Alice's blouse, starting from the top

177

and undoing each button slowly.

'If you wanted to make love you didn't have to do this,' Alice said, finding it difficult to conceal her growing excitement. She could feel the warmth in her pussy growing, her nipples were puckering, slowly becoming erect.

'Shut up!' Liza snapped. 'If you carry on talking I'll have to gag your pretty little mouth. I'll get my big black vibrator and strap it over your mouth, pushing it down your throat like a giant prick.'

'I'm sorry,' Alice whined, genuinely frightened by the threat. Something had come over Liza. Her aggressive manner no longer looked like playacting, her face had become hard, her lips pursed intently.

'You will be,' Liza promised, pulling open Alice's blouse. She hardly bothered to look at the bared breasts, the dark nipples already hard and erect. She turned and went over to the wardrobe, bending over to go through her suitcase.

'Please, I'll be quiet, I promise I will,' Alice pleaded. She managed to shift around to one side and then sat up awkwardly. Liza was bending over, the thin crutch of the denim shorts pulled impossibly tightly into the shallow groove between her rounded white arse-cheeks. Her legs were taut, smooth and flawless, the firm muscles of her long thighs standing out. In spite of her fear of being gagged with the vibrator, Alice still felt desire, a tingling heat in her pussy and an aching want deep within.

Liza stood up and turned to face Alice. In her hand she held another instrument, not the monstrous black vibrator that she had threatened. This was long and thin, tapering at one end, still phallic but not in the same exaggerated way as the other one. It was a dull creamy colour, with a kind of grip at one end.

Alice looked at the thing wide-eyed, shuffling painfully

far up the bed, trying to get away. Her blouse was open and her breasts hung loosely, warmed by the strong rays of the sun. Her proudly erect nipples gave the lie to the look of horror in her eyes.

Liza grabbed hold of Alice and pushed her down flat, on to her tummy. She checked the bonds quickly, pulling the knot to make sure there could be no escape. Alice's short skirt was in disarray; Liza merely tugged at it and it fell away. Next Liza pulled off Alice's panties, drawing them down around the ankles then using them to tie the ankles together.

Alice was breathing heavily, her hair falling over her eyes, beads of sweat running down her face. The space between her thighs was damp, thick drops of honey oozing from her sex. She waited, her whole being on edge, for Liza to begin.

'It's so hot,' Liza said calmly. She crossed the room again and got herself a drink, pausing to check her long golden hair in the mirror. She looked remarkably relaxed, smiling cheerfully, her face alternately kind and loving or cruel and vindictive. She took her time, finishing her drink slowly before returning to the bed.

'You've got a lovely backside,' Liza told Alice, running a hand up her thigh and massaging her arse-cheeks. She began to rub Alice's bottom with both hands, massaging her buttocks in a slow circular motion, pulling them apart at the bottom so that she could look directly into Alice's sex.

Alice buried her face in the pillow, her face red with shame. She could lie no longer. Her body gave her away, revealing the desire burning deep in her belly.

'Such a lovely backside,' Liza said wistfully, lingering over the view of Alice's parted cunny lips, the pink flesh within fully exposed. 'I bet your skin colours wonderfully, doesn't it?'

'Please let me go,' Alice cried weakly.

Liza leant back and removed her sandals, kicking one on to the floor and taking the other in her hand. She raised it high and then brought it down quickly, landing the stroke squarely on Alice's left buttock.

Alice screamed, through shock and pain. The blow left her skin burning, the stinging pain turning rapidly into a red-hot glow that seemed to seep inwards. A second blow fell, and then a rapid succession of hard strokes, each blow alternating, first on the right and then on the left buttock. The searing pain became incandescent, burning her skin and sending spasms of pure sensation running through her body. She was sobbing, tears falling uncontrollably down her face. It hurt so much, but then she froze, a tidal wave of pure pleasure breaking through her. She orgasmed, caught her breath, became lost in the swirling maelstrom of sensation.

When Liza stopped and rubbed her hand on Alice's backside Alice squirmed, trying to press herself against Liza's cool fingers. Her body was ablaze, the heat on her backside merging with the lava flow of energy burning in her pussy. She wanted more, ached to be hurt once more, to submit to Liza's punishment. She no longer cared for anything but the pleasure of submission and chastisement.

Liza bent down and touched her lips against Alice's burning backside, soothing the reddened flesh with coolness of her mouth. She rubbed her fingers just below Alice's sex, rubbing slowly back and forth, her fingers smeared with the thick flow of cunt-cream. Alice was moaning, lost in her private world of the senses.

Alice murmured softly when she was pulled up by the middle, lifting her backside high, offering herself for more punishment. She looked lost, a dazed expression on her face. When it came she cried out, a piercing shriek that filled the room and then faded to silence. Liza had taken the vibrator and pressed it deep into Alice's sex, sliding it in and out several times. The rush of penetration had taken Alice out of herself, making her body ache with pleasure-pain.

'Just relax now,' Liza whispered soothingly, kissing Alice on her trembling lips.

Alice tried to free herself again but failed. She was lying on her tummy and chest, arching her back so that her bottom raised high. Liza parted the reddened arse-cheeks with her fingers and then carefully guided the tip of the vibrator into Alice's tight arsehole.

Alice tried to wriggle free but a sharp slap made her stop. She felt herself being violated, her body invaded by the cool plastic hardness of the object. She realised that it had been lubricated with her pussy juices, and so was sliding slowly but easily into the tightness of her arsehole. It felt so alien, so horrible, but at the same time exciting, forbidden. Her arse was still stinging, alive with residual spasms of white-hot pain. The vibrator filled her, going deeper and deeper into her backside, the ring of muscle clenching tightly at the smooth phallic object.

'That looks lovely. I bet it feels great,' Liza said, sitting next to Alice. She passed a hand down the smooth curve of Alice's back, pressing firmly against the tender punished bottom cheeks. She was still clothed, and now she turned and opened her thighs, pressing a finger down between her thighs. 'Look,' she told Alice proudly, 'I'm wet.'

She sat up on her knees and wriggled out of her tight shorts, her breasts bouncing lightly as she moved. She sat on the pillow and parted her thighs, opening her sex with her fingers and pressing a finger into herself. She pressed the finger in deep and when she removed it it glistened with her pussy cream. She pressed the finger into Alice's mouth and Alice lapped at it greedily, licking it and swallowing the drops of pussy fluid with obvious relish.

Liza sat up on her knees and turned Alice on to her back. Alice cried out, the thing wedged into her anal hole moving slightly deeper.

'I want you to tongue me from here,' Liza touched a finger to her pussy lips, 'to here,' she moved the finger under herself and stopped at the dark eye of her arsehole. She sat herself down, opening herself over Alice's hungry mouth.

Alice closed her eyes. She was overcome with the flood of sensations: the cloying scent of Liza's sex, the view of her beautifully spread buttocks, the stinging of her own backside and the feel of the pseudo-penis pressed into her rear button. She opened her mouth and kissed Liza in the sex, pressing her tongue between the warmth of the pussy lips, sucking in the thick sex juices as if they were sweet nectar.

Liza leaned forward and pushed her head between Alice's thighs. She moaned softly, pressing her backside down fuller over Alice's face. She began to kiss Alice at the entrance to her pussy, at the same time taking hold of the vibrator in Alice's bumhole and moving it in and out slowly.

Alice cried out with pleasure, but her sound was swallowed deep in Liza's damp pussy. She thrashed her head, pressing herself deeper into Liza's sex, flicking her tongue over the pink cunt-bud. She was being pussy sucked by Liza, and at the same time frigged in the arse with the long thin vibrator. Her body was quivering, an electric glow of pleasure throbbing all over her.

Liza suddenly moved away, though keeping her mouth clamped tightly to Alice's pussy and increasing the piston motion of the vibrator in her rear hole. Alice opened her eyes, and saw a man standing over her. His thick prick was in his hand, hard and erect, the purple head glistening and the flesh veined with thin purple lines. The man was masturbating, moving his hand up and down his long hard prick.

Alice moaned, her lips parted to let the breath escape from her lungs. She knew that she was on the verge, that her body and soul were going to explode once more in a blissful golden orgasm.

The man gasped, moaning softly. He gripped his prick and pulled the skin hard, pulling the flesh so that it was white and the purple head suffused with a pink flush. Alice sighed at the same instant, opening her mouth, her eyes half-closed.

Thick drops of white sperm arced out from the man's prick, spurting out in long throbbing waves. The drops of thick warm cream fell over Alice's face, on to her cheeks and eyes, over her chin and lips and into her open mouth. The two of them were lost, overwhelmed in the moment of orgasm.

Liza sat up. She looked tired but happy, her lips drawn in a delighted smile. Martin sat on the edge of the bed, body slumped over, a look of sheer exhaustion on his drained face. Alice still looked dazed, her face flushed pink, her eyes almost bloodshot.

'Let me clean you up,' Liza told her softly, undoing the leather strap that had bound her so tightly. She stooped down and began to kiss away the drops of sperm that had splattered Alice's face.

Alice closed her eyes and swallowed the drops of come in her mouth, feeling the thick juices slide down her throat. She had so many questions, so many things to ask, to understand.

'Can we talk about it now?' she implored Liza, weakly.

'No, not now,' Liza said gently, kissing her on the mouth. 'We will talk,' she promised. 'But later, much later.'

ten

Alice staggered into the room, her whole body aching and stinging. Her backside still throbbed painfully, she wore no panties but even the flapping of her loose skirt as she walked caused tiny daggers of pain to jolt through her. She walked into the room and found Joanne waiting for her, sitting pensively by the door.

Joanne stood up, a look of shock marked clearly on her face. 'Are you all right?' she asked softly, her voice full of concern.

'Yes, I'm OK,' Alice lied. She caught sight of her reflection, hair unkempt, clothes a mess, her face a picture of exhaustion. 'I look worse than I feel,' she said, hoping to deflect Joanne's well-meaning concern.

'Do you want to talk about it?' Joanne asked.

'No, I'm fine,' Alice said again, managing to smile weakly. She was glad that Joanne was displaying such hesitation; the last thing she wanted was a big scene. If Joanne so much as touched her she knew she would break down and weep like a child, and she didn't want that. All she wanted was to stand under the shower and let the water wash over her, cool and cleansing. And then to sleep. To sleep for an age, to let the wounds on her body heal, and to let her dreams heal the wounds in her soul.

'If you're sure,' Joanne smiled, a note of relief in her

voice. She stepped back, sat down again, still looking pensive.

'I'm sure,' Alice said. She walked slowly to the bathroom trying not to limp or hobble, but unable to ignore the ache, or the tenderness between her thighs or the feeling of discomfort between her bottom cheeks.

'I didn't have much luck with what I was after,' Joanne said, just as Alice reached the bathroom door.

It took a moment but then Alice remembered the excuse that Joanne had given for leaving earlier. She looked at her with tired eyes, wondering whether Joanne wasn't suddenly feeling guilty. 'Did Amanda have anything to say?'

Joanne shook her head. 'No, I couldn't even find her. Apparently she left Paradise Bay today, at short notice. From what I found out, she and Andreas had a blazing row and then she left.'

'So what next?' Alice asked with an effort, leaning against the door frame for support.

'I have to find out where she's gone. I had a word with Nicky and he said that he'd find out for me.'

'What if she's gone to the mainland? How will you find her then?'

'I don't think she has. Nicky says that today isn't a ferry day, nobody arrives or departs that way. And I rang the airfield and they said that there were no flights in or out today either. She's on this island somewhere,' Joanne concluded confidently. 'And we're going to find her.'

'Yes,' Alice agreed. She was too tired to think or argue. She turned and went into the bathroom, wanting only to stand under the torrent of water and let it flow over her body.

The sun was blazing when Amanda finally pulled up outside Jean-Pierre's grand house. She stepped out of the jeep and grabbed her case, wanting to scream with anger and laugh at the same time. It had been ridiculous, so downright petty. At the last moment she realised that she hadn't enough cash or traveller's cheques to cover the inordinately high bill that Andreas had presented. If she had had the inclination she could have quibbled over the amounts and whittled it down, but really she didn't have the energy; nor was it something that she was accustomed to. Luckily, or so she had imagined, her credit cards would get her out of any difficulties.

Andreas, on the other hand, had decided to be as difficult and as petty as humanly possible. He had arrogantly rejected the cards she had offered and demanded either cash or equivalent payment. Even the reception staff looked astounded, and more than a little embarrassed, but Andreas was adamant. Amanda, furious but outwardly calm, had tried to reason with him but it was no good. In the end she had threatened to scream the place down before he relented, bellowing at her until he was red in the face and then storming off. The reception staff were more than apologetic but that was no good.

Amanda rang the doorbell, seething with anger and eager to spill the story to Jean-Pierre. It was laughable really; she just couldn't get under the skin of someone who could lower themselves to act so stupidly. What was Andreas thinking of? Anyone with any sense would have remained calm throughout. And it was a stupid move to put her out of the hotel and cut off her phone. Utterly stupid and self-defeating.

No one answered the door, and she rang again and again impatiently. What next? That was the question that she had asked herself during the long drive up from the hotel. In part it depended on what information Jean-Pierre had garnered from his numerous friends around the island. If it was really good then she wanted to pass the story on to friends in Athens. If it was scandal, then she would make sure Andreas was exposed on Greek TV for everyone to see. She knew that he was going to regret every indignity that he had forced upon her, every petty detail was going to be put down on paper.

There was still no answer so she tried the door and found it open. She stepped into the coolness of the hallway, glad to be out of the heat. She dropped her bags by the door and called out to Jean-Pierre. Her voice echoed through the silence of the big house, a silence that made her feel a little nervous. She called out again, this time louder, a note of alarm in her voice.

When there was no answer she headed straight for the big room, suddenly alarmed by the deathly silence. The room was empty. She crossed to the balcony and looked out over the pool but it was deserted. Had something happened? She looked beyond the pool and saw just how isolated the house was, nestling in the rock, partly shielded by the trees on the lower slopes of the mountain.

Andreas had shown himself to be ruthless and petty. Was he capable of more? The thought struck a chord of fear buried deep inside her. She and Jean-Pierre were strangers on this island, no matter how much Jean-Pierre boasted of his links to the people. Andreas was a powerful man in this small world, linked to the people with ties of blood, as well as by the mundane reality of being the largest employer on the island. If all of this was now in jeopardy, just how far was he willing to go? The islanders were notorious for their close-knit culture, and a vendetta was still passed down from father to son like a legacy, a family treasure to be nurtured on a diet of jealousy and blood.

Frantically Amanda returned to the room and picked up the nearest phone. It was dead, no dialling tone, no crackling of the line. She called out Jean-Pierre's name, hoping that he would suddenly appear, a jovial bear of

187

a man. She ran from room to room, searching for him, certain that her worst nightmares were coming true. At any moment she expected to find his body slumped in a corner, lying in a pool of blood, his face wearing a sickly death-smile. But there was nothing, only the enveloping silence and the coolness of the house.

She stopped at last, exhausted, shaking miserably with fear and dismay. Why had it turned out so badly? It had promised to be such a simple assignment, just another dull little island turning its face to the outside world.

The studio. She jumped up and raced down the stairs, her heels clattering on the rough stone steps. It was exactly as she remembered: the glass door open on to the pool, a shaft of cool air filtering into the long room, the stunning panoramic view of mountain and wood on the other side. The poolside was silent, the bluish water calm and still, catching the light and casting it back in strange geometric shapes. Jean-Pierre was nowhere to be seen.

Inevitably the sight of the studio stirred memories, vivid memories that had stayed with her, lurking below the surface, emerging in her dreams and imagination. She walked to the back of the studio, feeling slightly nervous. When she pulled away the filthy sheet, the beautiful white statue was there, as intensely beautiful as the image scored deep in her memory.

She touched it lightly, her fingertips dancing lightly over the carved stone, as light as the breeze from the pool that touched her own skin. It felt so good, so incredibly lifelike. Jean-Pierre was a master, an artist of the highest calibre, and the thought that something might have happened to him made her feel weak with fear and anger.

What next? The same question, but now this time with a greater urgency. She had to force herself to think about it, to picture the worst. If she was alone, without the support of Jean-Pierre what should she do? Could she trust the local police? Was there anyone at all that she could trust?

Amanda decided that she was alone. No, there was only one other person that sprang to mind, a woman that she had met briefly in Paradise Bay. She tried to remember her name, but couldn't. What she did remember was that the woman, beautiful, with blonde hair and brilliant blue eyes, was in some way connected to Paradise Bay but not to Andreas. Damn, if only she had remembered earlier. Perhaps something could have been done about Andreas. Amanda cursed herself, it was her fault, she had let that vital piece of information slip through her fingers.

She screamed suddenly, almost jumping out of her skin, her face ashen with horror and fear.

'I'm sorry... I'm...' Jean-Pierre stuttered apologetically, backing away.

'Jesus Christ,' Amanda said, gasping for breath, clutching her heart and feeling it thump wildly. She wanted to hug him and hit him at the same time. 'You frightened the life out of me. Where the hell have you been?'

'I went down to visit some friends, to see if my telephone was the only one not working. You have been here long?'

'I thought that something had happened to you,' she said, suddenly feeling very silly.

'To me?' Jean-Pierre laughed. 'What could happen to me? Who would dare to do anything to Jean-Pierre? No one!' He laughed again and then his manner changed. 'You were concerned,' he said softly, taking Amanda in his powerful arms and holding her close. 'Don't worry my dear, everything will be fine. They can do nothing to us.'

'I was just being silly, imagining all kinds of strange things,' Amanda explained, smiling again. She felt more relaxed, safe and secure now that he was close.

'I saw that you have brought your bags. You are staying, yes?'

'You don't mind, do you? Andreas was making things impossible for me. He couldn't wait to get me out of the place, and he made me pay, he cleaned me out of cash completely.'

'He is no man,' Jean-Pierre said gruffly. 'A man would not act that way. Only a . . . a . . . a child would act that way!'

'For a moment,' Amanda said, hands on hips, 'I thought you were going to say only a woman would act that way.'

'Me? I would never say such a thing! Never. You believe me, don't you?'

'Absolutely,' Amanda laughed. 'Now,' she said, suddenly serious again, 'what is it that you've found out?'

'I have no proof, you understand, none at all.'

'Yes, go on.'

'It is only a rumour, but a very good rumour. The man who told me this is like a brother. His word is iron, I cannot doubt that it is the truth . . .'

'Please Jean-Pierre, get to the point,' Amanda pleaded impatiently.

'Yes, yes. Andreas stole the money to buy all the land. And in fact not all the money has been paid so far.'

'That's it!' Amanda sounded overwhelmingly relieved, her face lit up with sudden excitement. 'That's great, just the story we need to nail him. What else?'

'As I understand it he got the money by stealing from his partner, and then using that to buy the first plots of land.'

'How does your friend know all this?'

'Because he has not been paid yet. He sold Karaplis a large plot of land on the other side of the island, an isolated piece of beach, very beautiful. I can take you there, if you wish.'

'Another time. What else?'

'Well my friend has not been paid and so he has been

to see Karaplis many times, to demand the money. At the last meeting Karaplis was drunk, in despair, crying like a child. He told my friend that he had approached another Englishman to join him as a partner, but this one was smarter than the first one, and had turned him down. He was saying that he would never find a partner like his first one, and that he couldn't steal any more from him.'

'So Andreas has been ripping off his partner, that's very interesting.'

'We call the police, yes?'

'No, not yet. We contact his partner first,' Amanda said decisively.

'But how? You have friends in England who can find him?'

'No, better than that. I know someone at Paradise Bay who knows the man personally.'

'Then we have Andreas. There is nothing he can do now,' Jean-Pierre said, his voice thick with relief.

'You've done very well,' Amanda said, taking his unshaven face in her soft hands and kissing him on the mouth. He took her by the waist and pulled her down on to him, holding her tightly, pushing his tongue into her mouth.

'When I saw you here I thought you had returned to worship the golden child,' he explained, holding her with one hand and brushing the other over the perfect form of the statue. His thick fingers moved deftly, tracing a line from the knee up to the base of the white stone erection, resting at the base of the thick prick, wrapped around the hand carved in stone.

'I still think you owe it to yourself to put your work on display,' Amanda said softly, putting her hand on his, her white skin closer to the tone of the statue than to his rough dark skin.

'I cannot, really I can't,' Jean-Pierre said wistfully.

'Do you know the story of Pygmalion?' Amanda asked, pressing herself closer to him.

'I think of it often,' Jean-Pierre admitted. 'I know how the ancient king of Cyprus loved his statue, I can feel the same emotion. But there is a difference. Galatea was brought to life, Aphrodite used her power to aid poor Pygmalion. In my case this is not an ideal image plucked from my soul but the image of a man who walks and lives and breathes.'

'But you love the image, you love the contours of pure white marble and not the flesh and blood.'

'Let me show you how I love this thing,' Jean-Pierre said, his voice hoarse with desire, dark eyes glittering.

He pulled away from Amanda and began to undress, unbuttoning the rough black peasant shirt to reveal his wide chest, the dark pattern of hair streaked in places with silver grey. He dropped his shirt and then undressed completely, his body covered all over with a fine layer of dark hair. He had a thick chest and a bulging belly, heavy arms and short muscular thighs. It was a peasant's build, tough and muscular, strong and masculine. He was alredy erect, his thick prick long and hard, its base surrounded by a dense bush of jet-black hair.

Amanda smiled. He wasn't good looking in the conventional sense, but his squat frame and dark raven eyes seethed with pure sensual power. She wore a simple white top and a long loose skirt that swirled around her as she walked. She pulled the top over her head and let the skirt fall around her ankles.

Jean-Pierre stepped closer and took her in his arms once more. They kissed, she felt his thick sensual lips on hers, his tongue snaking into her mouth. The thick hairs on his chest tickled her nipples, and his arms pulled her on to him, their bodies pressed close. She felt his prick pressing against her, hot and hard, sliding suggestively against the smooth pale skin of her upper thighs.

They kissed and kissed until she felt dizzy and breathless, the excitement making her pussy moist with urgent desire. His rough hands played over her body, with the same delicate touch that had caressed the white marble. His fingers touched her, running down her back, caressing her lightly between the thighs, flicking softly over her nipples.

Amanda managed to pull away from him for a second. She touched him with both hands, caressing his barrel chest before sinking to her knees in front of him. His prick towered before her eyes, thick and strong, the dark skin veined with thin purple lines, the glans wet with a smear of silvery fluid. She kissed him at the base of his prick, touching her lips softly against the dense brush of hair. His balls were cool and heavy in her hand, she took his prick with her other hand, squeezing it gently, feeling it flexing responsively.

She opened her mouth and took his glans into it, swirling her tongue around the very tip, sucking in the silky wetness that had made it glisten. She swallowed the first taste of him, letting it suffuse her mouth, his masculine essence settling on her tongue and slipping down her throat. She kissed him urgently, her lips caressing his swollen glans, her tongue sliding over the smooth flesh. He sighed, jerking forward, pushing his prick deeper into her sweet mouth.

Amanda closed her mouth over the tip of his prick and fell forward, taking it deep into the back of her throat, sucking her mouth in so that she could feel the length of it close on her inner mouth. Up and down she moved, sucking and licking, turning her mouth into a tight pussy over his hardness. She cradled his ball sac, holding him gently, wanting to increase his pleasure so that he could come in her mouth.

'No, not this way,' he whispered hoarsely, taking

Amanda by the arms and lifting her to her feet.

Amanda fell into his arms, her pussy wet, aching for him to fill her with his shaft. They kissed eagerly, passionately, the taste of his prick sucked out from her mouth and into his. She parted her thighs and collapsed into his arms, his strong fingers entering her deeply. She felt weak at the knees, alive to the pleasure caused by his probing fingers, sliding into her wet pocket of flesh. She sighed hotly, burying her face in his neck, her lips on the rough muscles of his throat and shoulder.

Jean-Pierre picked her up, his powerful arms grasping her around the waist. She looked a little shaky, but he lifted her effortlessly and moved her over the statue.

'No, I want you,' she complained, knowing what he was going to do.

'You will have me, deep inside your honey box,' Jean-Pierre said, his gravelly voice thick with desire and promise. He held her over the statue for a second then lowered her slowly.

A look passed between them, hesitation in her eyes and certainty in his. She swallowed her caution and reached down between her thighs, touching her pussy lips, flecked with the dew drops of her yearning desire. Very carefully she opened herself, gasping when the cool tip of the marble erection touched her inner flesh. Slowly Jean-Pierre let her down, watching her sit on the white stone penis, his eyes fixed on the vision of the inanimate stone entering her pure pink flesh.

Without wanting to Amanda found herself shifting, letting the cold stone prick enter her deeply, sliding into the moistness of her pussy. The cool stone shaft made her close her eyes blissfully, the incredible hardness brushing against her pussy-bud, powerful tremors of bliss passing from her pussy into her soul. She rocked slowly back and forth, eyes closed, her pussy rubbing deliciously against the statue.

Jean-Pierre still held Amanda. He released her slowly, taking her breasts in his large hands, covering each one with his fingers, as if moulding them from unfinished clay. His mouth was at her neck and then between her snow-white breasts, and seconds later he had a red-brown nipple between his thick sensual lips. He sucked and bit, pulling the erect nipple with his teeth and lips, rousing the pointed cherry and then soothing it with his tongue.

Amanda uttered a strangled cry, half sobbing with uncontrollable bliss. Her face contorted, wordless moans seeping from her open mouth, her lips blood-red against her pretty white skin. She was seized by the suddenness of the orgasm, crying out again and again, waves of pleasure reflected in the rolling of her eyes.

Jean-Pierre took her in his arms and carefully pulled her off the statue. She felt weak in his arms, her eyes fluttering, looking about her with a dazed expression. He reached down with one hand and pressed his fingers into the heat of her pussy. She sighed softly, alive to the renewed pleasure. He rubbed his fingers deep inside her and then withdrew for a moment. Amanda was too dazed to try to understand what he was doing; he seemed to twist his body away from her then he entered her with his fingers again. Two, three times it happened; then he sat her down on the cool thigh of the statue.

'Now you shall have me, deep inside you,' Jean-Pierre whispered in her ear.

Amanda turned to look at him, finding her bearings after the bitter ecstasy of climaxing on the cold stone penis. He took a step back, his face dark and intent, his eyes a little wild. He lifted himself up and then she understood what he was doing. She watched him open-mouthed, more than a little shocked by his behaviour.

Now it made sense. His professions of worshipping the

statue and paying homage to his creation were not just artistic metaphor, but the literal truth. He was balanced over the lap of the statue, his hand holding the marble prick and carefully guiding himself over it. Very slowly he lowered himself, balancing with one hand and guiding himself with the other. The stone prick glistened in the brittle light, wet with Amanda's pussy juice smeared all over it. That was what Jean-Pierre had been doing. He had smeared himself with her juices too, drawing the thick cream directly from her pussy with his fingers.

Amanda stood up and moved to one side. She watched silently, her face as intense as his. He had closed his eyes, poised as he was over the thick stone prick. Very slowly he lowered himself, the stone prick edging deep into his backside. He stopped once, opened his eyes, smiled at Amanda then finished. He let out a sigh, the thick prick wedged deep into his arsehole.

'Now you,' he said, extending a hand to Amanda.

Amanda hesitated. The sight of Jean-Pierre impaled sexually on his creation, his own prick seemingly doubled in size and potency, made her feel hot and nervous. But the fire in her belly was enough. She wanted him, wanted him deep in her pussy, wanted to feel his flesh on hers. She stepped forward and let herself be lifted up high.

Jean-Pierre kissed her passionately on the mouth, sucking at her breath, biting her lips so that she cried out. He lowered her on to his prick, and she felt herself open around him, the walls of her sex enveloping his heavy prick.

Their mouths locked tight, ferociously duelling. He held her under her bottom, a hand on each buttock, pulling her open so that he could score deeper. They began to move in unison, spiralling, moving to and fro, the cold penis deep inside his rear hole and his hot prick deep into her vagina. They moved fast, instinctively, breathing together, sighing, moaning, crying out with unbridled pleasure.

Amanda lost herself, dancing on his lovely stiff prick, his mouth on her mouth, his hands touching her between the bottom cheeks, touching her anal hole. She forced her breasts into his mouth, then bent down to bite him, sucking at his flesh. Their bodies were bathed in sweat, moving like the waves of the ocean, their pleasure bound up into one single movement, one entity.

Jean-Pierre gasped, his hands clutching Amanda's thighs. He buried his face between the twin perfection of her breasts. Amanda cried out also, sharing in the vital moment, in the single clear instant of elation. They froze, their bodies like the stone beneath them. Amanda felt Jean-Pierre pumping his thick cream into her and climaxed, the moment complete.

'I have to confront Andreas,' Joanne finally decided. She had spent most of the day pacing up and down the room, waiting for the phone to ring. Nicky had promised to find out where Amanda had disappeared to, but all he had done was come up with more details of her final departure.

'Are you sure?' Alice asked, her own hesitation evident in the look on her face.

'No, I'm not sure. But what else can I do?' Joanne said testily. She stood up and walked over to Alice, who had woken up only minutes earlier.

'Why not ring Philip now?' Alice suggested, making room for Joanne. 'You're going to have to tell him sooner or later.'

'Tell him what exactly? That his partner is buying up more land? That's hardly earth-shattering information.'

'And what will you tell Andreas?' Alice countered meekly.

'I'll tell him who I am, and that I know where Amanda has gone. I'll call his bluff.'

'Are you sure?'

'Of course I'm not sure,' Joanne repeated. She leaned across the bed and kissed Alice, breathing in the warm subtle scent of her skin. Alice responded, opening her lips, closing her eyes, twisting her head to one side. She was dressed only in bra and panties, her ample breasts prominently displayed and subtly perfumed. Joanne touched her hand on Alice's thigh and then pulled away.

'Do you want me with you when you see Andreas?' Alice asked, her face achingly attractive, her eyes reflecting the essentially reserved nature of her character.

'Yes, would you?'

Alice nodded, then stood up and padded across the room to get dressed. Joanne watched her go, eyeing her beautiful body, aware of the feeling of tenderness beating strongly in her heart. She still wondered what Alice and Liza had done together; the picture of Alice's exhausted countenance was still strong in her mind.

They walked across to the reception in silence, sharing only a strained smile as they entered the building. Joanne walked up to the reception desk, Alice trailing slightly, her stride less confident than Joanne's.

'Excuse me,' Joanne said loudly, ensuring that the young man behind the desk looked up from his stack of paperwork, 'I want to talk to Andreas Karaplis.'

'Perhaps I can help you, madam,' he smiled. He looked at Joanne and then at Alice, and his smile broadened, his thick lips drawn back over white uneven teeth.

'No, I want to talk to Andreas. Now.'

'But, madam,' the young man said patronisingly, 'Mr Karaplis is an extremely busy man. If you let me know what the problem is then perhaps I can take care of it.' He paused, then looked at Alice again. 'Does it involve your friend in some way?'

'Get me Karaplis now,' Joanne hissed, her eyes meeting

his leer head on. He looked at her for a moment and his smile faded.

'As you wish, madam,' he said and withdrew to the back office.

'Did that bother you?' Joanne asked, turning to face Alice.

'That little creep?' Alice said quietly, managing to sound almost scornful.

'Good,' Joanne smiled, glad that Alice was regaining the confidence that had all but disappeared.

'Yes, madam, how may I help you?' Andreas said. He looked tired and harassed, but he smiled gamely, his urbane voice as charming as usual.

'I'd like to speak with you in private,' Joanne said. She stood straight, her clear blue eyes fixed on Andreas.

He looked back at Joanne and then at Alice. 'As you wish, madam,' he said, signalling to the receptionist to make way for the two women.

Joanne and Alice followed Andreas into the small office behind the reception desk. He closed the door behind them and turned to Joanne. 'And what may I do for you two lovely ladies?'

'I've just come here to pass on kind regards from Philip,' Joanne said coolly, sitting casually on the edge of the desk, crossing one leg over the other.

'Philip?' Andreas repeated, his face blank with confusion.

'Yes, you must remember Philip. Philip who is part owner of Paradise Bay. Philip, your partner.'

Andreas's jaw dropped. 'How do you know Philip?' he asked, his eyes narrowed suspiciously.

'Well,' Joanne said, smiling, 'you could say that I'm his partner too. I happen to be married to him.'

Andreas collapsed into the nearest chair, beads of sweat forming all over his face. He seemed lost in confusion and bewilderment, whispering to himself, his eyes bulging.

'Philip thought it would be a good idea for me to spend my holiday here, quietly checking up on his little investment. And I've so much to tell him now.'

'You're lying,' Andreas finally decided, sitting up in his seat, the look of horror still fresh on his face.

'Why should I lie? I would guess that's your particular forte.'

'No, you are lying. Philip would never do this to me . . .'

'Let me see,' Joanne said, beginning to enjoy herself. 'You and Philip met at the airport bar in Copenhagen airport. You already had the plan for Paradise Bay worked out, you shook hands on the deal before he left for his flight. You came to my house for a summer party soon afterwards, I was away in London at the time. Do you want more?'

'What have you got to say about Paradise Bay? I trust you have found everything to your satisfaction, everything.' Andreas stood up. He tried to sound relaxed and amiable, but the smile around his lips was thin and his voice shaky.

'Amanda Trevelyan has a lot to say,' Joanne said, certain that the mere mention of Amanda's name would be enough.

'That stupid woman!' Andreas snapped angrily, banging his fist on the desk. 'That woman is a crazy woman, and that mad Frenchman she has picked up also. They are crazy, the two of them. Sick in the head, I tell you.'

'I think that Philip might like to talk to them, just to see for himself what state their sanity is in.'

'And does Philip know what his wife is up to in my hotel? Sleeping with another woman, shamelessly making love to her in front of everyone. And having sex with every man in sight, like a prostitute. I know all about it!'

'We've not kept it secret,' Joanne countered, trying to

cover her own sudden nervousness. She had expected Andreas to pull that trick, but still it made her feel uneasy.

'Like a slut. With every waiter and receptionist you could find. Sometimes with two at once. Have you no shame? Is that what you want your husband to find out?'

Joanne stood up. Andreas was shaking with rage, his voice raised high. 'If you think you can blackmail me then you're mistaken,' Joanne interrupted him. 'I think you're the one who has to worry, not me.'

'We can talk,' Andreas said, calming down quickly. He sat back down, wiping his face with a white handkerchief, his hands still shaking.

'No, let's go,' Joanne said, taking Alice by the arm. Alice smiled at her weakly.

'Please, we can talk,' Andreas begged. He stood up again, his eyes were dark with a sense of defeat. He looked like the world around him had collapsed, his shoulders were drooping, his skin white, the lines on his face scored deep.

Joanne took Alice by the hand and marched out of the room, passing the young receptionist who looked on open-mouthed at what had happened.

eleven

Joanne hardly slept. All night long she had debated calling Philip. She still had nothing concrete to go on, no final proof that Andreas was anything more than a slightly unscrupulous businessman. Against that, Andreas had the absolute truth about her and Alice. And about her and Nicky, and Petros.

The key to the whole thing lay with Amanda Trevelyan. It was inconceivable that she had been forced out over nothing; she represented the best hope Paradise Bay had of becoming well known, and Andreas would not have thrown the chance away over a mere trifle. She had dug out the truth from somewhere, and whatever it was it had caused him to throw her out. Joanne knew that she simply had to find Amanda. She was her only hope of salvaging something from the mess.

Joanne realised she had played her hand too early. She had revealed herself to Andreas before she really had the dirt on him, while he had the dirt on her, in fact. It had been a stupid move. Now she had to act fast to limit the damage. Andreas was no fool. He was certain to be busy covering up his tracks, obscuring whatever it was that he had done wrong. And all the time building up his story of her misdeeds. If he had any sense he would have called Philip himself, getting his story in before she got hers.

She had no choice. Dawn was breaking over the horizon, the sun rising above the blue haze where the sky met the sea. It was still cool, the sky still blue-white with cloud, clouds that would fade to nothing as the sun made its eternal ascent. She shivered, feeling cold for the very first time since arriving on Frixos. Beside her Alice stirred, her naked body pulled up tight, as if the cold had gotten to her also. She was sleeping, breathing slow and deep, her breasts rising and falling with a steady imperceptible rhythm.

'Alice,' Joanne whispered, bending over her and kissing her on the shoulder softly.

Alice half opened her eyes, sleep still fogging her brain. 'Yes,' she mumbled, snuggling closer to Joanne.

'I have something to tell you,' Joanne said, brushing Alice's long black hair back and kissing her on the cheek.

'What is it?'

'I'm going to call Philip this morning. It's time we told him what's going on.'

'No, you can't!' Alice cried, suddenly wide awake. She sat up, looking at Joanne anxiously.

'Don't look so alarmed. He has to find out sooner or later.'

'About everything? About us as well?'

'Yes, everything. Andreas will tell him even if we don't. It's only fair that he learns about it all. About Andreas and the hotel, and about you and me.'

'No, please,' Alice cried. She fell forward and began to cry, great wet tears streaming down her face, her body heaving with fearful sobs.

'Please don't cry,' Joanne said, bewildered by the unexpected tears. She didn't know what she expected of Alice. Embarrassment and shame probably, but not a sudden naked display of emotion. 'Everything will be all right, there's nothing to worry about.'

'There is,' Alice wailed. She looked up through tear-stained eyes, her lips trembling, her pretty face torn by a look of abject pain and sorrow. 'It'll be the end,' she cried. 'It'll be the end of us.'

'No it won't,' Joanne said, trying her best to console her. But inside, deep in her own heart she felt a stab of emotion too, the same fear and certainty that it was all going to finish.

'It will. I'll lose you, I know I will. Please, I love you, I don't want this to end.'

'I love you too,' Joanne whispered, holding Alice close, feeling the tears well in her own eyes, an unfamiliar lump in her throat. It was true. The dream was fading, coming to an unhappy end.

'I don't know what I'll do without you,' Alice was sobbing, drawing sharp breaths, her whole body shaking.

'You're wrong, honestly you are,' Joanne lied. 'I won't let it end this way, I promise. Go back to sleep, there's no need to cry. Just sleep.'

She held Alice in her arms and rocked back and forth gently, holding her tight, wanting to feel the warmth of her body. It wasn't going to end, she wasn't going to destroy the dream, she wouldn't. She held Alice tightly and silently vowed to keep it all together.

'Hello darling, how are you?' Joanne said as soon as Philip picked up the phone. The sound of his voice made her realise just how much she had missed him, and made her feel uncomfortably guilty.

'I'm fine. Busy. Missing you an awful lot. And how's your holiday?'

'I think you're going to find out sooner than expected,' Joanne said, smiling tightly at Alice who sat beside her, a fretful look on her face.

'What's wrong?' Philip asked, the crackling of the long-

204

distance phone line making his voice sound harsh and mechanical. 'You're not bored, are you?'

'No, far from it. Look, it's about Paradise Bay, I think you ought to come out here...'

'What about it?'

'Well, it seems as if Andreas isn't being very straight with you,' Joanne said, struggling to find the right words to describe the situation.

'Yes?' Philip waited, obviously anxious for more details.

'Well, it seems that he has been buying up lots of land all over Frixos. Good land at that, ripe for development. Now all this seems a bit odd as Paradise Bay has hardly broken records when it comes to profits.'

'Is there anything more?'

'I'm sorry, darling.' Joanne shook her head, as if Philip could see her. 'I think it best that you come out here and see for yourself.'

'Andreas hasn't been giving you a hard time, has he?' Philip asked suspiciously.

'I only told him who I was last night,' Joanne said. 'He was none too pleased by the news. But don't worry, I can handle him if I have to.'

'Are you sure you're telling me everything?'

'It's difficult over the phone,' Joanne said apologetically. 'There is more, you won't like everything you'll find when you get here. But you have to get here, we can't do this over the phone. I'm sorry.'

'This sounds serious. I'm sure I can catch a flight to Athens today or tonight. Do you think you could get Alice to charter a private plane to get me to Frixos from Athens?'

'I'm sure she can,' Joanne said, Alice nodding her agreement.

'How is Alice? Enjoying herself?'

'Yes, sort of. Please darling, I can't say any more,' Joanne said, the pained softness of her voice expressing a feeling of utter sadness and a grim foreboding of what was to come.

'In that case I'll probably see you tomorrow morning some time. Get Alice to pass the details of the flight to my office. And if you have any problems just call me, OK?'

'Yes, I will . . .'

'In fact do you want me to call Andreas now? I can have a word with him if you want me to.'

'No, please don't. I just want to see you first. You won't call him, will you? Promise me you won't.

'I promise. Is there anything else I can do?'

'No,' Joanne shook her head again. 'I'll see you tomorrow then. Bye, darling . . . I love you.'

'Yes, I love you too.'

Joanne put the phone down and stared across the room, shaking her head to herself. She felt awful, as if the full import of all that she had done was only just becoming apparent. Frixos, the sun and the sea, had obscured it all, turning everything hazy, blurring the edges like a shimmering mirage. But now the haze was clearing, and everything was being thrown sharply into focus, into full shocking clarity. What had she done?

Alice knelt down on the floor in front of her, looking up with dark soulful eyes. Joanne passed a hand through Alice's thick black hair. She felt torn, between her love for Philip and her love for Alice. She closed her eyes, unable to bear the thought of having to choose between them.

'Why didn't you tell him?' Alice whispered, resting her head on Joanne's knees.

'I couldn't, not over the phone like that. I just hope that Andreas doesn't decide to give him a call first.'

Alice looked away, falling silent. A moment later Joanne felt the warm teardrops falling on to her knees and thighs.

'Stop that! Stop that now, crying won't solve anything,' Joanne snapped, grabbing Alice by the shoulders and giving her a shake.

Alice looked up, the expression on her face seeming to change in character. It was the look in her eyes, the tearful despair gave way to a smouldering expression of passion, like a fire in her eyes. Desire and tears, Joanne felt herself responding, her heart beating faster, a powerful feeling of attraction rising up in her. She bent down and took Alice by the chin and kissed away her bitter tears, tasting the salty drops of silver sliding down the soft warmth of her face.

'Please, before this dies,' Alice said quietly, sitting on her knees in front of Alice, 'there is something I have to tell you. Something I tried to tell you before but couldn't.'

'It won't die, I won't let it,' Joanne said forcefully, willing herself to carry it through.

'I love you, I love you in a way I've never loved anyone else before. I love you, and I want you to hurt me,' Alice said, her voice aching with a deep and troubled yearning. She kissed Joanne on the knees softly, and then looked across the room, searching for something.

Joanne stood up and walked across the room. She wore red high heels, the heels capped with shining steel caps that smashed on to the floor with a sharp crack as she walked. She went over to the wardrobe and opened it, taking out a hanger with a smart black trouser suit on it. Very slowly, with her eyes fixed on Alice, she removed the trousers from the hanger and from them carefully removed the thick black belt.

She doubled the thick leather belt over and walked back across the room, her heels shattering the tense silence with a harsh metallic rhythm. Alice remained on the floor, looking up with an expression of fear and trepidation and desire. When Joanne stopped in front of her Alice bent down low and reverently kissed Joanne's shoes, pressing her full ruby lips against each sharp toe in turn.

'Strip down to your underwear,' Joanne ordered, thrilling to the strange feeling of power that overcame her. She knew that Alice was hers, and that she would submit to anything that was demanded.

Alice slipped her blouse over her head, not bothering to undo the buttons. She wore culottes and slipped them off, kicking off her own high heels at the same time. In seconds she was down to her black lacy bra and matching panties, her breasts cupped high by the bra.

'Put your hands behind your head, just like you did when you were a bad girl at school,' Joanne ordered, wanting to test the limits of her new role more than anything else.

Alice did as she was told. She straightened up, crossed her hands behind her head, and looked up at Joanne mournfully, sticking her chest forward and pulling her shoulders back.

'Good girl,' Joanne said, walking around Alice with cold deliberate menace. She let the belt hang loosely at her side, brushing it casually against Alice's back and side. The excitement was growing, making her wet between the thighs, her blood pulsing with a pure sexual high. 'Do you still love me?' she asked, and it was a challenge more than a question.

'Yes, of course I do,' Alice said, her hushed voice sounding shaky. She twisted round to look at Joanne standing at her side.

Joanne lashed out with the belt, striking a sudden blow against Alice's back, the snap echoing in the room and leaving behind it a vivid red smear on the soft flawless skin. Alice winced, cried out sharply and then fell silent, keeping her hands up and her chest out. 'Stay still! And call me miss, understand?' Joanne barked.

'Yes, miss,' Alice said, and the word sounded precious

on her lips.

'Unclip your bra,' Joanne ordered. 'Good, now cup your breasts with your hands, hold them up to me.'

Alice obeyed without question. She slipped off her bra, letting it fall to the floor beside her. Then she cupped her full round breasts in her hands, lifting them up temptingly, cradling her flesh in her upturned hands, her eyes downcast. Joanne stood in front of her, eyeing the delicious sight of the gorgeous breasts, the dark nipples peeping through Alice's fingers.

Joanne paused, unable to decide what to do next. The change in mood had been so sudden, there was no border between one mood and the next. All it had taken was a tone of voice, a certain look and then the atmosphere had shifted seamlessly. She let the belt, still bent double, dangle in front of her casually, knowing that it represented a promise and a threat to Alice. The very tip of it, where the thick band of leather was doubled up, rested between Alice's breasts, moving imperceptibly with her breath, rising and falling with the heaving of her chest.

'Kiss your breasts, take them in your mouth,' Joanne said, her voice cool and calm, hiding the raging excitement stirring within. She wanted to go further, to push Alice over the edge, but she also wanted to savour every moment, to prolong the tension until they lost control.

Alice bent forward, straining her neck, her hair falling over her face. She lifted her breasts higher, stretching the soft skin, forcing the nipples between her fingers. Her lips touched her breasts, slowly working towards the nipples, kissing herself tenderly. Joanne watched, fascinated by the display, knowing just how Alice's lips felt on her own nipples.

Alice took the nipple of her right breast into her mouth first, sucking it hard. When she took it out it was tinged with a pink flush, glazed in a thin layer of spit, erect and hardened. She twisted her head to the other side and did the same to the left nipple. Without looking up she began to alternate, sucking and kissing each breast in turn, lingering over her nipples, kissing herself, rousing her nipples, the pleasure clear on her face.

'Stop, now,' Joanne said imperiously. The erotic display had been too stimulating, making her wish for Alice's mouth on her own breasts, to suck and excite her own nipples.

Alice looked up, keeping her breasts held high in her hands, her nipples pointing up over her fingers.

Joanne raised the belt and brought it down flat and hard over the bare breasts, the stroke landing across both of them. Alice cried out, her startled cry merging with the snap of the belt. She looked down at her punished chest, a single red mark across the soft skin. The stroke had been above the nipples, a scarlet band above the dark-hued points of flesh. Joanne raised the belt again, bringing it down hard, this time scoring a vivid red impression right across the nipples.

Alice screamed, once, twice, three times, a cry of pain and shock each time the belt fell heavily across her chest. Each time she seemed surprised, as if unable to believe what Joanne was doing to her.

'Turn round, on your hands and knees,' Joanne snapped, quickening the pace, feeling the excitement rising faster within her. Each time the belt made impact, each time Alice cried out in pain, she felt a stab of fear and excitement inside her, a sharp dagger of emotion that connected to the fire in her belly.

Alice dropped down on to her hands, her reddened breasts hanging loose, the nipples pointing directly at the ground like little fingers of red flesh. She waited silently, on her hands and knees, her panties pulled tightly into her bottom.

'Now kiss my shoes properly,' Joanne ordered, standing tall, legs apart, the belt held in one hand, poised. She caught sight of herself in the mirror, long blonde hair falling loosely over her shoulders, blue eyes sparkling, her lips painted a brilliant red. Her skirt and shoes matched the lipstick, brilliant red, aggressive and sexy, the short skirt tight against her thighs.

Alice bent down low, her naked breasts touching the floor. She began to kiss one of Joanne's shoes, her lips tentatively brushing the shining patent-leather surface, then becoming more urgent, pressing her mouth against the smooth shining leather. She started at the toe and followed the shape of the shoe round to the heel, lovingly kissing every inch.

'The heel!' Joanne snapped and let loose with the belt, letting it crack down on Alice's lower back, just above the panties. Alice whimpered and her movement became more urgent, her mouth travelling over the full length of the high heel, passing over the silver stars studded on the outside.

Joanne released one end of the belt, keeping hold of the buckled end, and wielded it like a whip. She raised it high and made it whistle through the air before cracking thunderously on Alice's backside. She made Alice pull down her panties so her backside was naked, the bottom cheeks slightly parted by her position on the ground. Time and again she raised the belt, and each time it made contact a deep red line was scored deep into Alice's arse flesh, causing a spasm of pleasure to ripple through her. The contact, the moment when leather met flesh, also made Joanne sigh with pleasure, as if it were her own flesh that was touched by the wicked tongue of fire.

Alice was sighing and moaning, sucking the heel into her mouth as if it were an extension of Joanne. Her rear side was scarred by a lattice of thin red lines, burning into

211

her flesh.

'Stop that!' Joanne directed curtly. She pulled her foot away from Alice's mouth, then pushed her flat on to the ground. She stepped round, standing over Alice, feet parted, a wild look on her face. She was breathing fast, her heart pulsing manically, a smear of honey sliding from between her thighs. Almost without thinking she pressed her foot down between Alice's bottom cheeks, forcing her heel down between the chastised and reddened arse-cheeks.

'No, please no!' Alice cried urgently, a look of absolute horror on her face. She tried to scamper away but it was too late. Joanne had her pinned down. Desperately she tried to force Joanne's foot away, but couldn't, all she could do was twist and coil.

Joanne couldn't help herself, the fire in her belly was too much to resist. Alice's futile struggles, and her tone of injured pleading, only served to inflame her desire more. She looked down and saw that her heel was grazing Alice's pussy lips, just touching the parting of her sex. She swivelled her foot and pressed the heel down further.

Alice cried out, a tortured scream of denial that filled the room, but it had happened. Joanne forced her heel up and down, glad to see it sliding deep into Alice's damp pussy flesh. She moved her heel faster and faster, fucking Alice with her shoe, her own pussy raging, aching. It was her turn to cry out, to moan with pleasure, to close her eyes and give herself to the wave of ecstasy flowing through her body.

The two women climaxed together. Joanne touching herself through her wet panties, with the merest whisper of a touch from her fingertips. Alice writhing on the floor in near hysterics, Joanne's heel embedded deep in her pussy hole, her chastened bottom cheeks blazing red with a hundred scarlet lash-marks.

* * *

212

Liza opened the door and the young waiter stepped inside, glancing quickly over his shoulder as he did so. He stood nervously, hands clasped together in front of him, looking around the room as if searching for somebody.

'Hello, Nicky, my name's Liza. I've been speaking to a friend of yours,' she said, taking him by the hand and leading him gently into the room. She felt his reluctance, his body tensed up, his eyes darting around the room.

'Which friend is that, madam?' Nicky asked suspiciously.

'Just relax, there's no need to be nervous. I've been talking to your friend Joanne, she likes you a lot.'

'Yes, she is very nice,' Nicky said, with the kind of voice that gave nothing away.

Liza realised that she was going to have to do all the work, that it wasn't going to be as straightforward as she had hoped. She took Nicky's hands in her own and drew close to him. 'I'd like to get to know you as well as she does,' she purred softly, smiling at him purposefully.

For a moment he smiled back, his black-brown eyes glittering, but then he grew cautious once more. 'I have also been speaking to my friends,' he said. 'Will your husband pay me to make love to you?'

'Am I that ugly?'

'No, I didn't mean to make it sound like that. It's just that Marios told me. . .'

'If you want money I can get my husband to pay you. But it doesn't make me feel very nice, knowing that you are only making love to me because you wanted the money.'

'No. . .' Nicky stuttered, thrown off course by Liza's remarks. 'I'm sorry,' he smiled, relaxing at last.

Liza leaned forward and they kissed, their lips touching briefly, tasting each other for the first time. They parted and he began to undress, slowly removing his clothes, his

eyes fixed on her. She watched him, eager to see hi
attractive wiry body. He moved with an unselfcon
sciousness that made her smile; it seemed so at odds witl
his cautious nature, as if his true passionate self could b
revealed only when he was naked.

'If my husband comes into the room don't be nervous,
she whispered after they had kissed once more.

'Will he?'

'He might, but Marios must have told you that my
husband doesn't mind me making love with other men,
she said, whispering in his ear, kissing him all over th
face.

'Marios couldn't understand that,' Nicky said breath
lessly, 'and neither can I.'

'Forget that, forget him. Let's make love,' she said
She ran her hands over his body, lean and strong, his ches
smooth and hairless.

They moved on to the bed. She lay down and he lay
next to her, taking her in his arms. He kissed her pass
ionately, on the face, the eyes, the neck and the mouth
his lips searching every inch of her. His hands traced the
curves of her body, gliding down her back, over the
perfection of her rear, down the full unblemished lengtl
of her thighs.

She felt his hardness, his thick long prick, brush agains
her skin, pressing into her thighs. She touched him there
stroking him, making him press himself on her more
urgently. Her fingertips explored his body in turn, tracing
the definition of sinew and muscle down his back and over
his thighs. His stomach was hard with muscle, yet his skir
was soft and smooth. When she rubbed her fingers up and
down his long prick he sighed, his hot breath between her
breasts. She threw her head back, eager to let him moutl
her under the throat. Vaguely she was aware of a shadow
on the balcony, a dark form lurking in the corner of her

vision. In a moment the thought was gone, washed away by the sensation of Nicky's mouth sucking both her nipples together into his greedy mouth.

They lay in each other's arms, twisting and turning, exploring with fingers and mouths. He sucked her nipples, his tongue and lips making the points of flesh hard and sensitive, causing her to sigh and moan with pleasure. His fingers rubbed her between the thighs, rubbing the outside of the pussy, playing her pussy lips apart but never going further. His teasing was making her ache with desire, wanting to feel him pumping deep into her sex.

She moved down over his body, pressing him down flat on the bed with her hands. She licked her tongue over the length of his hardness, teasing him with her tongue just as he had done to her. He moaned, pushed himself against her mouth, she kissed him, lapped at his glans with pure delight. He was leaning up on one elbow, watching her, but when she swooped down and sucked his prick into her mouth he fell back, succumbing to the glorious ripple of sensation. She took him into her mouth, tasting his shaft properly, feeling it rub against the soft inside of her cheeks.

He moved up and down, rhythmically driving his prick in and out of her mouth. She revelled in the feeling of being fucked in the mouth, her tongue circling the tip of his prick or sliding down the underside of it. She could feel it crying dew drops of fluid on to her tongue, flexing and throbbing all the time. She knew when to withdraw, taking him to the very edge of orgasm then pulling away.

They kissed again and he moved round, taking her in his arms and laying her under him. He tried to move between her thighs, sliding his hand down into her pussy, his fingers dipping into the wetness inside her. She pushed him away gently, not rejecting him, but not letting him enter her either.

'In my bumhole,' she whispered hotly. 'I want you to

215

fuck me in my behind.'

Nicky sat back on his knees and watched her sit up an
get into position. She was on her hands and knees, on th
very edge of the bed, facing the open balcony door, th
sunlight falling over her like a golden skin. She looke
over her shoulder at him, smiling, her back arched so tha
her bottom cheeks were stretched tight and round, the dar
crease between visible. Her anal hole was stretched tigh
a dark petal between the white globes of her backside

He moulded himself around her, placing his knee
outside hers, his thighs in parallel. She felt his hardnes
press into her anal crease and shivered with anticipation
eager to have him enter deep into her body. 'I'm dry
she told him, 'wet me.'

Nicky moved back and parted her arse-cheeks fully wit
his hands, gazing adoringly at the parted pussy lip
revealing her pink flesh and at the inviting opening furthe
up. He bent down and kissed her very softly on the anu;
his mouth barely touching her anal lips. She sighed, urgin
him on, wanting his tongue not just his lips. He kisse
her again, this time more passionately, pressing his mout
down between her bottom cheeks, his tongue circling he
arsehole. He kissed her harder still, pressing his tongu
into the tight ring. She felt good, feeling her anal hole clo;
around his searching tongue, layer upon layer of sensatic
pulsing into her. She moved back, opening herself sti
further.

He tongued her deep, moving his tongue in and ou
wetting her hole with his spit. He pulled away eventually
Liza could feel his reluctance, he paused, looking at he
wistfully. She knew that he couldn't hold on much longe
that his prick was aching for release.

'Fuck me now,' she said, pressing her chest low an
her backside high. He moved closer, his thighs presse
against hers. She took his prick in her hands, it felt bi

and powerful, making her wonder how it would feel to have it wedged into her behind. She guided it, letting him rest it against her anal hole for a second. When he pushed forward she caught her breath, it slid into her tightly, forcing her arse cheeks apart. It felt too big, too strong, she held her breath, suddenly afraid that he would hurt her. It took forever, going deep into her, searing her, splitting her in half. It stopped. He breathed and she realised that he had been holding his breathe too.

Liza hardly dared to breathe. Nicky was inside her, his immense prick buried in her tight arsehole, the ring of muscle clamped tightly around the base of it. It felt too good, she wanted to scream just with the pleasure of having him inside her. Then he began to move, long slow strokes, in and out. The ripple of penetration seemed to last forever, driving her high with an intensity of pleasure that made her dizzy. He gained in confidence, his rhythm became regular, faster. He too was sighing and moaning, whispering to himself.

Suddenly Liza was aware of the shadow by the open balcony door. She had forgotten that, lost in the pleasure of being arse-fucked, her being focused on that single pleasure. With an effort she sat up, lifting her front up. Nicky took her by the shoulders, fucking her faster. She could feel his belly rubbing deliciously against her arse-cheeks, and she guessed that the feel of it was driving him faster too.

'I'm going to scream, as if it hurts me, but don't worry,' she whispered over her shoulder. 'It doesn't hurt much, it feels lovely, too good to stop...'

She screamed, the mirror across the room reflecting the distraught look on her face. Nicky just pumped harder, beads of sweat rolling down his face, his eyes half closed and his lips parted. Liza crossed her hands in front of her, holding them out as if chained by the wrists. She screamed

217

again and raised her hands over her head, a tortured look on her face matching her pose.

The shadow moved again and Martin emerged. He was naked, his prick was hard and swayed stiffly as he padded in from the balcony and across the room.

Liza looked at him, but he avoided her eyes, his gaze fixed on her body. He took her by the arms and pulled her up straight. His prick brushed against her belly, smearing her with a thick globule of sticky fluid. He bent down and took his prick in his hands and forced it between her thighs, then straightened up.

Liza cried out again, a genuine cry of pleasure and pain. Martin's prick was deep in her pussy, Nicky's deep in her arsehole. The two men were moving together, seemingly oblivious of each other. She was glad that Nicky was gripping her shoulders and Martin her hands; otherwise she felt she would collapse. The intensity of pleasure was unbelievable, like a searing white heat burning into her. Her pussy was dripping wet, burning, fuelled by the searing of two pricks inside her.

She came suddenly, her body overwhelmed with a series of waves of pure bliss, a trail of explosions inside her. She felt like she was a million people at once, that she was everywhere and nowhere. There was no time, no space, only the long falling through space.

Nicky climaxed first, he just froze, pressed his fingers painfully into her skin. Then he pumped his seed into her arsehole, his prick throbbing violently, her arse ring rippling with his prick. He pulled away, collapsed on to the bed, a look of absolute heaven on his sharp angular face.

Moments later Martin climaxed too. He held on to her, as if afraid that he was going to collapse. Desperately he sought her mouth, almost in a blind panic, but then he found her, joined their lips together. He froze for an instant then relaxed, jetting his come into her sopping wet pussy, sucking her breath from her mouth in a final frenzy.

Liza seemed to awake from a long dream, a dream where nothing had happened but that had made her feel powerful and fulfilled and special and everything.

She turned, remembering at once all that had happened. Martin was beside her, naked, smiling, waiting.

'Thank you,' he said softly.

'Was it good?' she asked, knowing from the look of gratitude what the answer was.

'I want to thank you, in the way that I think we'll both enjoy the most,' he said.

The sun was streaming into the room, and for the first time Liza saw that the sun matched his mood. 'How is that?'

'I want to suck you in the arsehole,' he said. 'I want to make you climax that way. Is that OK?'

Liza turned over on to her belly, resting her head in her arms and lifting her bottom high. The sun shone and everything was just as it had to be.

twelve

Alice and Joanne awoke just after the first light of dawn, emerging from the same dark dream into the pale light of morning. The atmosphere in the room was cold and mournful, funereal in all but name. Alice snuggled up close to Joanne, holding her tightly, sharing the warmth of her body, not wanting to let go.

They lay together for hours in cold silence, Alice unable to formulate the words to express her feeling of black despair. The last day had arrived, the end of the fantasy, and there was no saviour in sight, no hope of escaping the shattering of the illusion.

The still silence was eventually disturbed by a quiet knocking at the door. Joanne and Alice looked at each other questioningly. 'Yes?' Joanne said hesitantly.

The door opened a few inches and Nicky squeezed in, looking out into the corridor before closing the door softly behind him. He was dressed in a pair of faded jeans and a simple black tee-shirt. 'I have something for you,' he said, digging deep into his pocket.

Joanne got up and walked naked across the room, not caring to put on a robe or to cover herself up in any way. 'What is it?' she asked, unwilling to allow herself even to sound hopeful.

'A map,' Nicky said, pulling a crumpled piece of paper

from his pocket. He handed it over, smiling, his eyes scanning Joanne greedily.

'Good boy,' Joanne told him, almost snatching the paper from his hand with excitement. She turned and went over to the desk, studying the scrap of paper intently.

Alice reached out for her robe before getting up. She had none of Joanne's nonchalance; the idea of walking around naked in front of Nicky made her feel funny. To her nakedness meant desire and sex, but for Joanne it seemed as natural as drinking a glass of water.

'This is the village, right?' Joanne pointed at a thick black circle drawn in the centre of the map, which she had flattened out on the desk.

'Yes, that's right,' Nicky said, peering over her shoulder. 'This is the hotel,' he said, leaning over and pointing to a smaller circle.

'And x marks the spot,' Joanne laughed.

'Yes, that is where the Frenchman lives, in a big white house. Your friend Amanda Trevelyan is there with him,' Nicky said. 'But now I think Amanda Trevelyan isn't your friend, is she?'

'No, she isn't,' Joanne agreed sheepishly. 'I'm sorry to have lied to you like that. I couldn't tell you who I was, it would have made things very difficult.'

'Is it true you are the owner's wife?' he asked, eyeing her intently.

'Yes. My husband owns part of Paradise Bay. But I couldn't tell you that. If I had it would have made things too difficult. You would have treated me differently.'

'I'm sorry I ever spoke to you,' Nicky said sadly, backing away from her, a look of hurt in his dark eyes. 'Now I will lose my job. When Andreas tells him that I made love to his wife he will throw me out. Or if Andreas stays here he will throw me out for helping you.'

'No, Joanne won't let that happen,' Alice said, breaking

her silence. She felt strongly for Nicky, identifying herself with him, wondering what Philip was going to do when he found out that she had also been sleeping with Joanne

'Alice is right,' Joanne said brightly, the excitement shining in her eyes. 'We've still got a chance. Believe me Nicky, I won't forget how much you've helped me honestly I won't. Nothing will happen to you. In fact, you might even find yourself getting a nice pay rise at the end of all this.'

'I hope you are right,' Nicky said, smiling a little Joanne's confidence seeming to rub off on him. 'Besides, he said, 'I enjoyed making love to you very much.'

Joanne stood up and kissed him softly on the mouth. She lingered close to him for a second, letting him feel her nakedness close on his body. 'Now, we've got work to do,' she said breaking away. 'How far is the Frenchman's villa from here?'

'In kilometres?'

'No, in time.'

Nicky shrugged. 'An hour, maybe a little more or a little less.'

'What time is Philip scheduled to arrive?' Joanne asked turning to Alice.

'In three hours,' Alice said, looking at her watch.

'It's going to be tight, but we can make it.'

'I have to get to work,' Nicky said, also looking at his watch.

'Thank you, Nicky,' Joanne said, kissing him again, a longer searching kiss, her arms around his shoulders. Nicky held her too, moving his hands down her back. 'I'm sorry for lying to you before,' Joanne said once more, pulling away from him.

'Thanks for helping us,' Alice said, also moving close to him. He took her by the shoulders and kissed her on the mouth, slipping his tongue between her soft ruby lips.

222

She closed her eyes, felt the first stirring of desire flame briefly in her heart.

'I have to go now,' he said, releasing Alice and smiling broadly. He turned and left, looking out into the corridor to make sure the coast was clear before slipping out as furtively as he had come.

'We don't have much time,' Joanne said, quickly choosing her clothes from the wardrobe. 'We can't take any chances with Andreas. I want you to go and wake Liza and get her to hire a car in her name. I asked yesterday, Paradise Bay does have a car for use by guests, but mysteriously it was in for repair when I asked about it. I have a feeling that Liza may be luckier.'

'Do you think we can make it?' Alice asked, beginning to feel a faint flicker of hope.

'We will if we don't stand around asking too many questions,' Joanne said, smiling, the excitement etched in her face, her blue eyes sparkling with crystalline brilliance.

Alice smiled, breathed in deeply, felt the hope merge with desire. Joanne was at her best, impulsive, confident, beautiful.

Liza had complained good-naturedly about being woken up so early, but she had acted magnificently, ordering the car and then going down to pick it up. She seemed in a great mood, laughing and joking, her long blonde hair flowing like gold over her shoulders. Alice sensed that something had changed but couldn't tell what it was.

While Alice had gone with Liza to get the car Joanne had tried to catch Philip at Athens airport. She had been hoping to redirect him to Jean-Pierre's house, to keep him away from Andreas for as long as was necessary. It was a gamble, Alice didn't share her absolute faith that Amanda had the story. But it was a moot point. Joanne couldn't get hold of Philip at all. She had given up, throwing the phone down in frustration when Alice returned with Liza.

Together they all walked out to the car, a sporty open-top two-seater painted a dazzling white that gleamed in the sunshine. Liza tossed the car keys over to Joanne and kissed her good luck, then did the same with Alice. Joanne jumped into the driver's seat and Alice slipped in next to her. They left the hotel forecourt in a screech of rubber on concrete, Joanne's way of telling Andreas that she was far from beaten.

They followed the map as best they could, winding up unsigned roads, little more than gravel tracks in places. Alice kept catching her breath, certain that Joanne's manic driving was going to propel them over the sharp edged mountain roads down into the steep ravines below. The scenery was breathtaking; a brilliant sky above the sharp contours of mountains and trees, the sea never far from view, the sun playing on the blue surface so that it gleamed like gold or silver.

The car swung round the narrow mountain road, the tyres squealing momentarily, raising a cloud of dry brown dust. Joanne and Alice could see Jean-Pierre's house above them, a white geometric form nestling in the red brown hues of rock and stone. Higher still the slope of the mountains became carpeted with dense woods, and above them the bare peaks lost in the grey haze.

At last they drew up outside the imposing white house. Joanne jumped out of her seat, eager to meet Amanda, glancing at her watch all the time. Alice followed behind, checking the sky, also looking at her watch and wondering whether Philip wasn't going to come in early, the small plane arriving unheralded at the distant airfield.

Joanne rang the doorbell and waited.

'You!' cried Amanda opening the door a few moments later. She laughed out loud, her deep red lips open to reveal her straight white teeth. 'I've been trying to get hold of you, but I didn't know your name!'

'And we've been trying to contact you,' Joanne said, joining in the laughter, looking and sounding visibly relieved.

Amanda took her by the hand and almost pulled her into the house. Alice followed, feeling a little left out, slightly jealous of Amanda.

'Why didn't you just phone at the hotel?' Joanne asked.

'Our friend Andreas has screwed up our telephone, he has friends all over the place.'

'Well we're here now,' Joanne paused and waited for Alice to catch up. 'Amanda, this is my special friend Alice,' she said.

'Hello,' Amanda smiled. Her eyes darted from Joanne to Alice, as if she knew what kind of friend Joanne meant.

'Hello,' Alice said shyly, feeling a little embarrassed.

'Come on, I want you to meet Jean-Pierre. We've got a lot to tell you about your husband's partner.'

'That's why we're here,' Joanne remarked. 'We know the man is up to something, and we were hoping that you would know.'

'Absolutely,' Amanda laughed again. 'We've got all the gory details.'

Amanda led them all down a flight of bare stone steps, walking with a natural poise, an unstudied elegance that was familiar to both Joanne and Alice from Amanda's television appearances. 'This is Jean-Pierre's studio,' she explained quietly.

Jean-Pierre met them at the bottom of the stairs. Alice had never seen or heard of him before, but he was not how she imagined a great artist to be. She had expected a rather effete and sophisticated individual, not the powerful peasant that stood before them, with menacing eyes and a rough unshaven face.

225

'You'll never guess, Jean-Pierre,' Amanda said excitedly. 'But the mountain has come to Mohammed. This is the woman I told you about, and her friend Alice. I'm sorry,' she turned to Joanne, 'I still don't know your name.'

'Joanne,' she said. 'And my husband has the grave misfortune to be Andreas Karaplis's partner.'

'The man is a scoundrel!' Jean-Pierre boomed gruffly. He took Joanne by the hand and led her into the studio. The glass door to the pool was open and a cool breeze blew through, the sun was streaming in, suffusing the entire length of the studio with a bright golden light.

'Tell me, I want all the details,' Joanne said, glancing at her watch for the hundredth time.

'Karaplis is not worthy of a man, he is a thief, a man without honour. The way he has treated Amanda is intolerable, is it not? Believe me, my dear, your husband must be rid of this thing. If it were in my power I would have driven him from this island long ago ...'

'I'm sorry,' Joanne interrupted quietly, glancing nervously to Amanda for support, 'but I need to find out what he has done as soon as possible.'

'Philip, her husband, arrives by plane shortly. We need to know what has happened before Andreas can get to him,' Alice explained sombrely.

'I see,' Jean-Pierre said. 'Andreas Karaplis has been stealing from your husband from the day they signed their agreement. He has continued to steal throughout, he does it today. Your husband has acted as an unwitting banker while Karaplis has been buying up this island. If only your husband had paid closer attention, then perhaps all this would have been avoided. As it is ...'

'Yes Jean-Pierre,' Amanda cut him off gently, touching his hand with hers. 'Karaplis came up with the perfect scheme. He had a concept of an environmentally sound

226

holiday resort. All the building materials to construct it were to be of local origin. All labour was to be locally hired where possible. Food and supplies bought from local markets and to be locally produced. A brilliant concept. Except that Karaplis could control the local market. He set the prices of materials and labour, for food and wages. Your husband ended up paying far too much, Karaplis took a cut of everything. And he has carried on ever since. The food for the hotel costs twice as much as it does for everywhere else. The extra money goes into his pocket, not to the local people, by the way.'

'What a brilliant scheme,' Joanne said wistfully, her open admiration for Andreas's skills apparent again.

'Not brilliant,' Jean-Pierre corrected forcefully, 'devious. The man is a thief. Clever or not, that fact remains.'

'What was he going to do with all the land he bought?' Alice asked.

'Build more hotels, this time without the pretensions. He wanted to make money and lots of it. That's why he wanted to build his own airport. He wanted to fly tourists in and out on a regular service.'

'He wanted to rape Frixos, to destroy it forever. That's why he deserves to be thrown into the sea,' Jean-Pierre murmured darkly.

'Thanks,' Joanne said. 'We have to get back. What you've told us will be enough to sink Andreas Karaplis for good.'

Jean-Pierre and Amanda stood arm in arm and watched Joanne and Alice get back into the car. Suddenly Jean-Pierre looked up, shielding the sun from his eyes with his massive hand.

Alice looked up; she heard it before her eyes made out the silver point in the sky. 'It's Philip's plane,' she said, pointing it out to Joanne.

'Fuck it,' Joanne cursed, 'it'll be a race between him and us to see who gets to Paradise Bay first.'

'Joanne,' Alice said, 'we've got enough to sink Andreas. Do you think it's enough to save us?'

'I wish I knew,' Joanne said. The car roared to life and before Alice had time to turn back to Amanda and Jean-Pierre they were away, lost in the crunch of tyres on gravel and a thick cloud of dust.

The plane had disappeared even before the car had taken the first steep bend down the mountain track. Alice had thought the drive up to Jean-Pierre's had been manic, but it was nothing compared to the drive down. Joanne drove like a woman possessed, tearing around sharp bends with crazy abandon, the car screeching and squealing painfully.

'We're acting like the people Jean-Pierre wants to bring to Frixos,' Alice said, but the wind took her words away, and if Joanne heard she showed no sign of it.

Alice gripped her seat tightly, her knuckles white. She was flung from side to side, battered by the acceleration and deceleration, deafened by the roar of the wind and the car. Joanne wore smart black sunglasses and her long blonde hair flowed in the wind; she looked fabulous, her face white and impassive, her lips brilliant red. It made Alice feel happy just to sit back and look at her, like a young woman with a first lover.

The road flattened out, skirting the village altogether and following the curve of the shore and back up again towards the hotel. In the distance Alice spied the ferry anchored just outside the bay, the white hull floating low in the water. The launch was making its way out to meet it, leaving a white trail in its wake.

The car screeched round off the road and on to the drive leading to the hotel forecourt. They swerved suddenly, narrowly missing the battered blue taxi coming the other way. The old driver honked his horn angrily, gesticulating wildly, but Joanne carried on past him. Alice's heart sank, she knew what it meant — Philip had got to Paradise Bay before them.

Joanne stopped outside the entrance and ran up the steps and into the reception. Alice ran after her, heart beating wildly, suddenly feeling cold and afraid.

As soon as they stepped into the coolness of the lobby the two receptionists looked up at them, they didn't smile or say anything but they didn't need to. The look was enough. Joanne took her sunglasses off and turned to Alice, her eyes cold with grim determination. 'Go and wait for me in our room,' she said calmly, almost too calmly. 'I'm going in to see Philip and Andreas alone, I'm going to see this thing through to the end.'

'Are you sure you don't want me with you?' Alice asked tearfully. She hated confrontation, but for Joanne she would have done anything. Despite her reluctance she really did want to be with Joanne for the final showdown.

'No, I've got to do this alone,' Joanne said decisively. 'After all I started this whole mess. Now, go on, wait for me, it shouldn't take too long.'

Alice took Joanne by the shoulders and pulled her close and kissed her fervently on the mouth, one last loving kiss. The icy cold in Joanne's eyes melted and she seemed to relax, as if everything had been thrown into proportion.

'I love you,' Alice said tenderly.

'I love you too,' Joanne replied and then turned and marched uncompromisingly up to the reception desk. They made way for her immediately, leading her through to the back office.

Alice watched her go, then turned to go to their room. Her mind was in turmoil, her belly doing nervous somersaults. From their first arrival on Frixos the future had ceased to exist for them, and now it had returned with a vengeance. For Alice the future had been a dark ugly cloud at the back of her mind, a shadow that she had deliberately ignored. All that had mattered was the present, a present so intense that it had blocked out everything else. Now time had returned, and she had a past and a future also, and she feared that Joanne was going to disappear, leaving behind an emptiness that would be impossible to fill.

She couldn't face the idea of waiting alone in the silence of the room, surrounded by the brightest memories of her blissful time with Joanne. Instead she knocked gently at Liza's door, hoping that she was there, wanting beyond all else to have someone's shoulder to cry on.

'Can we talk now?' Alice asked when Liza opened the door.

'Sure,' smiled Liza. 'Where's Joanne?'

'With her husband and Andreas,' Alice said glumly, walking into the room. She looked around, glad to see that Martin was out.

'Don't look so worried. Everything's going to be wonderful, you'll see,' Liza said brightly.

'What makes you so sure? You seem very happy today. Has something happened?'

Liza poured herself and Alice a drink and gave it to her. 'This morning Martin made love to me,' she said, smiling wistfully at the memory.

'He still makes me feel uncomfortable,' Alice admitted, taking the drink. 'To be honest I don't understand what you see in him.'

'You mean you don't know yet?' Liza said, smiling quizzically.

'Know what?' Alice asked blankly.

'I can see why Joanne loves you so much. She mentioned how innocent you were, how girlishly naïve she found you. But I never realised just how true that was.'

'I don't understand. Is Martin your husband?'

Liza shook her head, a look of naked disbelief in her clear emerald eyes. 'No, not my husband or my boyfriend. He's just a patient of mine, or rather he was a patient, I seem to have sorted out his problem for good now.'

'A patient? I still don't understand ...'

'I'm a sex therapist,' Liza announced, sitting back in her seat, smiling proudly.

'A sex therapist ... Like a psychiatrist, sort of ...'

'Yes, sort of. I help people find themselves, help them to come to terms with their own deep feelings and desires.'

'But all the things we did ...' Alice's amazement seemed to turn inwards, a look of horror dawning on her face.

'Don't look so shocked. I enjoyed all our time together, didn't you? Joanne spent a long time with me, just talking, going through her feelings. With her talking was all it took, she had already come to terms with her feelings for you. But you were different.'

'What you did was horrible,' Alice said, looking hurt. 'You used me, didn't you? Working on me without even telling me what was happening.'

'No, it wasn't like that at all,' Liza said flatly. 'Joanne cares for you very much, and so do I. We wanted to help you, that's all.'

'So what's wrong with me?' Alice demanded.

Liza smiled, she got up and went over to where Alice was sitting. 'Nothing's wrong with you. I think you're finally coming to see yourself for what you really are.'

'Tell me, make it clear to me,' Alice said quietly. Her feeling of hurt had gone, she saw that Liza was right: they had wanted what was best and nothing more.

'You have very strong masochistic feelings, very strong indeed. Everyone has them, don't let anyone tell you that they don't. But in most people the masochist side of their

231

personality is balanced, hidden, denied. With you that feeling is very pronounced. It's only recently that you've even become aware of your feelings, only since you became involved with Joanne. Is that right?'

'Yes, it is.'

'You want Joanne to take control, to dominate you in every way. In that way you can give up responsibility for your feelings, you just hand it over to Joanne instead. And when you derive pleasure from being punished or being submissive, you don't have to admit that it's you, it's Joanne that is doing it.'

'But I don't want to be like this,' Alice whispered, recognising herself completely in the picture Liza had described. 'How can I stop it? Can you help me?'

'You can't stop it. Any more than you can stop breathing, or talking the way that you do, or thinking your thoughts. It's not something outside of you, something that you can control. This comes from deep inside your soul, somewhere hidden. It's you, it can't be separated or cut out. You have to accept it, it's as simple as that.'

'But I don't want to, I . . .'

'No, you do want it. Deep down it's all that you want. The guilt, the confusion, that's all part of it too. You won't get rid of those either, but then those feelings won't cover up your true desires.'

'So that's it? This is me?'

'And you're lovely, beautiful, mysterious, sensual, submissive. It's how you were made.'

'And if Joanne goes?' Alice voiced her uppermost concern, the thing she feared most of all.

'She won't, but if she did you'll find another mistress, sooner or later. Now that you know yourself I can't see how you can pretend otherwise.'

'Do you know,' Alice whispered, a lump in her throat, 'this hurts.'

'I know it does, darling. But would you rather live your life in ignorance, not even knowing who you are?'

'No, I guess not,' Alice replied, though in truth a small part of her longed for ignorance, longed for the simplicity of not knowing.

'And if it's any consolation,' Liza smiled, 'Joanne has had to go through the same feelings, the same process. You and she were made for each other, your desires complement each other's completely. Mistress and servant, dominant and submissive.'

The phone rang, startling Alice, its ring like a piercing shriek. Liza picked it up, listened for a second and put the receiver down. 'That was Joanne. She wants to see you now,' she said.

'Liza, I want to thank you. Just talking to you has helped me. I didn't understand at first, but you've made it clearer for me.'

'Look, before you leave Frixos I'll give you an address. We can meet again in London. I'll always be there if you need me.'

Alice kissed her on the cheek, and then on the mouth. She was about to turn to leave when she was seized by a sudden impulse. It felt silly but she knelt down in front of Liza and planted a single loving kiss on the tip of her shoe.

'Good girl,' Liza said, smiling happily.

Alice felt numb with fear and trepidation. The moment had come and there was no way of avoiding it. She stood and looked at the door to Joanne's room, unable to bring herself to enter. She was shaking, a cold sweat running down her back, her face frozen and expressionless.

'Come inside,' Joanne said, opening the door.

Alice was startled. She hadn't knocked or made a noise but Joanne had guessed that she was there. She entered

233

the room, not daring to utter a word, or to raise her eyes with a questioning look at Joanne.

Joanne closed the door and walked back into the room, her high heels sounding a staccato rhythm, each step coolly confident, the sound hypnotic to Alice's ears.

'Hello Alice,' Philip said, his voice firm and masculine. He was seated by the desk, facing Alice, a sober look on his face, with none of the warmth or good humour Alice remembered him for.

'Hello Philip,' Alice replied, her voice strained and hesitant. She walked into the room, edging into the patch of light that was reflected diagonally by the mirror. Joanne stood by Philip, to his side, her hand resting gently on his shoulder.

'Andreas is finished,' Joanne said, allowing herself a smile of triumph. 'We shall be contacting the police on the Greek mainland. Philip has brought a Greek lawyer with him and he assures us that Andreas will be in prison very shortly. Paradise Bay will fall entirely into our hands, to be run as we see fit.'

'Good, I'm happy about that,' Alice said, though she was unable to force a smile. She didn't feel happy, or even glad. The hotel didn't matter to her. Only one thing really mattered.

'Joanne has explained to me the relationship between you,' Philip said, glancing up at Joanne and then back to Alice. His face showed no sign of emotion; there was no fire of jealousy in his grey eyes, no flash of anger in his voice.

'We have discussed it, and we have an offer to make to you,' Joanne said, taking up the thread. 'You only have to say yes or no, there is no room for hesitation or doubt. Is that clear?'

Alice nodded, holding her breath, her heart beating wildly, she felt herself ready to explode, the blood pounding in her head.

'You will belong to us,' Philip said, his face breaking into a wry smile at last. 'To both of us. So long as you are with us you will do exactly as you are told, you can't refuse. We'll do what we like with you, use you as we want. You'll live with us, go where we go. And if we want to give you to our guests, or friends, then that's what we'll do. And if you ever want to leave, to refuse us in some way, then you'll be free to go.'

'But if you go, then you go for good,' Joanne added. 'As long as you are ours you cannot refuse. If you refuse, then you go cleanly, finally, with no turning back. Is that clear?'

'Yes,' Alice nodded, her mind thrown into utter confusion. There had been no plans, no thoughts for the future. But never in her wildest dreams had she imagined something so absolute and final.

'Then what's your answer?' Philip asked, his eyes fixed on her.

'If you need to think about it the answer has to be no,' Joanne said.

Alice looked at Joanne, trying to fathom what lay behind her glittering blue eyes. She wasn't smiling, there was not even any sign of hesitation. It was as if she knew what Alice's answer was going to be, just as Alice knew it. It was true, she didn't need to think about it, there was no doubt or hesitation, just the fear and excitement.

'My answer is yes,' Alice said, closing her eyes, feeling herself filled with a sense of crossing a barrier, because her life had suddenly changed forever. She felt afraid, but filled with a feeling of happiness, dark and mysterious, an intense bittersweet feeling that made her want to weep tears of joy.

'I told you to wait in this room for me, didn't I?' Joanne said sharply, in the stern tone of voice that Alice recognised at once.

'Yes, miss,' Alice said, her voice low, eyes averted, excitement growing in the pit of her belly.

'Then you disobeyed,' Philip said, his voice suddenly stern and cold also.

'Yes sir,' Alice agreed, finding herself attracted by his firm manner as well. The idea that she was going to be his also, to serve him like a slave, to submit to his demands with total abandon, suddenly struck home.

'Take your skirt and knickers down,' Philip said, in a tone that brooked no hesitation.

Alice felt herself blushing, growing red in the face, her eyes turned away from his. She felt vulnerable, embarrassed, the way she had with Joanne at the beginning. In a second her skirt was around her ankles and she slowly pulled down her snow-white panties, revealing herself before him for the first time.

Joanne watched, her face flushed with a look of excitement, her eyes ablaze. She was holding Philip by the shoulder, squeezing him, silently urging him on. 'Smack her hard,' she suggested, making sure that Alice could hear her. 'Her skin reddens so quickly, it looks wonderful.'

'Here, over my knee,' Philip said, uncrossing his legs, putting his knees together.

Alice stepped towards him, her heart pounding in her chest, looking at him with her dark eyes wide. She knelt down at his feet and he pulled her over his knees, resting her so that her bottom was over his lap. She felt his prick brush against her side, hard and erect. Her bottom was raised high, her buttocks slightly parted. She felt unsteady, touching the floor with her fingertips to stop herself falling on to the floor. Twisting her head round she saw Joanne looking at her, smiling greedily, looking stunningly beautiful.

The first slap resounded around the room. Alice caught her breath, but stopped herself from crying out. The pain was sharp and intense, but in seconds the sharpness turned to an oozing white heat, seeping into her flesh. She cried out with the next slap, as hard as the first, but on the other buttock. That was the signal, Philip raised his hand high and beat her in a slow methodical rhythm.

It felt as if every inch of her backside had been beaten, it seemed to burn with a wicked red heat, spreading into her body, igniting a burning fire in the heart of her pussy. Her eyes were closed but she felt as if she were outside herself, looking down on her partially clothed body being spanked by Philip.

Philip stopped and pushed Alice off his knees, letting her fall heavily to the floor, her red buttocks pressing flat on to the varnished floor.

'That was beautiful,' Joanne said. She bent down and kissed Philip on the lips. Alice watched, feeling her heart grow heavy with jealousy. She wanted to feel Joanne's lips on hers, to share her breath, to feel their tongues entwined.

Philip stood up and took Joanne in his arms, pulling her close, sucking at her mouth passionately. Alice saw what was happening. They were giving her a foretaste of what was to come.

Joanne stepped away from Philip and looked down at Alice. 'Undress me,' she ordered.

Alice stood up, catching sight of her punished backside in the mirror, her buttocks patterned red with Philip's fingermarks. It hurt when she walked, but she was also aware of the red heat in her sex, wet with moist expectation.

Joanne smelt perfect, her skin perfumed with a light scent that Alice recognised at once. She unbuttoned Joanne's blouse, carefully undoing each button, her hands

237

shaking. She removed the blouse, sliding it off Joanne's shoulders and placing it carefully on the desk. The feel of Joanne's smooth skin was driving her mad, it made her want to kiss Joanne, to hold her tightly, but she resisted. Next she unclipped Joanne's tight black skirt and let that fall to the floor. When she knelt down to gather it up she suddenly gave in to the temptation, planting soft loving kisses on Joanne's high heeled shoes.

Philip watched her, smiling when he saw her kissing Joanne's shoes so reverently. 'I like that,' he told Joanne excitedly.

'You won't regret this,' Joanne told him, passing her hand through Alice's long black hair.

Alice felt overwhelmed with happiness, like a surge of energy pulsing through her, an almost sexual feeling of pleasure. She stood up and unclipped Joanne's bra, her fingertips lightly brushing Joanne's nipples. Then she knelt down again and rolled Joanne's black panties down, her eyes gazing greedily at Joanne's sex, the lightly coloured bush of hair barely covering the pink-lipped opening. She was seized with an irresistible urge to bury her face in Joanne's sex, to tongue deeply between the pussy lips. It was too much to resist, so she bent forward and kissed her between the pussy lips, slipping her tongue into the wetness within, tasting Joanne's essence on her tongue.

'No, only when you're told!' Joanne snapped. She lifted her foot high and pushed Alice away, digging her heel into the soft flesh of her shoulder.

'Next time, you'll be punished for that,' Philip said, and his voice was thick with desire and excitement.

Philip undressed himself quickly, his body lean and muscular, the hair on his chest patterned with streaks of grey. His prick was hard, thick and strong. 'Taste me,' he told Alice, while kissing Joanne, running his hands over his wife's smooth body.

238

Alice crawled forward on her hands and knees, her shoulder stinging, marked with the imprint of Joanne's heel. She knew that she had done wrong, had known it even when she yielded to the temptation. But the punishment had been exciting also. The sudden stab of Joanne's steel-tipped heel had been like a stab of excitement, piercing her sex, making her dizzy with pleasure.

Still on all fours she raised her head and kissed Philip's prick, rubbing her lips on the outside of the firm shaft of flesh. He swivelled round slightly, still clinging to Joanne, his face buried between her breasts. Alice opened her mouth and took his prick into it, sliding down over the hardness, pressing her tongue on the ribbed underside. She rose and fell on his prick, inching it deeper every time, feeling it throb and twitch in the warmth of her mouth.

Joanne pushed Alice away and she and Philip fell on to the bed, wrapped in each other's arms. They were exploring each other with hands and mouths, rediscovering the pleasures of each other's body. He held her breasts and sucked at the nipples, she was rushing her hands through his hair and over his back.

Alice watched, not sure whether to turn away or whether to join in. What was the limit, was she intruding? There were new limits to learn, new rules of engagement. The complications hadn't disappeared, perhaps they had even become more complicated, more difficult to navigate than ever before.

Joanne fell on her side and pulled her knees up, her head thrown back. 'Fuck me Philip,' she said hoarsely.

Philip lay on his side also, pulling Joanne against him, his arms holding her tightly. He was kissing her on the neck and shoulder, sucking at her skin, biting her so that she squealed with pain and pleasure. He took his prick in his hands and pushed it down between Joanne's parted thighs. She sighed, letting the breath run between her lips.

His prick went in deep, sliding into the wetness of her sex. They moved together, rhythmically, back and forth, his prick driving in and out of her sex.

'Suck us here,' Joanne ordered, touching herself lightly under her sex.

Alice crawled on to the bed, flat on her belly. Both Joanne and Philip were on their sides, their bodies close, a single unit in loving motion. Joanne lifted her outer thigh, opening herself fully. Still moving in and out rhythmically, Philip did likewise. Alice stared, she had an unimpeded view of Philip fucking Joanne, she could see his thick prick, glistening with pussy-honey, sliding in and out of Joanne's parted pussy lips.

She edged in close and kissed Joanne on the sex, touching her lips against the engorged pussy lips. Then she started to suck and lick, passing her mouth over the parted sex, on to the thick wet prick, slipping her tongue into the sex as Philip drew in and out. She let her lips brush under Philip's prick, flicking her tongue under his balls and down over his rear crack, touching his anal hole with the very tip of her tongue. Philip's rhythm became more rapid, and Alice buried her face in the space between their thighs, vaguely aware of Joanne's breathless sighs and ecstatic moans.

Joanne climaxed, with Philip driving his hardness deep into her sex and with Alice tonguing the sensitive pussy lips wet with creamy sex juice. She became rigid, crying out wordlessly, her pussy suffused with waves of white cunt cream. She moved around, lifting herself from Philip's impaling prick. Quickly, her eyes blazing, she took Philip's prick in her hands and wanked him with her fingers. He caught his breath, clutching at Joanne with his hands, his body tensed. He orgasmed quickly, pumping thick drops of whitish come into Joanne's hand.

Alice pulled away, sat back on the floor, her punished

backside still smarting, her pussy wet and aching with pure naked desire. She knew that she was on the verge, could feet the great wave of passion building within.

Joanne leaned over the edge of the bed, her naked breasts red with Philip's bite-marks. She stretched out her hand to Alice, smiling to her.

Alice looked at Joanne's proffered hand, wet with a pool of white cream from Philip's prick, streaks of yellow and white in the thick jelly. She felt a stab of horror pass through her, a rising sense of shame. Was this it? Was this what she had willingly submitted to? Something seemed to click and it all made sense again. Automatically, even without thinking about it, she crawled forward. The questions faded into the background, her mind was clear once more. Her sex was pulsing, ready to explode into orgasm, to clear her mind of everything but the blinding white joy of submission.

Alice took Joanne's hand and sucked the thick cream into her mouth, letting the pool of come rest on her tongue. She swallowed it, eyes closed, her bottom smarting from the spanking. She felt the come sliding down her throat and then froze, climaxing, knowing that everything, absolutely everything had turned out right in the end.

NEXUS NEW BOOKS

To be published in September

DISPLAYS OF PENITENTS
Lucy Golden
£5.99

In this, the third volume of tales from Lucy Golden, the lives of ordinary people are turned upside down as they submit to the allure of a totally new experience. It may be a medical examination. It may be a drinking game with very wet forfeits. It may be a bet. It may be an encounter with friends, family, neighbours or colleagues that takes a turn for the bizarre. Whatever the circumstances, whatever aspects of pain, pleasure, domination and submission are encountered, these tales explore every facet of the wide world of perverse eroticism with a haunting power and intensity.

ISBN 0 352 33646 3

TEMPER TANTRUMS
Penny Birch
£5.99

Natasha Linnet has a weakness for dirty old men – hence her relationship with wine buff and accomplished spanker Percy Ottershaw. When Percy visits a former colleague, the louche Dr Blondeau, in France, Natasha tags along. Blondeau, figuring correctly that any girlfriend of his perverted old friend must be a willing submissive, has extreme ideas of his own, for which he considers Natasha fair game. Natasha sees right through his wiles, of course. But how can she give in, and still have the last laugh?

ISBN 0 352 33647 1

DARK DESIRES
Maria del Rey
£5.99

Sexual diversity is the hallmark of Maria del Rey's work. Here, for the first time in one volume, is a collection of her kinkiest stories – each one striking in its originality – with settings to suit all tastes. Fetishists, submissives and errant tax inspectors mingle with bitch goddesses, naughty girls and French maids in this eclectic anthology of forbidden games. A Nexus Classic.

ISBN 0 352 33648 X

To be published in October

CAGED!
Yolanda Celbridge
£5.99

Tucked away in the Yorkshire Dales is a women's corrective institution where uniforms and catspats are the order of the day, the first often shredded by the second! But are the bars and fences to keep the women confined, or the locals out?

ISBN 0 352 33650 1

BEAST
Wendy Swanscombe
£5.99

Without time to draw breath from the indignities already heaped on them, the three sisters of *Disciplined Skin* – blonde Anna, redhead Beth, reven Gwen – are plunged into the new tortures and humiliations gleefully devised for them by their mysterious leather-clad captor Herr Abraham Bärengelt. Putting its heroines through ordeals that range from mild to perversely bizarre, *Beast* is sure to confirm the reputation its author has already established for surreal erotic depravity that entertains as much as it arouses.

ISBN 0 352 33649 8

PENNY IN HARNESS
Penny Birch
£5.99

When naughty Penny is walking in the woods one day, she is surprised to find a couple pony-carting. Penny is so excited by watching this new form of adult fun that she has to pleasure herself on the spot. Realising how keen she is to discover for herself what it is all about, she begins to investigate this bizarre world of whips and harnesses. Will she ever be able to win the highest accolade in their world of kinky games – the honour of being a pony-girl? A Nexus Classic.

ISBN 0 352 33651 X

If you would like more information about Nexus titles, please visit our website at www.nexus-books.co.uk, or send a stamped addressed envelope to:

Nexus, Thames Wharf Studios,
Rainville Road, London W6 9HA

NEXUS BACKLIST

This information is correct at time of printing. For up-to-date information, please visit our website at www.nexus-books.co.uk

All books are priced at £5.99 unless another price is given.

MAIDEN	Aishling Morgan ISBN 0 352 33466 5	☐
NYMPHS OF DIONYSUS £4.99	Susan Tinoff ISBN 0 352 33150 X	☐
THE SLAVE OF LIDIR	Aran Ashe ISBN 0 352 33504 1	☐
TIGER, TIGER	Aishling Morgan ISBN 0 352 33455 X	☐
THE WARRIOR QUEEN	Kendal Grahame ISBN 0 352 33294 8	☐

Edwardian, Victorian and older erotica

BEATRICE	Anonymous ISBN 0 352 31326 9	☐
CONFESSION OF AN ENGLISH SLAVE	Yolanda Celbridge ISBN 0 352 33433 9	☐
DEVON CREAM	Aishling Morgan ISBN 0 352 33488 6	☐
THE GOVERNESS AT ST AGATHA'S	Yolanda Celbridge ISBN 0 352 32986 6	☐
PURITY	Aishling Morgan ISBN 0 352 33510 6	☐
THE TRAINING OF AN ENGLISH GENTLEMAN	Yolanda Celbridge ISBN 0 352 33348 0	☐

Samplers and collections

NEW EROTICA 4	Various ISBN 0 352 33290 5	☐
NEW EROTICA 5	Various ISBN 0 352 33540 8	☐
EROTICON 1	Various ISBN 0 352 33593 9	☐
EROTICON 2	Various ISBN 0 352 33594 7	☐
EROTICON 3	Various ISBN 0 352 33597 1	☐
EROTICON 4	Various ISBN 0 352 33602 1	☐

Nexus Classics
A new imprint dedicated to putting the finest works of erotic fiction
back in print.

AGONY AUNT	G.C. Scott ISBN 0 352 33353 7	☐
BOUND TO SERVE	Amanda Ware ISBN 0 352 33457 6	☐
BOUND TO SUBMIT	Amanda Ware ISBN 0 352 33451 7	☐
CHOOSING LOVERS FOR JUSTINE	Aran Ashe ISBN 0 352 33351 0	☐
DIFFERENT STROKES	Sarah Veitch ISBN 0 352 33531 9	☐
EDEN UNVEILED	Maria del Rey ISBN 0 352 33542 4	☐
THE HANDMAIDENS	Aran Ashe ISBN 0 352 33282 4	☐
HIS MISTRESS'S VOICE	G. C. Scott ISBN 0 352 33425 8	☐
THE IMAGE	Jean de Berg ISBN 0 352 33350 2	☐
THE INSTITUTE	Maria del Rey ISBN 0 352 33352 9	☐
LINGERING LESSONS	Sarah Veitch ISBN 0 352 33539 4	☐
A MATTER OF POSSESSION	G. C. Scott ISBN 0 352 33468 1	☐
OBSESSION	Maria del Rey ISBN 0 352 33375 8	☐
THE PLEASURE PRINCIPLE	Maria del Rey ISBN 0 352 33482 7	☐
SERVING TIME	Sarah Veitch ISBN 0 352 33509 2	☐
SISTERHOOD OF THE INSTITUTE	Maria del Rey ISBN 0 352 33456 8	☐
THE TRAINING GROUNDS	Sarah Veitch ISBN 0 352 33526 2	☐
UNDERWORLD	Maria del Rey ISBN 0 352 33552 1	☐

- - - - - - ✂ -

Please send me the books I have ticked above.

Name ....

Address ....

....

....

.... Post code ....

Send to: **Cash Sales, Nexus Books, Thames Wharf Studios, Rainville Road, London W6 9HA**

US customers: for prices and details of how to order books for delivery by mail, call 1-800-805-1083.

Please enclose a cheque or postal order, made payable to **Nexus Books Ltd**, to the value of the books you have ordered plus postage and packing costs as follows:

UK and BFPO – £1.00 for the first book, 50p for each subsequent book.

Overseas (including Republic of Ireland) – £2.00 for the first book, £1.00 for each subsequent book.

If you would prefer to pay by VISA, ACCESS/MASTER-CARD, AMEX, DINERS CLUB, AMEX or SWITCH, please write your card number and expiry date here:

....

Please allow up to 28 days for delivery.

Signature ....

- - - - - - ✂ -